PAUL JENNINGS'
FUNNIEST STORIES

ALSO BY PAUL JENNINGS

Unreal!
Unbelievable!
Quirky Tails
Uncanny!
Unbearable!
Unmentionable!
Undone!
Uncovered!
Unseen!

Tongue-Tied!

Paul Jennings' Weirdest Stories
Paul Jennings' Spookiest Stories
Paul Jennings' Trickiest Stories

The Cabbage Patch Fibs

The Cabbage Patch series
(illustrated by Craig Smith)

The Gizmo series
(illustrated by Keith McEwan)

The Singenpoo series
(illustrated by Keith McEwan)

Wicked! (series) and *Deadly!* (series)
(with Morris Gleitzman)

Duck for Cover
Freeze a Crowd
Spooner or Later
Spit It Out
(with Terry Denton and Ted Greenwood)

Round the Twist .
Sucked In . . .
(illustrated by Terry Denton)

For adults

The Reading Bug
. . . and how you can help your child to catch it.

For beginners

The Rascal series

Novel

How Hedley Hopkins Did a Dare . . .
The Nest

More information about Paul and his books can be found at
www.pauljennings.com.au and **puffin.com.au**

PAUL JENNINGS'
FUNNIEST STORIES

VIKING
an imprint of
PENGUIN BOOKS

VIKING

Published by the Penguin Group
Penguin Group (Australia)
250 Camberwell Road
Camberwell, Victoria 3124, Australia
(a division of Pearson Australia Group Pty Ltd)
Penguin Group (USA) Inc.
375 Hudson Street, New York, New York 10014, USA
Penguin Group (Canada)
90 Eglinton Avenue East, Suite 700,
Toronto ON M4P 2Y3, Canada
(a division of Pearson Penguin Canada Inc.)
Penguin Books Ltd
80 Strand, London WC2R ORL, England
Penguin Ireland
25 St Stephen's Green, Dublin 2, Ireland
(a division of Penguin Books Ltd)
Penguin Books India Pvt Ltd
11, Community Centre, Panchsheel Park, New Delhi -110 017, India
Penguin Group (NZ)
67 Apollo Drive, Rosedale, North Shore 0632, New Zealand
(a division of Pearson New Zealand Ltd)
Penguin Books (South Africa) (Pty) Ltd
24 Sturdee Avenue, Rosebank, Johannesburg 2196, South Africa

Penguin Books Ltd, Registered Offices: 80 Strand, London WC2R ORL, England

Individual stories Copyright © Lockley Lodge Pty Ltd
First published by Penguin Books Australia Ltd
Cow-dung Custard, Smart Ice-cream, Wunderpants and *Lucky Lips*, from *Unreal!*, 1985
The Gumleaf War and *One-shot Toothpaste* from *Unbelievable!*, 1987
Ufd and *Spaghetti Pig-out* from *Uncanny!*, 1988
Little Black Balls, Next Time Around, Yuggles, Smelly Feat and *Licked*, from *Unbearable!*, 1990
Little Squirt from *Unmentionable!*, 1991, *Moonies*, from *Undone!*, 1991
Too Many Rabbits, A Mouthful, Pubic Hare, Ringing Wet, Picked Bones, from *Uncovered!*, 1995
Squawk Talk and *Piddler on the Roof*, from *Unseen!*, 1998
Popping Off, Tongue-Tied and *Sniffex*, from *Tongue-Tied!*, 2002

This collection published by Penguin Group (Australia), 2005

This collection Copyright © Lockley Lodge Pty Ltd, 2005
Illustrations Copyright © Bob Lea, 2005

20 19 18 17 16 15 14 13

The moral right of the author and illustrator has been asserted.

Cover and text design by Adam Laszczuk © Penguin Group (Australia), 2005
Cover illustration by Bob Lea
Typeset by Midland Typesetters, Australia
Printed in Australia by Mcpherson's Printing Group, Maryborough, Victoria

National Library of Australia
Cataloguing-in-Publication data:
Jennings, Paul, 1943- .
Paul Jennings' funniest stories.
ISBN 978 0 670 02890 0
I. Title.
A823.3

penguin.com.au
puffin.com.au

Contents

Lucky Lips

Marcus felt silly. He was embarrassed. But he knocked on the door anyway. There was no answer from inside the dark house. It was as silent as the grave. Then he noticed a movement behind the curtain; someone was watching him. He could see a dark eye peering through a chink in the curtain. There was a rustling noise inside that sounded like rats' feet on a bare floor.

The door slowly opened and Ma Scritchet's face appeared. It was true what people said – she looked like a witch. She had hair like straw and her nose was hooked and long. She smiled showing pointed, yellow teeth.

'Come in,' she said. 'I have been waiting for you.'

Marcus was not going to let this old woman fool him. 'How could you be expecting me?' he answered. 'No one knew I was coming here.' He felt better now. He could see that it was all a trick. She was a faker. A phoney. Did she really expect him to believe that she knew he was coming?

'I knew you were coming,' she said. 'And I know why you have come.'

This time Marcus knew she was lying. He had not

told anyone about his problem. There was not one person in the world that knew about it, it was too embarrassing. The other kids would laugh if they knew.

He decided to go home. But first he would stir this old bag up a bit. 'Okay, Ma,' he said. 'Why have I come?'

She looked him straight in the eye. 'You are sixteen years old,' she told him. 'And you have never been kissed.'

Marcus could feel his face turning red. He was blushing. She knew – she knew all about it. She must be able to read minds. The stories that were told about her must be true. He felt silly and small, and he didn't know what to do.

Ma Scritchet started to laugh, a long cackling laugh. It made Marcus shiver. 'Come with me,' she said. She led him along a dark, narrow passage and up some wooden stairs. The house was filled with junk: broken TV sets and old bicycles, piles of books and empty bottles. The stair rails were covered in cobwebs. They went into a small room at the top of the house.

Inside the room was a couch and a chair. Nothing else. It was not what Marcus had expected. He thought there would be a crystal ball on a round table and lots of junk and equipment for telling fortunes. The room was almost bare.

2

Ma Scritchet held out her hand. 'This will cost you twenty dollars,' she said to Marcus.

'I pay after, not before,' said Marcus. 'This could be a trick.'

'You pay before, not after,' said Ma Scritchet. 'I only help those that believe in me.' Marcus looked into her eyes. They were cold and hard. He took out his wallet and gave her twenty dollars, and she tucked it inside her dress. Then she said, 'Lie down on the couch.'

Marcus lay on the couch and stared at the ceiling. A tiny spider was spinning a web in the corner. Marcus felt foolish lying there on a couch in this old woman's house. He wished he hadn't come; he wanted to go home. But there was something about Ma Scritchet that made him nervous. And now that he had paid his twenty dollars he was going to get his money's worth. 'Well,' he said. 'I suppose that you want me to tell you about my problem.'

'No,' said Ma Scritchet. 'I will tell you about it. You just stay there and listen.' Marcus did as she said.

'You have never kissed a girl,' said the old woman in a low voice. 'You have tried plenty of times. But they always turn you down. They think you are stuck up and selfish. They don't like the things you say about other people. Some girls go out with you once, but when you get home to their front door they always say, "Thank you" and go inside.'

Marcus listened in silence. Most of it was true. He knew he wasn't stuck up and selfish, but the rest of it was right. He tried everything he could think of. He would take a girl to the movies and buy her chocolates. He would even pay for her to get in. But then, right at the end when they were saying 'good night', he would close his eyes, pucker up his lips and lean forward, to find himself kissing the closed front door of the girl's house. It was maddening. It was enough to make him spit. And it had happened dozens of times. Not one girl would give him a kiss.

3

'Well,' said Marcus to Ma Scritchet. 'Can you help me? That's what I gave you the twenty dollars for.'

She smiled but said nothing. It was not a nice smile. It was a smile that made Marcus feel foolish. She stood up without a word and left the room, and Marcus could hear her footsteps clipping down the stairs. A minute or so later he heard her coming back. She came into the room and held out a small tube. 'Take this,' she said. 'It's just what you need. This will do the trick.'

Marcus took it out of her hand and looked at it. It was a stick of lipstick in a small gold container. 'I'm not wearing lipstick,' Marcus told her. 'You must think I'm crazy.' He sat up and jumped off the couch. This had gone far enough. He wondered if he could get his money back.

'Sit down, boy,' said Ma Scritchet in a cold voice. 'And listen to me. You put that on your lips and you will get all the kisses you want. It has no colour. It's clear and

4

no one will be able to see it. But it will do the trick. It will work on any female. Just put some of that on your lips and the nearest girl will want to kiss you.'

Marcus looked at the tube of lipstick. He didn't know whether to believe it or not. It might work. Old Ma Scritchet could read his mind; she knew what his problem was without being told. This lipstick could be just what he needed. 'Okay,' he said. 'I'll give it a try. But it had better work. If it doesn't, I will be back for my twenty dollars.'

'It will work,' hissed Ma Scritchet. 'It will work better than you think. Now it's time for you to go. The session is over.' She led Marcus down the narrow stairs and along the passage to the front door. He stepped out into the sunlight. It was bright and made him blink. As Ma Scritchet closed the door she told Marcus one more thing. 'This lipstick will only work once on each person. One girl: one kiss. That's the way it works.'

She closed the door in his face without saying another thing. Once more the old house was quiet.

4

Marcus kept the lipstick for a week before he used it. When he got home to his room with his record player and the posters on the wall, the whole thing seemed like a dream. The old house and Ma Scritchet were from another world. He wondered whether or not the visit had really happened, but he had the lipstick to prove that it had.

He held it in his hand. It had a strange appearance and he found that it glowed in the dark. He put it in a drawer and left it there.

Later that week a new girl started at Marcus's school. Her name was Jill. Marcus didn't waste any time; he asked her out for a date on her first day at school. She didn't seem too keen about going with him, but she was shy and didn't want to seem unfriendly, especially as she didn't know anyone at the school. In the end she agreed to go to a disco with him on Friday night.

Marcus arranged to meet Jill inside the disco. That way he wouldn't have to pay for her to get in. It wasn't a bad turn and Jill seemed to enjoy it. As he danced Marcus could feel the lipstick in his pocket. He couldn't forget about it; it annoyed him. It was like having a stone in his shoe.

At eleven o'clock they decided to go home. It was only a short walk back to Jill's house. As they walked, Jill chatted happily; she was glad that she had made a new friend so quickly. Marcus started to feel a bit guilty. He fingered the lipstick in his pocket. Should he use it? He remembered something about stolen kisses. Was he stealing a kiss if he used the lipstick? Not really – if it worked Jill would be kissing him of her own free will. Anyway, it probably wouldn't work. Old Ma Scritchet had probably played a trick on him. He would never know unless he tried it. He just had to know if the lipstick worked, and this was his big chance.

As they went inside the front gate of Jill's house, Marcus pretended to bend down and do up his shoelace. He quickly pulled out the lipstick and smeared some on his lips. Then he stood up. His lips were tingling. He noticed that Jill was looking at him in a strange way; her eyes were wide open and staring. Then she rushed forward, threw her arms around Marcus's neck and kissed him. Marcus was so surprised that he nearly fell over.

Jill jumped back as if she had been burned. She put her hand up to her mouth and went red in the face. 'I, I, I'm sorry, Marcus. I don't know what came over me. What must you think of me? I've never done anything like that before.'

'Don't worry about it. That sort of thing happens to me all the time. The girls find me irresistible.'

Jill didn't know what to say. She was blushing. She couldn't understand what had happened. 'I'd better go in,' she said. 'I'm really sorry. I didn't mean to do that.' Then she turned around and rushed into the house.

Marcus whistled to himself as he walked home. 'It works,' he thought. 'The lipstick really works.' He couldn't wait to try it on someone else.

5

It was not so easy for Marcus to find his next victim. None of the girls at school wanted to go out with him.

It was no use asking Jill again, as the lipstick only worked once on each person. He asked ten girls to go to the pictures with him and they all said 'no'.

He started to get cross. 'Stuck up snobs,' he said to himself. 'I'll teach them a lesson.' He decided to make the most popular girl in the school kiss him. That would show them all. Her name was Fay Billings.

The trouble was that he knew she wouldn't go out on a date with him. Then he had a bright idea: he wouldn't even bother about a date. He would just go around to Fay's house and ask to see her. He would put the lipstick on before he arrived, and when she came to the door she would give him a big kiss. The news would soon get around and the other kids would think he had something good going. It would make him popular with the girls.

Marcus grinned. It was a great idea. He decided to put it into action straight away. He rode his bike around to Fay's house and leaned it against the fence. Then he took out the lipstick and put some on his lips. He walked up to the front door and rang the bell with a big smile on his face.

No one answered the door. He could hear a vacuum cleaner going inside so he rang the bell again. The sound of the vacuum cleaner stopped and Mrs Billings appeared at the door. She was about forty. She had a towel wrapped around her head and had dust on her face from the housework she had been doing. She had never seen Marcus before; he was not one of Fay's friends.

Mrs Billings was just going to ask Marcus what he wanted when a strange look came over her face. Her eyes went large and round. They looked as if they were going to pop out. Then she threw her arms around Marcus's neck and kissed him on the mouth.

It was hard to say who was more surprised, Marcus or Mrs Billings. They sprang apart and looked around to see if anyone had seen what happened. Marcus didn't want anyone to see him being kissed by a forty-year-old woman. How embarrassing. 'My goodness,' said Mrs Billings. 'What am I doing? Kissing a perfect stranger. And you're so young. What has got into me? What would my husband think? Please excuse me. I must be ill. I think I had better go and have a little rest.' She turned around and walked slowly into the house. She shook her head as she went.

6

Marcus rode home slowly. He was not pleased. This was not working out the way he wanted. What if someone had seen him being kissed by an old lady like Mrs Billings? He would never live it down. He had had the lipstick for two weeks now and had only received one decent kiss. None of the girls would go out with him. And he couldn't wear the lipstick just anywhere – he didn't want any other mothers kissing him.

He decided to make Fay Billings kiss him at school,

in front of all the other kids. That would show them that he had something special. All the girls would be chasing him after that; he would be the most popular boy in the school.

He picked his moment carefully. He sat next to Fay for the Maths lesson the next day. She looked at him with a funny expression on her face but she didn't say anything. Miss White was late for the class. She was a young teacher and was popular with the students, but she was always late. This was the chance that Marcus had been waiting for. He bent down under the desk and put on some of the lipstick. Then he sat up in the desk and looked at Fay.

The lipstick worked. Fay's eyes went round and she threw herself onto Marcus and kissed him. Then she jumped back and gave a little cry. Marcus looked around with a grin on his face, but it did not last for long. All the girls' eyes were wide and staring. Tissy came up and kissed him. And then Gerda and Helen and Betty and Maria. They climbed over each other in the rush to get to him. They shrieked and screamed and fought; they scratched and fought and bit. Marcus fell onto the floor under a struggling, squirming heap of girls.

When all the sixteen girls in the class had kissed him there was silence. They were in a state of shock – they couldn't understand what had happened. They just sat there looking at each other. Marcus had his tie ripped off and his shirt was torn. He had a cut lip and a black eye.

Then Gerda yelled out, 'I kissed Marcus! Arrgghh ...' She rushed over to the tap and started washing her mouth out. All the girls started wiping their mouths as if they had eaten something nasty. Then everybody started laughing. The boys laughed, and the girls laughed. They rolled around the floor holding their sides. Tears rolled out of their eyes. Everybody laughed, except Marcus.

He knew that they were laughing at him. And he didn't think that it was funny.

7

After all the kissing at school everyone called Marcus 'Lucky Lips'. Nobody liked Marcus any better than before and the girls still stayed away from him. Everyone talked about the kissing session for a while; then they forgot about it and talked about other things. But Marcus didn't forget about it. He felt like a fool. Everyone had laughed at him. He was worse off now than he had been before.

He thought about taking the lipstick back to Ma Scritchet and telling her what he thought about it, but he was too scared. There was something creepy about that old lady and he didn't really want to see her again.

Marcus didn't use the lipstick again for about a month. None of the girls would go out with him and he wasn't going to risk wearing it just anywhere. Not after what happened at school that day. But he always carried the lipstick with him, just in case.

The last time he used it was at the Royal Melbourne Show. The whole class at school went there on an excursion. They had to collect material for an assignment. Marcus and Fay Billings and two other boys walked around together. The others didn't really want Marcus with them; they thought he was a show off. But they let him tag along. They didn't want to hurt his feelings.

The favourite spots at the show were the sideshows. There were knock-em-downs and rides on the Mad Mouse. There was a fat lady and a mirror maze. There was a ghost train and dozens of other rides. One of the side shows had a sign up saying 'BIG BEN THE STRONGEST MAN IN THE WORLD'.

They all milled around looking at the tent. It was close to one of the animal pavilions. There was a great hall full of pigs nearby. 'Let's go and look at the pigs,' said Fay.

'No,' answered Marcus. 'Who wants to look at filthy pigs. Let's go and see Big Ben. He fights people. Anyone who can beat him wins one thousand dollars and gets to kiss the Queen Of The Show.'

'That would be just the thing for Lucky Lips,' said Fay. They all laughed, except Marcus. He went red in the face.

'I could get a kiss from the Queen Of The Show,' he said. They all laughed again. 'All right,' said Marcus. 'Just watch me.' He paid his dollar and went inside Big Ben's tent. The others all followed him; they wanted to see what was going to happen.

Inside the tent was a boxing ring. Big Ben was standing inside it waiting for someone to fight him and try to win the thousand dollars and a kiss from the Queen Of The Show. She sat on a high chair behind the ring. Marcus looked at her. She was beautiful; he wouldn't mind a kiss from her. Then he looked at Big Ben. He was the biggest man Marcus had ever seen. He had huge muscles and was covered in tattoos. And he looked mean – very mean.

Marcus ducked around the ring to where the Queen Of The Show sat. He quickly put on some of the invisible lipstick, and at once the beauty queen jumped off her chair and kissed Marcus. Everyone laughed except Big Ben. He roared in fury. 'Trying to steal a kiss without a fight, are you?' he yelled. 'I'll teach you a lesson, my boy.'

Marcus tried to run away but he was not quick enough. Big Ben grabbed him and lifted Marcus high into the air. Then he walked outside the tent and across to the pig pavilion. Marcus wriggled and yelled, but it was no good; he couldn't get away. Big Ben carried Marcus over to one of the pig pens and threw him inside.

Marcus crashed to the floor of the pen. He felt dizzy. The world seemed to be spinning around. He tried to stand up, but he couldn't. The floor was covered in foul-smelling muck. In the corner Marcus could see the biggest pig that he had ever seen. It was eating rotten vegetables and slops from a trough. It was dribbling and slobbering as it ate. Its teeth were green. It turned around and looked at Marcus. It was a sow.

Marcus suddenly remembered something that Ma Scritchet had said about the lipstick. She had said: 'It will work on any female.' Marcus started to scream. 'Get me out. Get me out.'

But it was too late. The sow came over for her kiss.

Tongue-Tied

I'm standing here behind the toilet block. Talking to myself. You know, having a conversation in my head. The reason that I am talking to myself is out on the netball court. Giving me the silent treatment.

'Jill. Don't be like that. I'm sorry. I shouldn't have tried to kiss you.'

This is what I say to myself in my head. I am rehearsing a little speech.

'Say something, Jill. Please. Don't just stand there. Don't blink at me with that look on your face. I feel like a criminal.

'It's not like I'm a horrible person. I've never kissed a girl, you know. And you're the only one I would ever want to kiss. Say something. Please. Don't give me the silent treatment.

'All right, all right. Be like that. I don't care. Sulk. Tell your mum. Dob me in to the teachers. I'm not a murderer, am I? I didn't actually touch you, did I? I just closed my eyes and pouted my lips and leaned forward. So? Big deal.

'Still not going to talk? Okay, you can listen then. I'll tell you everything that happened. Right from the beginning.

'I always liked you. But I knew I didn't have a chance. Your dad is rich. My dad is poor. You are beautiful. I am ... well, you can see what I am. You are really smart. I am dumb.

'I'm clumsy. You are good at sport. You are always jogging and training. You even carry around one of those plastic squirt bottles of water. Imagine what my mum would say if I bought one of those.

' "Paying for water, Jeremy?" That's what she'd say. Or what she'd shout more like it. "What are you thinking of, boy? Water is free. You can get it out of the tap. What are you spending good money on it for?"

'Anyway, Jill, I knew when your birthday was. So I decided to buy you a present.

' "How much are those little wriggling guppies?" I said to the man in the pet shop.

' "Two hundred and ten dollars, son," he said. "And cheap at half the price."

' "Two hundred and ten dollars?" I yelled. 'Just for a fish?"

' "A very special fish," he said. "And there is someone else interested in it. You won't get another one anywhere."

'That was all the money I had from my paper rounds. Two years of getting up in the dark and rain. Riding around on a rusty bike. Up hill and down. Throwing papers on to rich people's front lawns. I was saving up for a bike with gears. To make the going a bit easier.

'I took the money out of my wallet and looked at it. I thought about that new bike. Then I thought about you. And your soft lips. My heart seemed to stop beating. I went all wobbly in the stomach. I admit it. I thought about kissing you. What's wrong with that?

'You really wanted a wriggling guppy. I heard you tell your friend Samantha. "They come from Japan," you said. "I would kill for one of those wriggling guppies."

'So I bought it. On your birthday. Today. You would kill for a wriggling guppy, you said. Well, my mum will kill me when she finds out my bike money is gone. Vanished like a fish down a drain.

'Why don't you say something, Jill? Cat got your tongue? Why don't you stop sipping out of your yuppy bottle of mineral water and speak to me?

'Anyway, to get back to the story, Jill. I walked home from the pet shop with the little wriggling guppy in a small glass fishbowl. "You will have to change the water every day," said the man. "Otherwise it will use up all the oxygen."

'So I kept it in my locker all day at school. Every chance I got I checked on the little wriggling guppy. To be quite honest I can't see the value, Jill. Okay, it looks pretty with its little orange and green spots. And it wriggles around in a funny way. But gees, you could get a good bike for that sort of money.

'After school I plucked up my courage. "Jill," I said. "Will you wait back after netball practice? I want to talk to you."

' "What about?" you said.

' "A secret," I told you.

'You nodded your head. You did. And don't deny it. You agreed to meet me here. Not with words. But with a nod.

'And you waited like I said. Just the two of us. Way out in the sale-yards car park after everyone had gone home. I had to walk all the way. I couldn't take a little glass fishbowl on my bike, could I? It took me an hour to walk here, Jill.

'So finally I held out my present. I was waiting for you to say, "Oh thank you, Jeremy. You shouldn't have. These are so rare. Where did you get it? All that money. You wonderful person."

'I was waiting for you to lean over and kiss me with those soft lips. Even a peck on the cheek would have been something.

'But you just left me standing there with my eyes closed, and you said nothing. You are good at saying nothing. Aren't you?

'Do you know how I felt? Stupid. Ridiculous. A total nerd. I could feel my face burning. You couldn't even bring yourself to say thanks.

'I was so embarrassed that I ran and hid behind the boys' toilets. Can you believe that? What a dork. The toilets were locked. But if I could have got inside I would have stuck my head in the dunny in shame.

'But then I stopped and thought, Hang on a bit. Okay,

okay. She has rejected me. But there is still the fish. There is still the stupid wriggling guppy. Jill can't expect to keep it. I will take it back to the man in the shop. He might give me my money back. But I had better get moving. Before it uses up all the oxygen.

'Oh gees. Hurry. Quick.'

2

I run out from behind the toilets on to the netball courts. And what do I find?

She has thrown my present on the ground. She has smashed the glass fishbowl. And still she won't say anything. What a mean, horrible, rotten stinking person. Standing there sipping out of her stupid yuppy water bottle.

'Guppy, guppy, guppy, where are you?'

I fall to the ground and search around on my knees. Has it gone down the drain? Is it in the grass? Has she chucked it on the roof?

All because I wanted a kiss.

Jill grabs me by the shoulders and pulls me to my feet. Boy, she is strong. She just stands there staring at me. A tear runs down her cheek. She takes another sip out of her bottle. Then she holds it out to me with a funny look on her face. It is too late for tears now. Two hundred and ten bucks. All for a kiss from a stupid girl.

She suddenly grabs me and pulls my face towards her. She presses her lips up to mine.

No, no. Not now. I don't want a kiss anymore. You are not worth it, Jill.

Oh shoot. She is pushing her tongue into my mouth.

What, what, what? It is soft and squirming around. I never experienced anything like this before. It is a tongue-tide. Oh gees. It feels like . . .

It feels like . . .

A little wriggling fish.

It is the guppy.

She had it in her mouth. It wasn't her tongue. It was the fish. And she has pushed it into my mouth.

She talks.

'Oh, Jeremy,' she yells. 'I am so sorry. I didn't know what to say. Such a generous present. I was shocked. I couldn't get any words out. Then you ran off behind the toilets. I started off after you but I tripped. And broke the fishbowl.'

I just stare at Jill and try not to swallow the fish. Jill shoves the water bottle into my hand. 'Fill your mouth with water,' she screams. 'I can't find a container anywhere. We have to keep the guppy alive.'

I gulp in water and blow out my cheeks. Jill looks around furiously for something to put the fish into. But there is nothing. Not even a rusty can. And there is no one to help. The netball courts are deserted.

'See if you can take the top off the water bottle,' she yells. 'We can put the fish in there but I can't open it.'

I twist at the little squirting cap and shake my head.

I can't talk because the guppy is swimming around inside my cheeks. The water fills my mouth. I can't speak. I am tongue-tied.

'Pass the fish to me,' Jill says. She sucks some water into her mouth from the bottle and then pouts her lips. I press my lips against hers and push the guppy back into her mouth with my tongue. Gees, it feels good. Her lips are really soft.

'We have to get to a tap,' I gasp. 'Twenty steps each and then we pass back the fish.'

Jill nods. She is smiling.

So we walk back down the road, passing the fish to each other with our lips. Each time the fish gets a new mouthful of water. And I get a kiss. A fish kiss. We walk slowly.

Finally, after many fish kisses, we reach a tap.

I decide to confess. 'Jill,' I say. 'I really could have got the top off the bottle. I felt it move.'

She grins and pulls my head to hers. It is my last turn to have the guppy.

'Don't worry about it,' she says when she finally comes up for air. 'I swallowed the silly fish five minutes ago.'

Spaghetti Pig-out

Guts Garvey was a real mean kid. He made my life miserable. I don't know why he didn't like me. I hadn't done anything to him. Not a thing.

He wouldn't let any of the other kids hang around with me. I was on my own. Anyone in the school who spoke to me was in his bad books. I wandered around the yard at lunch time like a dead leaf blown in the wind.

I tried everything. I even gave him my pocket money one week. He just bought a block of chocolate from the canteen and ate it in front of me. Without even giving me a bit. What a rat.

After school I only had one friend. My cat – Bad Smell. She was called that because now and then she would make a bad smell. Well, she couldn't help it. Everyone has their faults. She was a terrific cat. But still. A cat is not enough. You need other kids for friends too.

Even after school no one would come near me. I only had one thing to do. Watch the television. But that wasn't much good either. There were only little kids' shows on before tea.

'I wish we had a video,' I said to Mum one night.

'We can't afford it, Matthew,' said Mum. 'Anyway, you watch too much television as it is. Why don't you go and do something with a friend?'

I didn't say anything. I couldn't tell her that I didn't have any friends. And never would have as long as Guts Garvey was around. A bit later Dad came in. He had a large parcel under his arm. 'What have you got, Dad?' I asked.

'It's something good,' he answered. He put the package on the loungeroom floor and I started to unwrap it. It was about the size of a large cake. It was green and spongy with an opening in the front.

'What is it?' I said.

'What you've always wanted. A video player.'

I looked at it again. 'I've never seen a video player like this before. It looks more like a mouldy loaf of bread with a hole in the front.'

'Where did you get it?' asked Mum in a dangerous voice. 'And how much was it?'

'I bought it off a bloke in the pub. A real bargain. Only fifty dollars.'

'Fifty dollars is cheap for a video,' I said. 'But is it a video? It doesn't look like one to me. Where are the cables?'

'He said it doesn't need cables. You just put in the video and press this.' He handed me a green thing that looked like a bar of chocolate with a couple of licorice blocks stuck on the top.

'You're joking,' I said. 'That's not a remote control.'

'How much did you have to drink?' said Mum. 'You must have been crazy to pay good money for that junk.' She went off into the kitchen. I could tell that she was in a bad mood.

'Well at least try it,' said Dad sadly. He handed me a video that he had hired down the street. It was called *Revenge of the Robots*. I pushed the video into the mushy hole and switched on the TV set. Nothing happened.

I looked at the licorice blocks on the green chocolate thing. It was worth a try. I pushed one of the black squares.

The movie started playing at once. 'It works,' I yelled. 'Good on you, Dad. It works. What a ripper.'

Mum came in and smiled. 'Well what do you know,' she said. 'Who would have thought that funny-looking thing was a video set? What will they think of next?'

2

Dad went out and helped Mum get tea while I sat down and watched the movie. I tried out all the licorice-like buttons on the remote control. One was for fast forward, another was for pause and another for rewind. The rewind was good. You could watch all the people doing things backwards.

I was rapt to have a video but to tell the truth the movie was a bit boring. I started to fiddle around with the handset. I pointed it at things in the room and pressed the buttons. I pretended that it was a ray gun.

'Tea time,' said Mum after a while.

'What are we having?' I yelled.

'Spaghetti,' said Mum.

I put the video on pause and went to the door. I was just about to say, 'I'm not hungry,' when I noticed something. Bad Smell was sitting staring at the TV in a funny way. I couldn't figure out what it was at first but I could see that something was wrong. She was so still. I had never seen a cat sit so still before. Her tail didn't swish. Her eyes didn't blink. She just sat there like a statue. I took off my thong and threw it over near her. She didn't move. Not one bit. Not one whisker.

'Dad,' I yelled. 'Something is wrong with Bad Smell.'

He came into the lounge and looked at the poor cat. It sat there staring up at the screen with glassy eyes. Dad waved his hand in front of her face. Nothing. Not a blink. 'She's dead,' said Dad.

'Oh no,' I cried. 'Not Bad Smell. Not her. She can't be. My only friend.' I picked her up. She stayed in the sitting-up position. I put her back on the floor. No change. She sat there stiffly. I felt for a pulse but I couldn't find one. Her chest wasn't moving. She wasn't breathing.

'Something's not quite right,' said Dad. 'But I can't figure out what it is.'

'She shouldn't be sitting up,' I yelled. 'Dead cats don't sit up. They fall over with their legs pointed up.'

Dad picked up Bad Smell and felt all over her. 'It's no good, Matthew,' he said. 'She's gone. We will bury her in the garden after tea.' He patted me on the head and went into the kitchen.

Tears came into my eyes. I hugged Bad Smell to my chest. She wasn't stiff. Dead cats should be stiff. I remembered a dead cat that I once saw on the footpath. I had picked it up by the tail and it hadn't bent. It had been like picking up a saucepan by the handle.

Bad Smell felt soft. Like a toy doll. Not stiff and hard like the cat on the footpath.

Suddenly I had an idea. I don't know what gave it to me. It just sort of popped into my head. I picked up the funny-looking remote control, pointed it at Bad Smell and pressed the FORWARD button. The cat blinked, stretched, and stood up. I pressed PAUSE again and she froze. A statue again. But this time she was standing up.

I couldn't believe it. I rubbed my eyes. The pause button was working on my cat. I pressed FORWARD a second time and off she went. Walking into the kitchen as if nothing had happened.

Dad's voice boomed out from the kitchen. 'Look. Bad Smell is alive.' He picked her up and examined her. 'She must have been in a coma. Just as well we didn't bury her.' Dad had a big smile on his face. He put Bad Smell down and shook his head. I went back to the lounge.

I hit one of the licorice-like buttons. None of them

had anything written on them but by now I knew what each of them did.

Or I thought I did.

3

The movie started up again. I watched it for a while until a blowfly started buzzing around and annoying me. I pointed the hand set at it just for fun and pressed FAST FORWARD. The fly vanished. Or that's what seemed to happen. It was gone from sight but I could still hear it. The noise was tremendous. It was like a tiny jet fighter screaming around in the room. I saw something flash by. It whipped past me again. And again. And again. The blowfly was going so fast that I couldn't see it.

I pushed the PAUSE button and pointed it up where the noise was coming from. The fly must have gone right through the beam because it suddenly appeared out of nowhere. It hung silently in mid-air. Still. Solidified. A floating, frozen fly. I pointed the hand set at it again and pressed FORWARD. The blowfly came to life at once. It buzzed around the room at its normal speed.

'Come on,' yelled Mum. 'Your tea is ready.'

I wasn't interested in tea. I wasn't interested in anything except this fantastic remote control. It seemed to be able to make animals and insects freeze or go fast forward. I looked through the kitchen door at Dad. He had already started eating. Long pieces of spaghetti dangled from his mouth. He was chewing and sucking at the same time.

Now don't get me wrong. I love Dad. I always have. He is a terrific bloke. But one thing that he used to do really bugged me. It was the way he ate spaghetti. He sort of made slurping noises and the meat sauce gathered around his lips as he sucked. It used to get on my nerves. I think that's why I did what I did. I know it's a weak excuse. I shivered. Then I pointed the control at him and hit the PAUSE button.

Dad stopped eating. He turned rock solid and just sat there with the fork halfway up to his lips. His mouth was wide open. His eyes stared. The spaghetti hung from his fork like worms of concrete. He didn't blink. He didn't move. He was as stiff as a tree trunk.

Mum looked at him and laughed. 'Good one,' she said. 'You'd do anything for a laugh, Arthur.'

Dad didn't move.

'Okay,' said Mum. 'That's enough. You're setting a bad example for Matthew by fooling around with your food like that.'

My frozen father never so much as moved an eyeball. Mum gave him a friendly push on the shoulder and he started to topple. Over he went. He looked just like a statue that had been pushed off its mount. Crash. He lay on the ground. His hand still halfway up to his mouth The solid spaghetti hung in the same position. Only now it stretched out sideways pointing at his toes.

Mum gave a little scream and rushed over to him. Quick as a flash I pointed the remote control at him and pressed FORWARD. The spaghetti dangled downwards. Dad sat up and rubbed his head. 'What happened?' he asked.

'You had a little turn,' said Mum in a worried voice. 'You had better go straight down to the hospital and have a check up. I'll get the car. Matthew you stay here and finish your tea. We won't be long.'

I was going to tell them about the remote control but something made me stop. I had a thought. If I told them about it they would take it off me. It was the last I would see of it for sure. If I kept it to myself I could take it to school. I could show Guts Garvey my fantastic new find. He would have to make friends with me now that I had something as good as this. Every kid in the school would want to have a go.

Dad and Mum came home after about two hours. Dad went straight to bed. The doctor had told him to have a few days' rest. He said Dad had been working too hard. I took the remote control to bed with me. I didn't use it until the next day.

4

It was Saturday and I slept in. I did my morning jobs and set out to find Guts Garvey. He usually hung around the shops on Saturday with his tough mates.

The shopping centre was crowded. As I went I looked

in the shop windows. In a small cafe I noticed a man and a woman having lunch. They were sitting at a table close to the window. I could see everything that they were eating. The man was having a steak and what was left of a runny egg. He had almost finished his meat.

It reminded me of Dad and the spaghetti. I took out the remote control and looked at it. I knew that it could do PAUSE, FORWARD and FAST FORWARD. There was one more button. I couldn't remember what this last button was for. I pushed it.

I wouldn't have done it on purpose. I didn't really realise that it was pointing at the man in the shop. The poor thing.

The last button was REWIND.

Straight away he began to un-eat his meal. He went backwards. He put his fork up to his mouth and started taking out the food and placing back on his plate. The runny egg came out of his mouth with bits of steak and chips. In, out, in, out, went his fork. Each time bringing a bit of food out of his mouth. He moved the mashed-up bits backwards on his plate with the knife and fork and they all formed up into solid chips, steak and eggs.

It was unbelievable. He was un-chewing his food and un-eating his meal. Before I could gather my wits his whole meal was back on the plate. He then put his clean knife and fork down on the table.

My head swirled but suddenly I knew what I had to do. I pressed FORWARD. Straight away he picked up his knife and fork and began to eat his meal for the second time. The woman sitting opposite him had pushed her fist up into her mouth. She was terrified. She didn't know what was going on. Suddenly she screamed and ran out of the cafe. The man didn't take any notice. He just kept eating. He had to eat the whole meal again before he could stop.

I ran down the street feeling as guilty as sin. This thing was powerful. It could make people do things backwards.

I stopped at the corner. There, talking to his mean mate Rabbit, was Guts Garvey. This was my big chance to get into his good books. 'Look,' I said. 'Take a squizz at this.' I held out the remote control.

Guts Garvey grabbed it from my hand. 'Yuck,' he growled. 'Green chocolate. Buzz off bird brain.' He lifted up the remote control. He was going to throw it at me.

'No,' I yelled. 'It's a remote control. From a video. You press the black things.' Guts Garvey looked at me. Then he looked at the control. He didn't believe me but he pressed one of the buttons.

Rabbit was bouncing a basketball up and down on the footpath He suddenly froze. So did the ball. Rabbit stood there on one leg and the ball floated without moving, halfway between his hand and the ground. Guts Garvey's mouth dropped open. He rubbed his eyes and looked again. The statue of Rabbit was still there.

'Press FORWARD,' I said, pointing to the top button.

Guts pressed the control again and Rabbit finished bouncing the ball. I smiled. I could see that Guts was impressed. He turned and looked at me. Then he pointed the remote control straight at my face. 'No,' I screamed. 'No.'

But I was too late. Guts Garvey pressed the button. He 'paused' me. I couldn't move. I just stood there with both arms frozen up in the air. My eyes stared. They didn't move. Nothing moved. I was rock solid. Guts and Rabbit laughed. Then they ran off.

5

People gathered round. At first they laughed. A whole circle of kids and adults looking at the stupid dill standing there like a statue. Someone waved their hand in front of my face. A girl poked me. 'He's good,' said someone. 'He's not moving a muscle.'

I tried to speak. My mouth wouldn't move. My tongue wouldn't budge. The crowd got bigger. I felt an idiot.

What a fool. Dozens of people were staring at me wondering why I was standing there posed like a picture on the wall. Then I stopped feeling stupid. I felt scared. What if I stayed like this forever? Not breathing. Not moving. Not alive, not dead. What would they do with me? Put me in the garden like a garden gnome? Stash me away in a museum? Bury me alive? It was too terrible to think about.

Suddenly I collapsed. I puddled onto the ground.

Everyone laughed. I stood up and ran off as fast as I could go. As I ran I tried to figure it out. Why had I suddenly gone off pause? Then I realised what it was. I remembered my Uncle Frank's video. If you put it on pause and went away it would start up again automatically after three or four minutes. The movie would come off pause and keep going. That's what had happened to me.

I looked ahead. I could just make out two tiny figures in the distance. It was Rabbit and Guts Garvey. With my remote control. I had to get it back. The dirty rats had nicked it. I didn't care about getting in Guts Garvey's good books any more. I just wanted my controller back.

And revenge. I wanted revenge.

I ran like a mad thing after them.

It was no good. I was out of breath and they were too far away. I couldn't catch them. I looked around. Shaun Potter, a kid from school, was sitting on his horse, Star, on the other side of the road. I rushed over to him. 'Help,' I said. 'You've got to help. Guts Garvey has pinched my remote control. I've got to get it back. It's a matter of life and death.'

Shaun looked at me. He wasn't a bad sort of kid. He was one of the few people in the school who had been kind to me. He wasn't exactly a friend. He was too scared of Guts Garvey for that. But I could tell by the way he smiled and nodded at me that he liked me. I jumped from foot to foot. I was beside myself. I had to get that remote control back. Shaun hesitated for a second or two. Then he said, 'Okay, hop up.'

I put one foot in the stirrup and Shaun pulled me up behind him onto Star's back. 'They went that way,' I yelled.

Star went into a trot and then a canter. I held on for grim death. I had never been on a horse before. I bumped up and down behind Shaun. The ground seemed a long way down. I was scared but I didn't say anything. I had to catch Guts Garvey and Rabbit. We sped down the street past all the parked cars and people crossing the road.

'There they are,' I yelled. Guts and Rabbit were in a line of people waiting for a bus. Shaun slowed Star down to a walk. Guts Garvey looked up and saw us. He pulled the remote control from his pocket. 'Oh no,' I yelled. 'Not that.'

6

I don't know whether or not Star sensed danger. Anyway, he did what horses often do at such times. He lifted up his tail and let a large steaming flow of horse droppings fall onto the road. Then he took a few steps towards Guts and the line of people.

Guts pointed the remote control at us and hit the REWIND button. 'Stop,' I screamed. But it was too late. Star began to go into reverse. She walked a few steps backwards. The pile of horse droppings began to stir.

It twisted and lifted. Then it flew through the air – back to where it came from.

The line of people roared. Some laughed. Some screamed. Some ran off. How embarrassing. I was filled with shame. Poor Star went into a backwards trot. Then, suddenly she froze. We all froze. Guts had hit the PAUSE button. He had turned Shaun, Star and me into statues.

While we were standing there like stiff dummies the bus pulled up. All the people in the queue piled on. They couldn't get on quickly enough. They wanted to get away from the mad boys and their even madder horse.

After four or five minutes the pause effect wore off. We were able to move. I climbed down off Star's back. 'Sorry,' I said to Shaun. 'I didn't know that was going to happen.'

Shaun stared down at me. He looked pale. 'I think I've just had a bad dream,' he said. 'In the middle of the day. I think I'd better go home.' He shook his head slowly and then trotted off.

7

'Rats,' I said to myself. Everything was going wrong. I had lost the remote control. Guts Garvey had nicked it and there was nothing I could do about it. I was too scared to go near him in case he put me into reverse again. I felt terrible. I walked home with slow, sad footsteps.

When I got home Dad was mad because the remote control had disappeared. I couldn't tell him what had happened. He would never believe it. I had to spend most of the weekend pretending to help him look for it. The video wouldn't work without the control.

On Monday it was back to school as usual. Back to wandering around with no one to talk to.

As I walked around the schoolyard my stomach rumbled. I was hungry. Very hungry. I hadn't had anything to eat since tea time on Friday night. The reason for this was simple. This was the day of The Great Spaghetti Pig-out. A competition to see who could eat the most spaghetti bolognaise in fifteen minutes.

The grand final was to be held in the school hall. The winner received a free trip to London for two and the entrance money went to charity. I had a good chance of winning. Even though I was skinny I could eat a lot when I was hungry. I had won all the heats. My record was ten bowls of spaghetti bolognaise in fifteen minutes. Maybe if I won the competition I would also win the respect of the kids. I was going to give the tickets to London to Mum and Dad. They needed a holiday badly.

I didn't see Guts Garvey until just before the competition. He kept out of my sight all day. I knew he was cooking up some scheme but I didn't know what it was.

There were four of us up on the platform. Me, two

girls and Guts Garvey. The hall was packed with kids and teachers. I felt confident but nervous. I knew that I could win. I looked at Guts Garvey and saw that he was grinning his head off. Then I saw Rabbit in the front row. His pocket was bulging. Rabbit had something in his pocket and I thought I knew what it was.

They were up to no good. Guts and Rabbit had something cooked up and it wasn't spaghetti.

The plates of steaming spaghetti bolognaise were lined up in front of us. Everything was ready for the starter to say 'go'. My empty stomach was in a knot. My mind was spinning. I tried to figure out what they were up to. What if I ate five plates of spaghetti and Rabbit put me into reverse? I would un-eat it like the man in the cafe. I would go backwards and take all of the spaghetti out and put it back on the plate. My knees started to knock.

I decided to back out of the competition. I couldn't go through with it.

'Go,' yelled Mr Stepney, the school Principal. It was too late. I had to go on.

I started shovelling spaghetti into my mouth. There was no time to mix in the meat sauce. I just pushed in the platefuls as they came. One, two, three. The winner would be the one to eat the most plates in fifteen minutes.

I watched Guts and the others out of the corner of my eye. I was already ahead by two bowls. In, out, in, out. Spaghetti, spaghetti, spaghetti. I was up to seven bowls, Guts had eaten only four and the two girls had managed two each. I was going to win. Mum and Dad would be pleased.

Rabbit was watching us from the front row. I noticed Guts nod to him. Rabbit took something out of his pocket. I could see that it was the remote control. He was going to put me on rewind. I was gone.

But no. Rabbit was not pointing the control at me. He pointed it at Guts. What was going on? I soon found out. Guts began eating the spaghetti at enormous speed. Just like a movie on fast forward. His fork went up and down to his mouth so quickly that you could hardly see it. He licked like lightning. He swallowed at top speed. Boy did he go. His arms whirled. The spaghetti flew. Ten, eleven, twelve bowls. Thirteen, fourteen, fifteen. He was plates ahead. I didn't have a chance to catch up to Guts the guzzling gourmet. He fed his face like a whirlwind. It was incredible. Inedible. But it really happened.

Rabbit had put Guts on FAST FORWARD so that he would eat more plates than me in the fifteen minutes. It wasn't fair. But there was nothing I could do.

The audience cheered and shouted. They thought that Guts was fantastic. No one had ever seen anything like it before. He was up to forty bowls. I had only eaten ten and the two girls six each. The siren blew. Guts was the winner. I was second.

He had eaten forty bowls. No one had ever eaten forty bowls of spaghetti before. Rabbit hit FORWARD on the control and Guts stopped eating. Everyone cheered Guts. I looked at my shoes. I felt ill and it wasn't just from eating ten plates of spaghetti. I swallowed. I had to keep it all down. That was one of the rules – you weren't allowed to be sick. If you threw up you lost the competition.

8

Guts stood up. He looked a bit funny. His face was a green colour. His stomach swelled out over his belt. He started to sway from side to side. Then he opened his mouth.

Out it came. A great tumbling surge of spew. A tidal wave of swallowed spaghetti and meat sauce. It flowed down the table and onto the floor. A brown and white lake of sick. Guts staggered and tottered. He lurched to the edge of the stage. He opened his mouth again and let forth another avalanche. The kids in the front row screamed as the putrid waterfall splashed down. All over Rabbit.

Rabbit shrieked and sent the remote control spinning into the air. I jumped forward and grabbed it.

I shouldn't have done what I did. But I couldn't help myself. I pointed the control at Guts and the river of sick.

Then I pressed REWIND.

After that Guts Garvey was not very popular at school. To say the least. But I had lots of friends. And Mum and Dad had a great time in London.

And as to what happened to the remote control. Well … That's another story.

Smart Ice-cream

Well, I came top of the class again. One hundred out of one hundred for Maths. And one hundred out of one hundred for English. I'm just a natural brain, the best there is. There isn't one kid in the class who can come near me. Next to me they are all dumb.

Even when I was a baby I was smart. The day that I was born my mother started tickling me. 'Bub, bub, bub,' she said.

'Cut it out, Mum,' I told her. 'That tickles.' She nearly fell out of bed when I said that. I was very advanced for my age.

Every year I win a lot of prizes: top of the class, top of the school, stuff like that. I won a prize for spelling when I was only three years old. I am a terrific speller. If you can say it, I can spell it. Nobody can trick me on spelling. I can spell every word there is.

Some kids don't like me; I know that for a fact. They say I'm a show-off. I don't care. They are just jealous because they are not as clever as me. I'm good looking too. That's another reason why they are jealous.

Last week something bad happened. Another kid got

one hundred out of one hundred for Maths too. That never happened before – no one has ever done as well as me. I am always first on my own. A kid called Jerome Dadian beat me. He must have cheated. I was sure he cheated. It had something to do with that ice-cream. I was sure of it. I decided to find out what was going on; I wasn't going to let anyone pull a fast one on me.

It all started with the ice-cream man, Mr Peppi. The old fool had a van which he parked outside the school. He sold ice-cream, all different types. He had every flavour there is, and some that I had never heard of before.

He didn't like me very much. He told me off once. 'Go to the back of the queue,' he said. 'You pushed in.'

'Mind your own business, Pop,' I told him. 'Just hand over the ice-cream.'

'No,' he said. 'I won't serve you unless you go to the back.'

I went round to the back of the van, but I didn't get in the queue. I took out a nail and made a long scratch on his rotten old van. He had just had it painted. Peppi came and had a look. Tears came into his eyes. 'You are a bad boy,' he said. 'One day you will get into trouble. You think you are smart. One day you will be too smart.'

I just laughed and walked off. I knew he wouldn't do anything. He was too soft-hearted. He was always giving free ice-creams to kids that had no money. He felt sorry for poor people. The silly fool.

There were a lot of stories going round about that ice-cream. People said that it was good for you. Some kids said that it made you better when you were sick. One of the teachers called it 'Happy Ice-Cream'. I didn't believe it; it never made me happy.

All the same, there was something strange about it. Take Pimples Peterson for example. That wasn't his real name – I just called him that because he had a lot of pimples. Anyway, Peppi heard me calling Peterson 'Pimples'. 'You are a real mean boy,' he said. 'You are always picking on someone else, just because they are not like you.'

'Get lost, Peppi,' I said. 'Go and flog your ice-cream somewhere else.'

Peppi didn't answer me. Instead he spoke to Pimples. 'Here, eat this,' he told him. He handed Peterson an ice-cream. It was the biggest ice-cream I had ever seen. It was coloured purple. Peterson wasn't too sure about it. He didn't think he had enough money for such a big ice-cream.

'Go on,' said Mr Peppi. 'Eat it. I am giving it to you for nothing. It will get rid of your pimples.'

I laughed and laughed. Ice-cream doesn't get rid of pimples, it *gives* you pimples. Anyway, the next day when Peterson came to school he had no pimples. Not one. I couldn't believe it. The ice-cream had cured his pimples.

There were some other strange things that happened

too. There was a kid at the school who had a long nose. Boy, was it long. He looked like Pinocchio. When he blew it you could hear it a mile away. I called him 'Snozzle'. He didn't like being called Snozzle. He used to go red in the face when I said it, and that was every time that I saw him. He didn't say anything back – he was scared that I would punch him up.

Peppi felt sorry for Snozzle too. He gave him a small green ice-cream every morning, for nothing. What a jerk. He never gave me a free ice-cream.

You won't believe what happened but I swear it's true. Snozzle's nose began to grow smaller. Every day it grew a bit smaller. In the end it was just a normal nose. When it was the right size Peppi stopped giving him the green ice-creams.

I made up my mind to put a stop to this ice-cream business. Jerome Dadian had been eating ice-cream the day he got one hundred for Maths. It must have been the ice-cream making him smart. I wasn't going to have anyone doing as well as me. I was the smartest kid in the school, and that's the way I wanted it to stay. I wanted to get a look inside that ice-cream van to find out what was going on.

I knew where Peppi kept his van at night – he left it in a small lane behind his house. I waited until about eleven o'clock at night. Then I crept out of the house and down to Peppi's van. I took a crowbar, a bucket of sand, a torch and some bolt cutters with me.

There was no one around when I reached the van. I sprang the door open with the crowbar and shone my torch around inside. I had never seen so many tubs of ice-cream before. There was every flavour you could think of: there was apple and banana, cherry and mango, blackberry and watermelon and about fifty other flavours. Right at the end of the van were four bins with locks on them. I went over and had a look. It was just as I thought – these were his special flavours. Each one had writing on the top. This is what they said:

HAPPY ICE-CREAM for cheering people up.

NOSE ICE-CREAM for long noses.

PIMPLE ICE-CREAM for removing pimples.

SMART ICE-CREAM for smart alecs.

Now I knew his secret. That rat Dadian had been eating Smart Ice-cream; that's how he got one hundred for Maths. I knew there couldn't be anyone as clever as me. I decided to fix Peppi up once and for all. I took out the bolt cutters and cut the locks off the four bins; then I put sand into every bin in the van. Except for the Smart Ice-cream. I didn't put any sand in that.

I laughed to myself. Peppi wouldn't sell much ice-cream now. Not unless he started a new flavour – Sand Ice-cream. I looked at the Smart Ice-cream. I decided to eat some; it couldn't do any harm. Not that I needed it – I was already about as smart as you could get. Anyway, I gave it a try. I ate the lot. Once I started I couldn't stop. It tasted good. It was delicious.

I left the van and went home to bed, but I couldn't sleep. To tell the truth, I didn't feel too good. So I decided to write this. Then if any funny business has been going on you people will know what happened. I think I have made a mistake. I don't think Dadian did get any Smart Ice-Cream.

2

It iz the nekst day now. Somefing iz hapening to me. I don't feal quite az smart. I have bean trying to do a reel hard sum. It iz wun and wun. Wot duz wun and wun make? Iz it free or iz it for?

EHEE! HAAHA!

One-Shot Toothpaste

'I'm afraid this tooth will have to be filled,' said Mr Bin. 'It's badly decayed.'

Antonio's knees started to knock as he looked at the dentist's arm. He knew that Mr Bin was hiding a needle behind his back. 'Not an injection. Not that,' spluttered Antonio. But it was too late. Before he could say another word the numbing needle was doing its work.

Antonio could feel tears springing into his eyes. He stared helplessly out of the window at the huge, white tooth that was swinging in the breeze. On the side of it was written:

M. T. BIN

DENTIST

The needle seemed to be taking years to go in. Mr Bin held Antonio's mouth open with one hand and slowly pushed the plunger with the other. 'Try not to move,' he said. 'You're shaking like a leaf.'

At last it was over. The dreaded needle came out. 'Rinse,' ordered Mr Bin. Antonio took a mouthful of water from the glass and tried to spit it out but his mouth was numb and he dribbled most of it down his T-shirt.

Antonio fought back the tears as Mr Bin started up the drill. He mustn't cry. It wouldn't be right for a thirteen-year-old boy to cry at the dentist's. He stared out of the window again at the giant tooth sign and opened up his mouth.

What are you going to do for a job when you leave school?' asked Mr Bin.

'A dustman,' answered Antonio. 'I've always wanted to be a dustman.'

Mr Bin put down the drill with an amazed look on his face. 'A dustman. Did you say a dustman? Now isn't that funny. I always wanted to be a dustman when I was a boy.'

'Well, how come you ended up a dentist then?' Antonio asked.

The dentist looked around the room and then went over and shut the door. He spoke in a very soft voice. 'If you promise not to tell anyone, I'll tell you the story, seeing that you want to be a dustman too. But you must give me your solemn promise not to tell any other person. Not a soul. Do you promise?'

Antonio nodded. He couldn't say a word because Mr Bin had started drilling away inside his mouth. He closed his eyes and listened.

'When I was a boy,' said Mr Bin, 'I loved looking in rubbish bins. I just couldn't walk past one without opening it. I mean there are really some wonderful things to be found in the garbage.

'I once found a dead pig's head in our neighbour's bin. I took it home and put it on an ants' nest. They ate all the flesh off and I was left with just the skull. Next I drilled a hole in the top of it and gave it to my mother for a sugar container. She liked it so much that she never used it. She hid it away in a special place and then forgot where it was.

'All the bins in our street had something interesting about them, but Old Monty's rubbish was the strangest. I used to look in his garbage tin every Wednesday and Friday and it was always filled with the same thing. Empty toothpaste tubes. Dozens and dozens of them. They weren't your everyday tubes either. They always had the same label: ONE SHOT TOOTHPASTE was written on every one.

'I could never work out why one old man who lived all alone would use so many tubes of toothpaste. He couldn't have spent all day cleaning his teeth. Or I should say tooth, for he only had one fusty, old, green tooth right in the middle of his mouth. In fact his tooth was so scungy that I am sure he had never cleaned it since the day it first grew.

'I couldn't stop thinking about old Monty and his empty toothpaste tubes. I just had to find out what was going on. I knew it would be no good trying to talk to him because he hated children (actually, I think he hated everyone). If you said "good morning" to him he would just tell you to clear off. In the end I decided to sneak up to his house at night and peek in the window.'

2

'One night, after my parents had gone to bed, I crept up to the side of Monty's house. It was a ramshackle, tumble-down old joint with a rusty tin roof and cobwebs all over the windows. It was a dark night and a cold wind was blowing. I was covered in goose bumps, but they weren't from the cold. I was scared stiff.

'I stumbled around until I found a window which had a chink between the curtains. Then I stood on tip-toe and peered inside. All was black inside and at first I couldn't see anything. After a minute or two, however, I noticed something eerie, something strange, something I had never seen before. Teeth. I saw teeth.

'About twenty sets of teeth were glowing palely in the dark. They were so white that they shone like tiny, dim light globes in the blackness. They hovered in the air at various heights above the floor like fierce kites on strings.

'They were opening and shutting and waving around as if they belonged to invisible heads. That was when I realised the teeth did have heads. And bodies. I just couldn't see them because it was dark. The teeth were so clean that they gave off their own light.

'There were large pointed teeth and tiny, sharp ones.

There was every type of cruncher and chomper that you could think of except one. None of them belonged to people. There were no human teeth. I could tell that at once.

Just then someone lit a candle and an amazing sight met my eyes. I saw a room filled with animals. There were rabbits, dogs, kangaroos, wallabies and cats. Each one was in its own cage and each one possessed the whitest pair of teeth I had ever seen. But the poor things – they all looked so sad. I could tell they hated being kept in those small cages. And even more, they hated what was about to happen next.

'Monty strode across the room with an evil grin on his face and a candle in his hand. "Tooth time, boys," he croaked. I could almost feel the poor animals shiver as he said it. He put the candle on a table and went over to a large cupboard and opened it. Inside were thousands of tubes of toothpaste. He took down one of the tubes. "Number 52A," he said. "Let's see if this is the mix that will make my fortune."

'Monty went over to the cage of a small rabbit and pressed a button. A red light flashed inside the cage and the rabbit poked its head out of a hole in the wire. The rabbit screwed up its nose and bared its teeth. Monty put some of the toothpaste on a brush and scrubbed away at them. I could tell that the toothpaste tasted terrible. When Monty had finished he threw a dirty old carrot to the rabbit but the poor thing couldn't eat.

It was too busy trying to get the nasty taste out of its mouth.

'This was terrible. This was monstrous. How cruel. That mean old man was cleaning the teeth of animals with some foul-tasting toothpaste. He was trying it out on them to see if it was any good. I didn't think of my own safety. I didn't think of anything except those frightened creatures. I raced around to the front door and banged on it as hard as I could. "Let me in," I screamed. "Let me in and let those animals go."'

3

'The door swung open and there stood Monty, grinning at me with his fusty, green tooth. He seemed pleased to see me. "Just what I need," he said. "A cheeky brat of a kid. Come in, boy, and welcome."

'I burst into the house and ran into the room where the animals were kept. "What are you doing?" I yelled. "Why are you cleaning these animals' teeth?"

'"I am inventing One Shot Toothpaste," grinned Monty. "And I am nearly there."

'"What's One Shot Toothpaste?" I shouted.

'"It's toothpaste that you only use once in your life. One go and you never need to clean your teeth again. Everyone will buy it once it's invented. All those brats who won't clean their teeth. Their parents will all buy it and I will be rich. Every time I make a new batch I have to try it out. That's why I have the animals."

'"Let the animals go," I said. "It's cruel. Try your rotten old toothpaste out on yourself."

'"I couldn't do that," said Monty. "It tastes horrible. But now I don't need the animals any more. I have you." He looked at me with a sneaky smile and pointed to an empty cage.

'Before I had a chance to move he jumped on me and grabbed me with his skinny hands. He was thin but very strong. We rolled over and over on the floor and crashed into the cupboard. Hundreds of tubes of toothpaste fell out of the cupboard and showered all over us. As we struggled on the floor many of the tubes burst open and squirted long worms of toothpaste into the air. Soon we were both covered in every colour of toothpaste you could think of. They all got mixed up and the different types smeared into horrible, smelly puddles.

'Monty grabbed the toothbrush and dipped it into the mixture. "See how you like this, boy," he hissed as he tried to shove the brush into my mouth.

'There was no way I was going to let him put mixed-up toothpastes on my teeth. I pushed Monty backwards and he fell against the wall with a grunt. He was winded and lay there gasping for breath. "Have a bit of your own medicine," I said. I plunged the toothbrush into Monty's mouth and brushed at his fusty old green tooth.'

4

'He didn't like it. Not one bit. He rolled around on the floor screaming and yelling and holding his hands up to his neck. It must have tasted foul.

'Then something happened I will never forget. Monty's tooth started to grow. It swelled up and started to stick out of his mouth. Soon it was as big as his head. A whopping, big green, fusty tooth. And as it grew Monty started to shrink. It was just as if the tooth was sucking his innards out. Monty shrivelled up like a slowly collapsing balloon as the tooth grew bigger and bigger. Soon it was bigger than he was. It wasn't Monty and a tooth. It was a tooth and Monty.

'The tooth continued to feed on Monty until it was as big as a full-grown man and he was only the size of a pea on the end of it. Then there was a small "pop" and he was gone altogether. The super tooth lay there alone on the floor.

'I was in a daze. I didn't know what to do. I staggered over to the cages and let the animals out one at a time. Each one bounded out of the door in a panic. The last to go was a big kangaroo. The poor thing was in such a fright that it knocked over the table with the candle on it. In a flash the curtains caught on fire and the room was alight. The animals had all fled into the night, so I grabbed the huge tooth and lugged it out onto the lawn. The house burned to the ground before the fire brigade could even get there.'

5

'And that,' said the dentist to Antonio, 'is the end of the story. And your filling is finished. It didn't hurt much, now, did it?'

'No,' said Antonio, 'I didn't feel a thing. 'But what happened to the giant tooth?'

Mr Bin looked up at the large tooth swinging in the breeze outside with

M. T. BIN

DENTIST

written on it and said, 'That is a secret which I can't tell even you.'

Antonio walked outside and looked at the large tooth sign. It was painted white but on one corner the paint was peeling off. Underneath he could see that it was a fusty green colour. He turned round and walked home, shaking his head as he went.

Mr Bin went back into his surgery. A small girl was sitting in the chair crying. 'No needles, please,' she whimpered.

'What are you going to do for a job when you grow up?' asked Mr Bin.

'A ballet dancer,' said the little girl.

Mr Bin put down the needle with an amazed look on his face. 'A ballet dancer. Did you say a ballet dancer? Now isn't that funny? I always wanted to be a ballet dancer when I was a boy.'

'Well, how come you ended up a dentist?' the girl asked.

Mr Bin looked around the room and then went over and shut the door. He spoke in a very soft voice. 'If you promise not to tell anyone, I'll tell you the story,' he said as he picked up the needle.

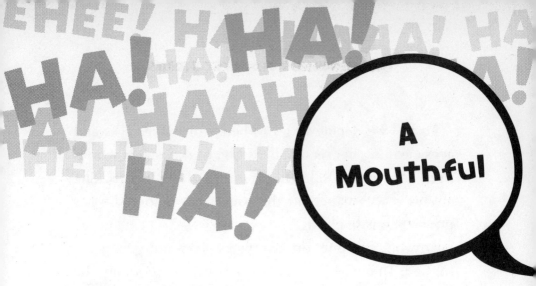

A Mouthful

Parents are embarrassing.

Take my dad. Every time a friend comes to stay the night he does something that makes my face go red. Now don't get me wrong. He is a terrific Dad. I love him but sometimes I think he will never grow up.

He loves playing practical jokes.

This behaviour first starts the night Anna comes to sleep over.

Unknown to me, Dad sneaks into my room and puts Doona our cat on the spare bed. Doona loves sleeping on beds. What cat doesn't?

Next Dad unwraps a little package that he has bought at the magic shop.

Do you know what is in it? Can you believe this? It is a little piece of brown plastic cat poo. Pretend cat poo. Anyway, he puts this piece of cat poo on Anna's pillow and pulls up the blankets. Then he tiptoes out and closes the door.

I do not know any of this is happening. Anna and I are sitting up late watching videos. We eat chips covered in sauce and drink two whole bottles of Diet Coke.

Finally we decide to go to bed. Anna takes ages and ages cleaning her teeth. She is one of those kids who is right into health. She has a thing about germs. She always places paper on the toilet seat before she sits down. She is *so* clean.

Anyway, she puts on her tracky daks and gets ready for bed. Then she pulls back the blankets. Suddenly she sees the bit of plastic cat poo. 'Ooh, ooh, ooh,' she screams. 'Oh look, disgusting. Foul. Look what the cat's done on my pillow.'

Suddenly Dad bursts into the room. 'What's up, girls?' he says with a silly grin on his face. 'What's all the fuss about?'

Anna is pulling a terrible face. 'Look,' she says in horror as she points at the pillow.

Dad goes over and examines the plastic poo. 'Don't let a little thing like that worry you,' he says. He picks up the plastic poo and pops it into his mouth. He gives a grin. 'D'licioush,' he says through clenched teeth.

'Aargh,' screams Anna. She rushes over to the window and throws up chips, sauce and Diet Coke. Then she looks at Dad in disgust.

Dad is a bit taken aback at Anna being sick. 'It's okay,' he says, taking the plastic poo out of his mouth. 'It's not real.' Dad gives a laugh and off he goes. And off goes Anna. She decides that she wants to go home to her own house. And I don't blame her.

'Dad,' I yell after Anna is gone. 'I am never speaking to you again.'

'Don't be such a sook,' he says. 'It's only a little joke.'

It's always the same. Whenever a friend comes over to stay Dad plays practical jokes. We have fake hands in the rubbish, exploding drinks, pepper in the food, short-sheeted beds and Dracula's blood seeping out of Dad's mouth. Some of the kids think it's great. They wish their Dad was like that.

But I hate it. I just wish he was normal.

He plays tricks on Bianca.

And Yasmin.

And Nga.

And Karla.

None of them go home like Anna. But each time I am so embarrassed.

And now I am worried.

Cynthia is coming to stay. She is the school captain. She is beautiful. She is smart. Everyone wants to be her friend. And now she is sleeping over at our house.

'Dad,' I say. 'No practical jokes. Cynthia is very mature. Her father would never play practical jokes. She might not understand.'

'No worries,' says Dad.

Cynthia arrives but we do not watch videos. We slave away on our English homework. We plan our speeches for the debate in the morning. We go over our parts in the school play. After all that we go out and practise shooting goals because Cynthia is captain of the netball team. Every now and then I pop into the bedroom to check for practical jokes. It is best to be on the safe side.

We also do the washing-up because Cynthia offers – yes *offers* – to do it.

Finally it is time for bed. Cynthia changes into her nightie in the bathroom and then joins me in the bedroom. 'The cat's on my bed,' she says. 'But it doesn't matter. I like cats.' She pulls back the blankets.

And screams. 'Aargh. Cat poo. Filthy cat poo on my pillow.' She yells and yells and yells.

Just then Dad bursts into the room with a silly grin on his face. He goes over and looks at the brown object on the pillow. 'Don't let a little thing like that worry you,' he says. He picks it up and pops it into his mouth. But this time he does not give a grin. His face freezes over.

'Are you looking for this?' I say.

I hold up the bit of plastic poo that Dad had hidden under the blankets earlier that night.

Dad looks at the cat.

Then he rushes over to the window and is sick.

Cynthia and I laugh like mad.

We do love a good joke.

Cow Dung Custard

A lot of kids have nicknames. Like Mouse, or Bluey, or Freckles. Those sort of nicknames are okay. My nickname was the Cow Dung Kid. Can you imagine that? The Cow Dung Kid. What a name to get stuck with.

It was all my father's fault. Him and his vegetable garden.

Don't get me wrong, though. Dad was a good bloke. A real good bloke. He brought me up all on his own. I didn't have a mother so he can take all the credit for the way I turned out.

Dad loved to grow vegetables. His vegetable garden was his pride and joy. Every year he went into a competition. He always won lots of prizes for the best vegetables. He won prizes for the biggest pumpkins and the juiciest tomatoes. He grew the biggest and best vegies in the whole town. He once grew a pumpkin that was so big it took four men to lift it. His peas were as big as golf balls and his beans were as long as your arm. No kidding.

The whole yard was filled up with vegetables. He had long rows of them. Every row had a little sign at the end. On each sign was the name of the vegetable that was growing. And the batch number. This batch number told which type of manure he had used.

Batch twenty-four meant three shovels of cow dung and one shovel of horse droppings. Batch fourteen was two shovels of horse droppings, one shovel of sheep droppings and three shovels of pig droppings.

Dad had every type of manure that you could think of. He had duck and goose. He had kangaroo and wombat. He had bat and emu. He even had snake droppings.

And guess who had to help him collect it. You are not wrong. It was me.

2

Every weekend I had to go and collect cow dung. Every weekend without fail. We lived right in the middle of the town. I had to get a wheelbarrow and walk out to the country. Then I had to fill it up with cow dung. And it had to be fresh. 'Nice and sloppy,' Dad would say. 'Make sure that it's nice and sloppy.'

Then I had to walk back through the town, with a wheelbarrow full of sloppy cow dung. I wasn't on my own, though. Oh no. I had company. About five thousand flies came with me. They were like a black cloud following me along the street.

Everyone could see me. It felt like the whole town was watching me and my flies.

I got my nickname of the Cow Dung Kid on one of these trips. It was on Christmas Day. Dad's boss at work grew vegetables too. But they were never as good as Dad's. He didn't have a son to go and get manure. So Dad had a bright idea. He decided to give the boss a surprise. A Christmas present. He wanted me to go and get manure for his boss. 'Just tip it out and leave it for him to find,' said Dad. 'He will be tickled pink. I might even get a rise out of this.'

'But Dad,' I pleaded. 'Not on Christmas Day. Everyone will be looking. I can't do it. I just can't.'

He gave me one of his sorrowful looks. He shook his head and said, 'After all I've done for you, Greg. And you won't even help me out with one little thing.' I gave in and went. I didn't want to spend all Christmas feeling guilty.

I set out at the crack of dawn. I didn't even open my presents. I wanted to get it over and done with before people were out of bed.

But it was no use. All the kids in town were up early. They followed me and my cow dung along the street. They were all on new bikes and scooters that they had got for Christmas.

They thought it was a great joke. 'Look what Santa brought Greg,' shouted some bright spark. Everyone laughed. As I went along, more and more kids started following me. After a while there were about fifty of them.

Someone else yelled out, 'King of the Flies. Greg is King of the Flies.'

'The Cow Dung Kid,' said another voice. Another laugh went up. They all started yelling it out. 'Cow Dung Kid, Cow Dung Kid.' It was embarrassing, I can tell you that.

I ran faster and faster. Some of the cow dung fell out. But I didn't care. I just kept running. At last I reached the boss's house. I tipped out the cow dung on his doorstep. Right against the door. That way he would get a surprise when he opened the door. And Dad would get all the glory.

Anyway, that's how I got the name of the Cow Dung Kid. And after all that trouble Dad's boss wasn't even grateful. He said something about cow dung all over his carpet. There is just no understanding some people. He didn't even say thanks.

3

Flies, flies, flies. They hung around our house all day and all night. It was the smell of the manure. The smell attracted them. There were flies everywhere; they came down the chimney and under the doors. People had no trouble finding our house. If anyone asked where we lived they were always told the same thing. 'Just stop at the house with the flies.'

The neighbours didn't like the flies. They were always going crook. So Dad gave them vegetables to keep them quiet. He gave them giant carrots and potatoes. They liked them so much that they only complained about the really bad days. This usually happened when Dad made a very smelly batch, like batch seventy-two.

Dad kept each batch of manure in a large rubbish bin. He had at least two hundred of them in the back yard. The worse they smelt, the more flies hung around them. The ones with the really bad smell were kept down near the back fence, away from the house. Mr Farley lived in the house at the back. He didn't like us much – he never spoke to us. He was a pretty crabby bloke. I could never figure out why.

The trouble all started with batch seventy-two. It was the strongest batch that Dad had ever made. It had bat droppings, rabbit droppings and wombat droppings. There was also a bit of lizard and potaroo. But the main ingredient was cow dung.

Dad also threw in some rotten pumpkins. They were bright yellow. He added water and stirred the mix up. It all went smooth and yellow. 'It's like custard,' I said. 'Cow-dung custard.'

It was a smelly batch, very smelly. It was the worst one that Dad had made. 'Good,' said Dad, 'The more it smells, the better it works. I'll grow some great potatoes with this batch.' He took out a pen and wrote Cow Dung Custard on the side of the bin. The flies were already starting to gather so I decided to go inside out of the way. The smell was bad and it was getting worse.

I could smell batch seventy-two as I went to bed, even though it was at the bottom of the yard. I knew there was going to be trouble with the neighbours over this. Batch seventy-two looked like custard. But it sure didn't smell like it.

4

The next morning I woke early. I knew that something was wrong. I could hardly breathe and I felt sick. It was the smell of the Cow Dung Custard. It was the most terrible smell I had ever come across. It was so bad that you could almost see it. Every breath was painful.

I put a handkerchief over my mouth and rushed to the window. All the neighbours were up. They were outside our house. Nobody could sleep. They were all dressed in their pyjamas, and they were all holding handkerchiefs over their noses. Some of them were making groaning noises. They were trying to shout. Some people were waving their fists at the house. They were all mad at us.

I went and woke Dad up. He has a poor sense of smell. He was the only person in the street who was still asleep. He looked out of the window. 'Amazing,' he said. 'Amazing. Look at that. There is not one fly to be seen.' He didn't even notice the people – he was looking for flies. I couldn't believe it. But what he said was true. There were no flies hanging around. They were all dead. The ground was covered in dead flies. They were like a black carpet all over the lawn.

The smell was so bad that it had killed all the flies. 'You had better do something,' I told him. 'That stuff might be dangerous. And everyone is mad at us. The neighbours are all angry.' He looked out of the window. Everyone was running away. The smell was so awful that they couldn't stand it.

'You're right,' said Dad. 'You stay here. I will go and see what I can do.' He walked down to the bottom of the yard. I could hear the bodies of the dead flies crunching under his feet. I was glad he had told me to stay inside. I think I would have fainted if I had gone any closer to that smell. It was lucky for Dad that he couldn't smell very well.

I watched him out of the window. He drove our old truck into the back yard. He tried to lift the Cow Dung Custard onto it, but it was too heavy. He had to tip it out into a lot of buckets. Then he lifted them up onto the truck. After he had put all the buckets onto the truck he came back to the house. He had yellow stuff all over his dressing gown. 'Don't come in,' I shouted. 'Please don't come in.'

He yelled at me through the window, 'I'm going down to the sea with it. I can't think of anywhere else to put it. You stay here, Greg.' He needn't have worried. There was no way I was going anywhere near that Cow Dung Custard.

Then I noticed something terrible. Dad's hair had

fallen out. He was completely bald. He did not have one hair left on his head – even his eyebrows had fallen out. That Cow Dung Custard was strong. Too strong.

Dad jumped into the truck and drove out the front gate. I watched him drive down the road. There wasn't a person in sight. They were all inside with their heads under their pillows. As he went by the dogs in the street ran off yelping with their tails between their legs.

5

Dad tipped the Cow Dung Custard over a cliff and into the sea. For the next two weeks there were dead fish floating around everywhere. The town we lived in is called Lakes Entrance. It is a fishing town. All the fishermen were cross with Dad, for killing the fish.

The people in the street were mad at him too. The smell hung around for weeks. Dad took a lot of vegetables around to them, trying to make it up. Mr Jackson lived next door. He told Dad to go away, 'I don't want your vegetables,' he said. 'And I don't want your manure, or your smells. Why don't you go and live out on a farm? Then you can be as smelly as you want.'

He had a point. I was getting sick of it too. The kids at school called me the Cow Dung Kid. Everyone knew us and where we lived. All the houses in the street had 'For Sale' notices in the front yard. No one wanted to live near us, and I didn't blame them.

'Listen, Dad,' I said. 'Let's go and live somewhere

else – on a farm. Then I won't have to go and get manure. You will have all you want. And there won't be any neighbours to complain.'

Dad looked sad. He nodded his bald head. 'I would like to move to a farm, Greg. But we can't afford it. Farms cost a lot of money, and we're broke. We will have to stay here. But I will do one thing for you – I'll get rid of the smell. I'll find a way to stop the manure smelling. It will be called Batch One Hundred. Batch One Hundred will have no smell. And it's the only one I will use.'

I went off shaking my head. Poor old Dad. He meant well. But I knew he couldn't do it. How could anyone make up a batch of manure that didn't smell?

Dad tried everything he could think of to make Batch One Hundred. He put in flowers. He put in soap. He put in perfume. But he just couldn't stop the manure smelling.

Our house was as smelly as ever. Even the school bus wouldn't come down our street any more. One good thing did happen – Dad's hair started growing back. It was as thick and black as it had always been.

Then one day he did it. He made Batch One Hundred. You couldn't smell a thing. It wasn't like the Cow Dung Custard – you didn't even know it was there. I was rapt. I thought our problems were over.

But I was wrong. Batch One Hundred had other problems. It was the worst one ever.

6

People couldn't smell Batch One Hundred, but the flies could. Flies can smell better than people can. It's something like a dog whistle. Dogs can hear them and people can't. Well, flies could smell Batch One Hundred when people couldn't.

The flies came in their thousands. In their millions. The air was thick with them. The sound of their buzzing was terrible to hear. They crawled all over your face, and into your nose and ears. They were so thick that you couldn't see the sun. After a while it started to grow dark, and it was only lunch time.

Dad and I were in the back yard. After a while we couldn't see the house, or the back fence. The flies were too thick. I had never seen anything like it before. There were so many flies in the air that I couldn't find Dad. 'Greg,' he shouted. 'Go back to the house. Quickly. This is dangerous.' I couldn't see where he was. I couldn't see where anything was.

I looked down at the ground. There were so many flies in the air that I couldn't see my feet. I had to squint to stop them getting into my eyes. I started to walk slowly to where I thought the house was. I bumped into something large. It was the truck. I could tell what it was by the feel of it. I was going the wrong way. I turned around and tried a different direction. Then I heard Dad's voice. I could just make it out over the buzzing of the flies. 'Greg, Greg, this way,' he called.

I followed the sound of his voice. I walked very slowly to make sure I didn't bump into anything. At last I reached Dad. I couldn't see him but I could feel him. He was standing on the door step.

'Get ready,' he shouted. 'I'm going to open the door. When I say "go", rush in as quick as you can. I'll slam the door after us.'

'Go,' he yelled. We both fell into the room. I couldn't see anything, but I heard the door shut with a bang. 'Put on the light,' said Dad.

I switched on the light. The room was full of flies, but it wasn't as bad as outside. At least we could see. I looked at the window. It was black. Millions of flies were crawling all over it. 'Quick,' said Dad. 'Block up all the cracks under the doors. I'll cover up the chimney. We've got to stop them coming in.'

I started stuffing towels and rags under the door. Dad covered up the fireplace with a piece of cardboard. When we had all the cracks blocked up he found some fly spray. We had plenty of fly spray in the house – it was something we used a lot of. It took three cans to kill them all.

We ran upstairs to look out of the top windows. They were all black too. We couldn't see outside at all. We were trapped in our own house by millions and millions of flies.

7

Dad was upset. 'This is bad, Greg,' he said. 'Very bad. Batch One Hundred is much too strong. Every fly in the country must be here, and it's all my fault. We've got to get rid of those flies.'

Just then the phone rang. Dad picked it up. It was Mr Jackson. He was shouting. I could hear every word even though the flies were making such a loud noise outside. 'You've done it this time, Moffit,' he yelled. 'The whole town is blacked out with flies. Nobody can get out of their house. It's pitch black in the middle of the day. It's all your fault, you and your manure. You'd better do something, and quick. You brought the flies here. Now you get rid of them.' The phone went dead. He had hung up.

'What can we do?' said Dad. 'How can we get rid of them?' He hung his head in his hands. The poor bloke – I really felt sorry for him. We both sat there thinking. Outside the flies were getting thicker and thicker.

'Fly spray,' I said.

'No good,' he told me. 'There isn't enough fly spray in the world to kill this lot. We need something stronger. Something really powerful.'

We sat there looking at each other. We both thought of the answer at the same time. 'Cow Dung Custard,' we shouted together.

'That's it,' said Dad. 'The smell is so strong that it kills flies. I'll mix up a special batch.'

'But what about the smell, Dad?' I asked.

'We can't help the smell. This is an emergency. The whole town is blacked out with flies. We have to do something.'

'But how can we make it?' I asked him. 'You can't see a thing out there. You can hardly breathe. The flies get into your nose and mouth. You wouldn't be able to make the Cow Dung Custard. It's as black as pitch.'

We both fell silent again. We just sat and looked at each other. Then Dad had an idea. 'The bee-keeper's outfit,' he yelled. 'I can wear the bee-keeper's outfit.' Once Dad used to keep bees. He still had the outfit for smoking out the bees. It had a hat and net to stop the bees from stinging him.

'What about me? You can't do it on your own. You'll have to make a heck of a lot. I'll have to come too.'

'Your wet suit. You can wear your wet suit. And put on the goggles. You can wear the snorkel to stop the flies getting into your mouth.'

We dressed up in our outfits. Dad had his hat and bee net. I had my wet suit, goggles and snorkel. I felt silly. But, as Dad said, this was an emergency. We tied a rope to each other so that we didn't become lost. Then we walked over to the door and opened it.

8

A million flies poured into the room. Everything went black. The light was on but we couldn't even see it.

I felt a pull on the rope. Dad was moving out into the back yard. I couldn't see him so I just followed the rope. The flies swirled around us in one huge, black cloud.

We walked slowly. We didn't want to fall over. At last we reached the back fence. I felt Dad's hand on my arm. He was shouting at me. It was difficult to hear him because of the loud buzzing of the flies. 'Help me tip over Batch One Hundred,' he yelled. 'Then we will empty another fifteen bins. We will need at least sixteen bins of Cow Dung Custard to kill all these flies. They must be covering the whole town.'

We struggled over to Batch One Hundred. The flies were all trying to get to it. They were so thick that it was like walking through a river. I plunged my arm through the sea of flies and pushed over the bin. A billion flies rose into the air as it tipped over. The buzz was so loud that it hurt my ears, and the wind from their wings blew me over.

We stood up and felt our way to the other bins. It took a long time to push them all over and empty out the manure. In the end we had sixteen empty bins. I felt Dad's hand on my arm again. 'We will have to untie the rope,' he shouted. 'It will take a long time to mix up sixteen bins of Cow Dung Custard. We have to hurry. The flies are getting thicker. Every fly in Australia will be here soon.'

'I'm scared, Dad,' I told him. 'I might get lost if you untie the rope.'

'Feel your way along the fence,' he said. 'When you get to the manure heap try to fill up the wheelbarrow with cow dung. Put ten shovelsful into each bin. I'll put in the rest of the mixture.' His voice was shaking; I knew that he was scared too. So I undid the rope and followed the fence to the manure heap.

It took a long time, but at last I managed to put cow dung in every bin. The flies kept bumping into my goggles – it felt as if someone was throwing rice at me. Every now and then I bumped into Dad. He was tipping all sorts of things into the bins. Once he dropped a rotten pumpkin onto my foot.

Then something wonderful happened. A shocking stink filled the air. It was the first batch of Cow Dung Custard. 'Hooray,' I shouted. I was really happy even though the smell was so bad. I didn't know whether it was working. I couldn't tell if it was killing the flies. There seemed to be just as many as ever.

Dad came over to me. 'Go back to the house,' he yelled. 'If this works there are going to be dead flies everywhere. You might get buried if you stay here.'

'No way,' I told him. 'I'm staying with you.'

9

After a while we had two bins of Cow Dung Custard mixed up. The stink grew stronger and stronger. I felt ill, but I had to keep going. We made one bit at a time. By the time we had made ten bins the smell was so strong we had to stop.

'We can't go on,' said Dad. 'I'm going to faint, if I don't get away from this smell.'

'Hey!' I suddenly shouted. 'I can see you.' I could just make out the shape of Dad in his bee net. There were not so many flies in the air. The Cow Dung Custard was working – it was killing some of the flies.

I looked at the ground. It was covered in flies. Some of them were dead, but some were lying on their backs kicking their legs in the air. There was a thick carpet of flies all over the lawn. Then I felt my head. My hair was full of dead flies. They were starting to fall down out of the sky. It was raining flies.

'Quick,' said Dad. 'Back to the house. We will be buried alive if we don't hurry.'

We ran back to the house. Flies were pouring down all around us. The dead bodies were so deep that we couldn't move properly. They came up to my ankles and then up to my knees. Dad reached the door first. He pushed it open and fell inside.

'Help!' I screamed. 'I'm stuck.' The flies were up to my armpits and they were still falling. I was scared out of my wits. I didn't want to drown in a sea of flies. I couldn't move backwards or forwards.

Dad still had the rope wrapped around his waist. He started to undo it. 'Quick, I'm going under,' I yelled. The flies were getting deeper and deeper – they were nearly up to my mouth. He threw the rope over and I grabbed the end of it. But it was too late. The dead flies were right over my head. I was buried under the bodies of the flies.

It was lucky that I had the goggles and snorkel on. The snorkel poked above the pile of flies. It enabled me to breathe, but I couldn't see a thing. Everything was black. Then I felt strong hands pulling me up. It was Dad. He had followed the rope and dug down to me. He dragged me across the top of the flies and into the house. Then he slammed the door.

10

It was much better in the house. The flies were only knee deep. At least we could walk around. We went upstairs as quickly as we could and looked out of the window. It was still raining flies, but it was starting to ease off. At last it stopped. Every fly was dead. The Cow Dung Custard had killed the lot. The smell of it was terrible.

Our place was on the top of a hill. We could see the whole town. Every house was covered in dead flies. They covered the road and the cars, the trees and the gardens. It looked just like a snow-covered village, but with black snow. There was not a person in sight. Everyone was trapped inside their houses. The whole town was silent. And over it all hung the terrible smell of Cow Dung Custard.

Dad looked at me. 'Good grief, Greg,' he said. 'All of

your hair has gone.'

I felt the top of my head. It was smooth. I was as bald as a badger. I rushed to the mirror. 'Oh no,' I groaned. 'Not that. Not bald.' Then I looked at Dad. He was bald again too. All of his new hair had fallen out.

'It's the Cow Dung Custard,' I said. 'It's so strong that it makes hair fall out.'

I looked out of the window again. It was still very quiet, but four or five people were out. They were trying to clear the flies away from their front doors. It was hard work – they were up to their armpits in flies. I looked at them more closely. There was something strange about them but I couldn't work out what it was. Then I got a shock. They were all bald. I knew there was going to be big trouble over this.

A bit later we heard the sound of a motor. It sounded like a tractor, but it wasn't. It was a bulldozer. It was clearing the streets. It pushed the flies to the side of the road in huge banks. Behind the bulldozer was a police car. They came slowly up our street. People were following them, lots of bald people. Men, women and children. They were angry. They were mad. They were yelling and screaming at us.

The bulldozer stopped at our house. It turned around and came through our garden. It cleared a path up to the front door; then it stopped. A bald policeman stepped down from it. He had a handkerchief tied around his nose to stop the smell. He came into the house without knocking. 'Quick,' he said. 'Get into the police car. I'll have to get you out of here before the mob gets you. I don't know what they will do if they get their hands on you. They might tear you to pieces.' He was worried – very worried. So was I.

He pushed us into the car and started driving down the street. Crowds of bald people surrounded the car. They threw things at the car and tried to open the doors. They wanted to pull us out. Some even threw handfuls of flies at the car.

I could see why they were mad. Everyone was bald, even the dogs and cats. Not one person in the town had a hair left anywhere on their body.

In the end the police got us safely through the town. They took us down to Melbourne, which was a long way away. Then they let us go. Dad and I were both upset. We knew one thing for sure – we could never go back to Lakes Entrance again.

11

There was a big fuss about the whole thing. It was in all the papers and on the TV. Dad and I changed our names so that nobody could find us. Then it all died down and people started to forget about it. There was a shortage of wigs in Australia for a while. But after a couple of months everybody's hair grew back. As time passed people started to think it was funny.

I'm writing this next to the swimming pool on our

farm. Dad is out the front cleaning our Rolls Royce. Things worked out quite well for us in the end. Dad made a lot of money out of an invention. It's yellow stuff for getting rid of hair. People buy it in tubes. They put it on their legs. It works really well and it smells lovely.

It's called CDC Hair Remover. Everybody likes it. They think it's wonderful. But nobody knows what CDC stands for.

Licked

Tomorrow when Dad calms down I'll own up. Tell him the truth. He might laugh. He might cry. He might strangle me. But I have to put him out of his misery.

I like my dad. He takes me fishing. He gives me arm wrestles in front of the fire on cold nights. He plays Scrabble instead of watching the news. He tries practical jokes on me. And he keeps his promises. Always.

But he has two faults. Bad faults. One is to do with flies. He can't stand them. If there's a fly in the room he has to kill it. He won't use fly spray because of the ozone layer so he chases them with a fly swat. He races around the house swiping and swatting like a mad thing. He won't stop until the fly is flat. Squashed. Squished – sometimes still squirming on the end of the fly swat.

He's a dead-eye shot. He hardly ever misses. When his old fly swat was almost worn out I bought him a nice new yellow one for his birthday. It wasn't yellow for long. It soon had bits of fly smeared all over it.

It's funny, the different colours that squashed flies have inside them. Mostly it is black or brown. But often there are streaks of runny red stuff and sometimes bits of blue. The wings flash like diamonds if you hold them up to the light. But mostly the wings fall off unless they are stuck to the swat with a bit of squashed innards.

2

Chasing flies is Dad's first fault. His second one is table manners. He is mad about manners.

And it is always my manners that are the matter.

'Andrew,' he says. 'Don't put your elbows on the table.'

'Don't talk with your mouth full.'

'Don't lick your fingers.'

'Don't dunk your biscuit in the coffee.'

This is the way he goes on every meal time. He has a thing about flies and a thing about manners.

Anyway, to get back to the story. One day Dad is peeling the potatoes for tea. I am looking for my fifty cents that rolled under the table about a week ago. Mum is cutting up the cabbage and talking to Dad. They do not know that I am there. It is a very important meal because Dad's boss, Mr Spinks, is coming for tea. Dad never stops going on about my manners when someone comes for tea.

'You should stop picking on Andrew at tea time,' says Mum.

'I don't,' says Dad.

'Yes you do,' says Mum. 'It's always "don't do this, don't do that". You'll give the boy a complex.' I have never heard of a complex before but I guess that it is something awful like pimples.

'Tonight,' says Mum. 'I want you to go for the whole meal without telling Andrew off once.'

'Easy,' says Dad.

'Try hard,' says Mum, 'Promise me that you won't get cross with him.'

Dad looks at her for a long time. 'Okay,' he says. 'It's a deal. I won't say one thing about his manners. But you're not allowed to either. What's good for me is good for you.'

'Shake,' says Mum. They shake hands and laugh.

I find the fifty cents and sneak out. I take a walk down the street to spend it before tea. Dad has promised not to tell me off at tea time. I think about how I can make him crack. It should be easy. I will slurp my soup. He hates that. He will tell me off. He might even yell. I just know that he can't go for the whole meal without going crook. 'This is going to be fun,' I say to myself.

3

That night Mum sets the table with the new table-cloth. And the best knives and forks. And the plates that I am not allowed to touch. She puts out serviettes in little rings. All of this means that it is an important meal. We don't usually use serviettes.

Mr Spinks comes in his best suit. He wears gold glasses and he frowns a lot. I can tell that he doesn't like children. You can always tell when adults don't like kids. They smile at you with their lips but not with their eyes.

Anyway, we sit down to tea. I put my secret weapon on the floor under the table. I'm sure that I can make Dad crack without using it. But it is there if all else fails.

The first course is soup and bread rolls. I make loud slurping noises with the soup. No one says anything about it. I make the slurping noises longer and louder. They go on and on and on. It sounds like someone has pulled the plug out of the bath. Dad clears his throat but doesn't say anything.

I try something different. I dip my bread in the soup and make it soggy. Then I hold it high above my head and drop it down into my mouth. I catch it with a loud slopping noise. I try again with an even bigger bit. This time I miss my mouth and the bit of soupy bread hits me in the eye.

Nothing is said. Dad looks at me. Mum looks at me. Mr Spinks tries not to look at me. They are talking about how Dad might get a promotion at work. They are pretending that I am not revolting.

The next course is chicken. Dad will crack over the chicken. He'll say something. He hates me picking up the bones.

The chicken is served. 'I've got the chicken's bottom,' I say in a loud voice.

Dad glares at me but he doesn't answer. I pick up the

chicken and start stuffing it into my mouth with my fingers. I grab a roast potato and break it in half. I dip my fingers into the margarine and put some on the potato. It runs all over the place.

I have never seen anyone look as mad as the way Dad looks at me. He glares. He stares. He clears his throat. But still he doesn't crack. What a man. Nothing can make him break his promise.

I snap a chicken bone in half and suck out the middle. It is hollow and I can see right through it. I suck and slurp and swallow. Dad is going red in the face. Little veins are standing out on his nose. But still he does not crack.

The last course is baked apple and custard. I will get him with that. Mr Spinks has stopped talking about Dad's promotion. He is discussing something about discipline. About setting limits. About insisting on standards. Something like that. I put the hollow bone into the custard and use it like a straw. I suck the custard up the hollow chicken bone.

Dad clears his throat. He is very red in the face. 'Andrew,' he says.

He is going to crack. I have won.

'Yes,' I say through a mouth full of custard.

'Nothing,' he mumbles.

Dad is terrific. He is under enormous pressure but still he keeps his cool. There is only one thing left to do. I take out my secret weapon.

4

I place the yellow fly swat on the table next to my knife.

Everyone looks at it lying there on the white tablecloth. They stare and stare and stare. But nothing is said.

I pick up the fly swat and start to lick it. I lick it like an ice-cream. A bit of chewy, brown goo comes off on my tongue. I swallow it quickly. Then I crunch a bit of crispy, black stuff.

Mr Spinks rushes out to the kitchen. I can hear him being sick in the kitchen sink.

Dad stands up. It is too much for him. He cracks. 'Aaaaaagh,' he screams. He charges at me with hands held out like claws.

I run for it. I run down to my room and lock the door. Dad yells and shouts. He kicks and screams. But I lie low.

Tomorrow, when he calms down, I'll own up. I'll tell him how I went down the street and bought a new fly swat for fifty cents. I'll tell him about the currants and little bits of licorice that I smeared on the fly swat.

I mean, I wouldn't really eat dead flies. Not unless it was for something important anyway.

The Gumleaf War

The park ranger looked out of the train window and said, 'It's a hot summer. We'll have bushfires this year for sure.'

No one in the carriage answered him. They were all too busy looking at me and my nose. They weren't looking straight at me. They were straining their eyeballs by trying to look out of the corner of their eyes. I didn't pay any attention to them. If they wanted to be sticky-beaks, that was their business and there was nothing I could do about it. I was used to people staring at me but it still made me embarrassed. After all, I couldn't help it. I didn't ask to have the longest nose in the world. It happened by accident and it wasn't my fault.

Actually, I had only had the nose for three months. But three months is a long time when your nose has been stretched to seven centimetres long. Every day is filled with humiliation and pain because of people staring and smiling to themselves.

It all started one night when I went down to the kitchen to get myself a snack from the pantry. Dad and Mum were asleep so I crept down the stairs as quietly as I could. The pantry had two swinging doors which closed in the middle. I opened them a few centimetres and poked my nose through, looking at all the goodies within. Suddenly, someone pushed me from behind and I fell onto the doors, slamming them shut. The only problem was, my nose was stuck between them. The pain was terrible and there was blood everywhere. My screaming just about brought the house down and Dad and Mum rushed into the kitchen. Dad shoved me in the car and raced me off to hospital while Mum stayed home and told my little brother off for pushing me in the back and causing all the trouble.

The damage to my nose was monstrous. It was stretched from its normal three centimetres to seven. It stuck out on the front of my face like the bonnet of a car in front of the windscreen. I could see my own nose quite clearly without even using a mirror or going cross-eyed. And to make matters worse, the doctors said nothing could be done for another three years when I had stopped growing. They weren't willing to operate on it for three whole years. Three years of walking around with my own personal flagpole. I felt ill at the thought of it.

I only lasted one day back at school. Most kids were pretty good about it. They tried not to stare at me and only peered at my nose when they thought I couldn't see them. But people have to look at you when you talk and I could see some of them were having a hard time not to crack up laughing. And then there were those who were downright mean. One girl made a smart remark about the only boy in the world who had to blow his nose with a bedsheet.

When I got home from school I gave it to Mum straight. 'I'm not going back to school,' I said. 'No way. I've finished with school for three years. I'm not going to be the laughing stock of Terang High.'

Mum and Dad tried everything to get me back at school. They tried bribes, but I wouldn't take them. Dad lifted me into the car and dumped me at the school gate but I just walked home again. They brought in a psychologist, a nice bloke who spent hours and hours talking to me. But nothing worked. In the end they decided to send me for a holiday with Grandfather McFuddy who lived all alone in a shack high in the mountains. They thought a spell in the country might bring me back to my senses.

So there I was, sitting in the train on the way to Grandfather McFuddy's with a carriage load of people staring at me out of the corner of their eyes. Besides the ranger there was a clergyman with a white dog-collar around his neck, an old woman of about thirty-five and a girl about my age. The girl was biting her tongue trying to stop herself from laughing at my nose. In fact the only passenger who wasn't interested in my nose was the park ranger. He just kept mumbling to himself about how dry it was and how there were going to be bad bushfires this year.

2

Grandfather McFuddy was waiting for me at the station with a horse and trap. A horse and trap. That gave me a surprise for a start. I didn't think anyone drove around in a horse and trap any more. But that was nothing compared with what was to come. Grandfather McFuddy turned out to be the strangest old boy I had ever met. He was dressed in dirty trousers held up with a scungy pair of braces. He had a blue singlet and a battered old hat which was pulled down over his whiskery face. His false teeth were broken and covered in brown tobacco stains. He cleared his throat and spat on the ground. 'Git up here, boy,' he said. 'We have to git back before dark.'

I don't know how Grandfather McFuddy recognised me because I had never met him before. I guess he recognised my nose from Mum's letters. We rattled along the dusty road which wound its way through the still gum forest. 'Thanks for having me for a holiday, Grandfather,' I said.

Grandfather grunted and said, 'Call me McFuddy.' He wasn't a great one for talking. I told him all about my nose and what had happened at school but he made no comment. Every now and then he would cough terribly and spit on the ground. He was a fantastic spitter. He could send a gorbie at least four metres. A couple of times he stopped the horse and rolled himself a cigarette.

After a while the trees turned into paddocks and the road started to wind its way upwards. There was only one house, if you could call it a house, on the whole road. It was really a tumble-down old shack with a rusty iron roof and a rickety porch. McFuddy stopped the cart before we reached the shack. 'Cover your ears, boy,' he said to me.

'What?' I asked.

'Block your ears. Put your hands over your ears while we go past Foxy's place,' he yelled.

'Why?' I wanted to know.

'Because I say so,' said McFuddy. He put his hand in his pocket and fished out a dirty wad of cotton wool. He tore off two pieces and stuffed them in his ears. Then we went slowly past the old shack, me with my hands over my ears and McFuddy with cotton wool sticking out of his. The horse was the only one of us who could hear. An old man ran out onto the porch of the shack and started shaking his fist at us. He was mad about something but I didn't know what. I was shocked to see that the old man had cotton wool in his ears as well. There was one thing for sure, I told myself: this was going to be a very strange holiday.

McFuddy stood up in the cart and started shaking his fist back at the other old man. Then he sat down and drove on, grumbling and mumbling under his breath.

I looked round at the shack to see what the angry old man was doing. All I could see was the top of his bald head. He was bending over, peering through a telescope set up on the porch. It was pointed at another old shack higher up the mountain.

'He's looking at my place,' said McFuddy. 'That's my place up there.' My heart sank. Even though McFuddy's shack was about a kilometre away I could see it was a ramshackle, neglected heap. There were rusty cars, old fridges and rubbish all around it. The weatherboards were falling off and the last flake of paint must have peeled off about a hundred years ago.

We went inside the shack and McFuddy showed me my room. It was the washroom. It had a broken mangle and an empty trough. On the floor was a dusty, striped mattress and an old, grey blanket. The whole place was covered in cobwebs and the windows were filthy dirty. In the kitchen I noticed a telescope pointing out of a window. A little patch had been cleaned on the window pane to allow the telescope to be aimed down the hill at Foxy's shack.

'I'm going to put in some fenceposts in the top paddock,' said McFuddy. 'You can have a look around if you want, boy, but don't go down near Foxy's place. And don't git lost.' He went out into the hot afternoon sun, banging the door behind him.

I wandered around McFuddy's farm, which didn't take long, and then decided to go and explore a small forest further up the hill. I saw a brown snake and a couple of lizards but not much else. In the distance I could hear McFuddy banging away at his fenceposts. Then I heard something else quite strange. It was music. Someone was playing a tune but I couldn't work out what sort of instrument it was. Then it came to me. It was a gumleaf. Someone was playing 'Click Go The Shears' on a gumleaf.

I sat down on a log and listened. It was wonderful listening to such a good player. The tune wafted through the silent gum trees like a lazy bee. I strained my eyes to see who it was but I couldn't see anyone. Then, suddenly, I felt a pain in my left hand. I looked down and saw a deep scratch. It was bleeding badly. I wondered how I had done it. I thought I must have scratched it on a branch. I forgot all about the music and ran back to the shack as fast as I could.

McFuddy was sitting in the kitchen having a cup of tea. He was as angry as a snake when he saw the cut. 'How did you do it?' he yelled.

'I don't know,' I answered. 'I just noticed it when I was sitting on a log.'

'Was there music?' he shouted. 'Did you hear music?'

'Yes, someone was playing a gumleaf. A good player too.'

McFuddy went red in the face. 'They were playing "Click Go The Shears" weren't they?' he said. I nodded. He jumped out of his chair and ran over to the wall and took down a shotgun. 'That rat Foxy,' he spluttered. 'I'll get him for this. I'll fix him good.' He ran over to the door and fired both barrels of the shotgun somewhere in the direction of Foxy's shack. It went off with a terrific bang that rattled the windows.

I ran outside and looked down the mountainside. Far below I could see Foxy's shack. A tiny figure was standing on the porch and pointing something up at us. There was a small flash and then the dull sound of another shotgun blast echoed through the hills.

'Missed,' said McFuddy. 'Missed by a mile.' He went back in the kitchen chuckling to himself. I wasn't surprised that Foxy had missed. I wasn't surprised that either of them had missed. Shotguns aren't meant to be used over long distances. There was no way they could have hit each other.

'What's going on?' I asked. 'Foxy didn't give me the scratch. There was no one near me at all. I didn't see one person the whole time I was away. It wasn't his fault. It was an accident.'

McFuddy didn't answer for a while. He was eating a great slab of bread covered in blackberry jam. He pushed his false teeth between his lips and fished around under them with his tongue, cleaning out the blackberry seeds. When he had finished he said, 'Don't git yerself into something yer don't understand. Foxy is lower than a snake's armpit. He caused that cut and that's that.'

'But,' I began.

'No buts. And don't go wandering off again without my permission.'

That was the end of the discussion. He just wouldn't say any more about it. That night I went to bed on the old mattress. I tossed and turned for a while but at last I went off to sleep.

3

In the morning McFuddy had a terrible cold. He was coughing and sneezing and spitting all the time. His nose was as red as a tomato. He was in a bad temper. 'Foxy's been here,' he yelled. 'He's given me the flu. He came when I was in bed and I couldn't git out quick enough.

'Didn't yer hear it boy? Didn't yer hear the gumleaf playing?'

'No,' I said. 'And I don't believe Foxy gave you the flu. You can't catch colds through closed windows.' I walked out of the front door to get away from his coughing. That's when I saw the note. A crumpled dirty envelope was lying on the porch. It said:

To the boy, with the long nose.

I tore it open. Inside was a message for me.

Sorry about the scratch, boy. I thought you was McFuddy.

McFuddy tore the note out of my hand. 'I knew it. I just knew it,' he spluttered. 'That low-down ratbag was up here last night and he gave me the rotten flu.' He ran inside and came out with the shotgun again. Once again he fired off both barrels down at Foxy's shack. The shot was answered straight away by another dull bang from Foxy in the valley below.

I tried to get McFuddy to explain what was going on but he was in a bad mood and wouldn't say anything about it. 'I'm straining a fence today,' he said. 'And I need your help. Grab one end of that corner post and we'll take it down to the bottom paddock.'

We staggered down the hillside with the heavy post. I was surprised at how strong McFuddy was. He didn't stop once but he coughed and spat the whole way. Then, just as we neared the fence line McFuddy stepped in a pat of fresh cow dung and slipped over. 'Ouch,' he screamed. 'My ankle. My ankle.' I rushed over to him and looked at his ankle. It was already starting to swell and turn blue.

'I'll help you back to the house,' I said. 'This looks serious.' I looked at his face. It was all screwed up with pain. Then, suddenly, a change swept over him and he grinned.

'Good,' he said. 'It hurts like the dickens. Just what I wanted.' He started to cackle like a chook that had just laid an egg. 'Go git me a stick boy. This is the best thing that's happened for a long while.' I found him a stick and he used it to help him hobble off to the road. He limped badly and I could see his ankle was hurting.

'Where are you going?' I asked him. 'You can't go off down the road with that ankle.'

'I'm going to the old twisted gum,' he called back over his shoulder. 'And then I have some other business. You can go back to the house, boy, and don't you try to follow me.' He limped slowly down the road and finally disappeared round a bend in the road.

The whole thing was crazy. These two old men shooting at each other. And blaming each other for things they couldn't have done. And sneaking around playing tunes on a gumleaf in the middle of the night. I had to find out what was going on. So I followed McFuddy down the road, making sure I kept behind bushes where he couldn't see me.

4

I found it easy to keep up with him because he went so slowly on account of his twisted ankle. After about an hour he reached the old twisted gum he had pointed out to me the day before. I noticed all of the lower branches were stripped bare of leaves as if stock had been grazing on them. McFuddy hit at a branch with his stick and a leaf fell off. He put it up to his lips and blew. A strong musical note floated up the road. McFuddy laughed to himself and put the leaf in his pocket. Then he headed off down the road. I knew where he was going.

Sure enough, after about another hour of hobbling, McFuddy reached Foxy's shack. Foxy was peering into his telescope which was pointed at our place. McFuddy crept on all fours along a row of bushes so he couldn't be seen. When he was quite close to the shack, but still out of sight, he grabbed the gumleaf and started to play a tune. I couldn't hear what it was because a strong wind was blowing but I found out later that it was 'Click Go The Shears'.

As soon as the first few notes sounded, Foxy jumped up in the air as if he had been bitten. Then he clapped his hands over his ears and ran inside screaming out at the top of his voice. McFuddy turned and ran for it. He bolted out to the road like a rabbit. I had never seen him move so fast. It took me a few seconds to realise he wasn't limping. His sprained ankle was cured. It wasn't swollen and it didn't hurt.

Foxy came out onto the porch carrying a shotgun which he fired into the air over McFuddy's head. 'You're gone, McFuddy,' he shouted. 'I'll have you for goanna oil.' He tried to chase McFuddy up the road but he couldn't. He had a sprained ankle.

5

My head started to spin. This was the weirdest thing I had ever come across. These two old men seemed to be able to give each other their illnesses and cure themselves at the same time. By blowing a gumleaf where the other person could hear it. I decided to find out what was going on and I followed McFuddy up the dusty, winding road.

I caught up to him under the old twisted gum tree where he was sitting down for a rest. He was laughing to himself in his raspy voice. I could see he thought he had won a great victory. 'That's fixed him,' he said.

'That'll slow him down for a bit.' McFuddy didn't seem to care about me following him. In fact he seemed pleased to have someone to show off to.

'What's happened to your sprained ankle?' I demanded. 'And how come Foxy's got one now and he didn't have before?'

McFuddy looked at me for a bit and then he said, 'You might as well know the truth, boy. After all, you are family. It's this tree. This old twisted gum tree. When you play "Click Go The Shears" on one of its leaves, it passes your illness on to whoever hears it. But it only works for leaves on this tree. And the only tune that makes it work is "Click Go The Shears".'

It seemed too fantastic to believe but I had seen it work with my own eyes. 'Why does it only work with leaves from this old twisted gum tree?' I asked.

'I don't know,' he said. 'I've tried it with hundreds of other trees but it never works. It only works with this tree.' He gave an enormous sneeze and spat on the road. His nose was still red and his eyes were watering.

'Well, how come you've still got your cold?' I asked. 'Why didn't Foxy get that back just now when you passed on the sprained ankle?'

'You can't get it back again. The same thing can only be passed on once. After that you are stuck with it. I will just have to wait for the cold to go away on its own. And Foxy can't give me the sprained ankle back. He will have to wait for it to get better in the normal way. That's the way it works.' McFuddy took the gumleaf out of his pocket and threw it on the ground. I picked it up and tried to make a noise. Nothing came out. Not a peep.

'Save your breath, boy,' said McFuddy. 'Each leaf only plays once. After that it don't work any more.'

'Well, I think it's the meanest thing I've ever heard of,' I said. 'Fancy making another person sick on purpose. How long has this been going on?'

'Over sixty years, boy. And it's not my fault. Foxy first gave me the measles when we were at school. But I found out and I gave him a toothache back. That's how it all got started and it's been going on ever . . .' McFuddy stopped in mid-sentence. He was twisting up his nose and sniffing the hot, north wind. 'Smoke,' he yelled. 'I can smell smoke.'

He jumped up and started running up the road. 'Quick, boy,' he called out over his shoulder. 'There's a bushfire coming. Back to the house.' We both sped up the road as fast as we could go. We were only just in time. A savage fire swept over the top of the hill and raced through the dry grass towards the shack. Smoke swirled overhead and blocked out the sun.

'Git up on the roof, boy,' McFuddy yelled. 'Block up the downpipes and fill up the spouting with water. I'll close up the house.' I put a ladder up against the wall and filled up the spouting with buckets of water. McFuddy went around closing all the windows and doors. Then he started up a portable generator and started spraying the house with a hosepipe connected to his water tank. Soon the house was almost surrounded by fire. Sparks and smoke swirled everywhere. Spot fires broke out in the front yard and at the back of the house. Then the back door caught on fire. I beat at it with a hessian bag that I had soaked in water but it was getting away from me. McFuddy couldn't help. He was fighting a fire that had broken out under the front porch.

It looked hopeless. I couldn't hold the fire at the back door and I knew that at any moment the whole house would explode into a mass of flames. Then, without any warning, an old Holden utility sped through the front gate and stopped in a swirl of dust. It was Foxy. He jumped out of the car, put on a back-pack spray and rushed over to the back door. He soon had the flames out. Then he ran around to the front and started helping McFuddy on the porch.

The three of us fought the flames side by side for two hours until the worst of it had passed. Then we just stood there looking at the shack, which had been saved with Foxy's help, and the burnt grass and trees which surrounded us. The shack was saved but it was surrounded by a desert of smouldering blackness.

6

McFuddy looked at his old enemy who was still limping when he walked. He held out his hand. 'Thanks, mate,' he said. 'Thanks a lot.'

Foxy paused for a second, then he shook the outstretched hand. 'It's okay, McFuddy,' he answered. 'I would have done the same for a wombat.'

McFuddy grinned. 'Come over and have a beer. You've earned it.' They both went into the kitchen and McFuddy opened two stubbies of beer and a can of Fanta for me. They were soon joking and laughing and talking about what a close shave it had been.

'I'm glad to see you're friends at last,' I said after a while. 'Now neither of you will have to visit the old twisted gum again.'

They both sprang to their feet as if someone had stuck a pin in them. 'The old twisted gum,' they shouted together. Both of them ran outside and jumped into the utility. I only just had time to climb into the back before it lurched off down the hill. I hung on for grim death and stared at the blackened, leafless trees that sped by us on either side. The car screeched to a halt and we all climbed out.

I was pleased to see the old twisted gum had been burnt in the fire. It was a black and twisted corpse. The leaves had all gone up in smoke. Except one. High up on the top, well out of reach, one lonely, green leaf pointed at the sky. We all stood there looking at it and saying nothing. Then, without a word, Foxy ran over to the utility and drove off down the hill as fast as he could go. 'Quick,' shouted McFuddy. 'He's gone to git a ladder. Come and help me, boy. We must git that leaf before he does. It's the last one. Come and help me carry the ladder.'

'No way,' I said. 'I wish every leaf had been burnt. Passing on your sickness to someone else is a terrible thing to do. Carry your own ladder.'

'Traitor,' he yelled as he hurried off.

I sat there beside the blackened countryside looking up at the leaf. It was too high up for me to climb up and get it and anyway, the tree was still hot and smouldering. So I just sat there and waited.

I had been sitting there for quite some time when something happened. The leaf fell off its lonely perch and slowly fluttered to the ground. It landed right at my feet. I picked it up and put it in my pocket.

7

I was only just in time. At that very moment McFuddy and Foxy arrived carrying a ladder each. Foxy's car had conked out from overheating and both men were staggering under their heavy burdens. They dumped their ladders down and stared at the tree with their mouths open. Then they fell onto their hands and knees and started scrabbling around in the burnt debris at the bottom of the tree. 'The last leaf,' moaned Foxy. 'The very last leaf.'

'Gone, gone,' cried McFuddy. They scratched and searched everywhere but to no avail. They both became covered in black soot and dust. They looked like two black ghosts hunting around in a black forest.

After a while they slowed down in their search. McFuddy looked at me. 'The boy,' he said suddenly. 'The boy's got it. Give it here, boy.' They both started walking towards me slowly with outstretched hands. Their eyes were wild circles of white set in their black faces. They looked mean. Real mean. I felt like a rabbit trapped by two starving dingoes. I could see they would tear me to pieces to get their leaf. I pushed it deeper into my pocket and backed away.

I had to get rid of it. I wasn't going to give either of them the chance to get one last shot at the other. But I didn't know what to do. I was cornered. One of them was coming from each direction on the road and the paddocks were still hot and smouldering. Then I remembered what McFuddy had told me. Each leaf would only play one tune and then it wouldn't work any more. I decided to use up its power by playing it. I put it to my lips and blew. But nothing happened. Not a squeak. I tried again and a loud blurp came out. It was working. I tried to think of a tune to play but my mind was a blank. I was so nervous I couldn't think of one single tune. Except 'Click Go The Shears'. So that is what I played. It wasn't very good – there were a lot of blurps and wrong notes but it was 'Click Go The Shears', no worries.

McFuddy and Foxy fell to the ground screaming with their hands up over their ears. Then they put their hands over their noses. And so did I. My nose was normal. It had gone back to three centimetres long. And McFuddy and Foxy both had long, long noses. They had both copped my poor broken, stretched nose and mine was normal again.

McFuddy looked at Foxy's nose and started to laugh. He rolled around in the dirt laughing until tears made little tracks through the soot on his face. Then Foxy saw McFuddy's nose and he started to laugh too. Soon all of us were rolling around in the dirt shaking with laughter.

8

McFuddy and Foxy didn't seem to mind their long noses and they made friends again once they realised there were no leaves left. I explained that both of them could have operations to shorten their noses but neither of them seemed very interested. 'I'm not trying to impress the girls at my age,' was all McFuddy said.

The next day I got on the train to go home. I wanted to get back to school again now I had a normal nose. It was a short holiday but it had turned out to be a good cure.

So there I was sitting in the train with the same people that I had arrived with. They were all staring at me out of the corners of their eyes trying to work out if I was that funny-looking kid they had travelled with before.

The ranger was the only one not taking any notice of me. He was staring out of the window at the blackened forest. No one was listening to him except me. And I didn't like what he was saying.

'Never mind,' he rambled on. 'It will be green again this time next year. Gum trees usually spring back to life after a bushfire.'

See, no one had ever seen a yuggle before. And no one's ever seen one since. Where they came from and how they exploded has never been explained. Anyway, I'm getting a bit ahead of myself. I'd better start at the beginning.

This boy called Pockets was visiting his little sister Midge in hospital. Pockets called in every day to try and cheer her up. The poor little kid – she was really sick. Mostly she just lay with her head on the pillow looking at you sadly with those big brown eyes. It was pretty hard getting a smile out of her.

'The prize is an Easter egg,' said Pockets. 'The biggest bloomin' Easter egg in the world.' He stretched out his hands like a fisherman telling lies about his catch. 'It's covered in little chocolate angels,' he went on. 'Hundreds of 'em.'

Something unusual happened when Pockets said this. Midge smiled. Only a little smile, filled with pain. But a smile all the same. 'I'd sure like to see that egg,' whispered Midge. 'I'd love to see those angels.'

Well, this was enough for Pockets. 'If you want that

egg, Midge,' he said, 'me and Cactus will get it for you.'

Pockets' mate Cactus stood at the end of the bed. He smiled back at Midge. But inside he wasn't smiling. He was wondering how they were going to keep Pockets' promise.

2

'How are we going to win that egg?' said Cactus as they walked home from the hospital. 'Now you've gone and got her hopes up. What if we don't come first? There's only one prize.'

'We'll win,' said Pockets. 'All we have to do is collect more mushrooms than anyone else.'

'Everyone else wants to win too,' said Cactus. 'The whole school is after that Easter egg. Everyone'll be searching.'

'No one wants to win more than us,' said Pockets. 'We'll search all day. And we'll search all night. That way we're sure to find the most.'

'All night,' yelled Cactus. 'My dad won't let me out at night. Nor will yours.'

'What they don't know won't hurt 'em,' said Pockets. He was like that, was Pockets. Didn't care what happened if it was something for poor little Midge.

Well, Pockets and Cactus searched all day for mushrooms. And they found plenty. They trudged through the paddocks in the pouring rain. They walked and walked until their feet grew blisters as big as eggs.

Their bag of mushrooms was so heavy they could hardly carry it.

But they kept going. On and on. Bending. Picking. Searching. Running over to each new clump of mushrooms as if it might vanish before they got there.

Just before tea, they saw something bad. In the next paddock. It was Smatter, the school bully. He and his mate Johnson were looking for mushrooms too. And they carried a large sack of mushrooms.

'Oh no,' said Pockets. 'Look at that sack. They've nearly got as many as us.'

3

That's how it was that Pockets and Cactus came to be out in the paddocks at night. In the dripping rain. It was their only chance to make sure they found more mushrooms than Smatter and Johnson. In the feeble light of their torches they stumbled through the grass. Every now and then finding a sodden but precious mushroom.

The sack grew heavier and heavier. 'Let's leave it here for a while,' said Pockets. 'We can come back and get it later.' He dumped the precious sack down under a dark tree. The two boys set off carrying only a small bucket. They didn't notice another torch flashing between the bushes. Nor did they know that more than mushrooms were growing in the cold, wet night.

Luck was against them. Cactus and Pockets searched

and stumbled through the wet grass. But they found nothing. Not a single mushroom. Not so much as the smell of one.

'It's okay,' said Pockets wearily. 'We've got enough already. Smatter can never get as many as us now. I can't wait to see the look in Midge's eyes when she sees that Easter egg. Let's get the sack and go home.' With squelching feet they made their way back to the tree. 'Where's the sack?' grumbled Cactus. His dying torch beam searched the wet grass. The sack wasn't there.

'Is this the right tree?' said Pockets. His voice shook as he spoke.

Cactus shone the torch up into the branches. 'There it is,' he yelled. 'Someone's thrown it up into the tree. Give me a bunk up.' Cactus scrambled up the wet gum tree. Dripping leaves mopped his face. Water trickled down his back. Suddenly Cactus slipped. He slithered down, scraping the skin off his knee. He swung for a moment from a bucking branch. Then, slowly, painfully, he hooked one leg over the branch and dragged himself up. He climbed carefully to where the sack dangled from a fork in the branches.

Cactus just managed to hook the sack with one finger and pull it towards him. It came away easily. Lightly. He peered into the sack and gasped. There was only one little mushroom in the sack. Otherwise, it was empty. 'They're gone,' he shouted down through the branches.

'Someone's nicked 'em,' yelled Pockets. Rage choked his words. They had worked all day. And all night. For nothing. Now Midge would never get the giant chocolate Easter egg. The thought of his little sister lying in hospital was too much for Pockets. He punched the tree with his fist and skinned his knuckles. Blood ran down his fingers. He wiped his eyes with a knuckle. It made the tears on his cheek turn red.

Far off, along a ridge of darkness, two torches twinkled between the trees. 'After 'em,' yelled Cactus. 'We can catch 'em at the road.'

4

The two friends charged into the night. They plunged across a small creek and headed up the hill to the road. Just in time. Two large figures loomed out of the shadows. They carried an enormous sack. Pockets and Cactus could smell freshly picked mushrooms.

'Drop those mushrooms,' yelled Pockets. 'You pinched 'em out of our sack.'

Smatter and his off-sider stopped and peered at their enemies. They were the biggest kids in the school. They were tough. Real tough. 'Prove it,' said Smatter. 'These are ours. We picked every one ourselves.' He bunched up his fist.

Pockets wanted to fight them. He felt anger growling in his throat. But he knew it was useless. They were just too big. There was no way he and Cactus could beat the bullies.

Smatter knew that he'd won. He laughed cruelly. 'Wimps,' he chortled as he headed off into the night.

By now the rain had stopped and the sun was rising over the bush. A kookaburra laughed. But Pockets and Cactus didn't join in.

'It's hopeless,' said Cactus. 'Even if we could find more mushrooms it's too late. The competition ends at ten o'clock. There's not enough time left.'

Pockets didn't answer. He was thinking about little Midge. Poor kid. She'd been in hospital most of her life. If you could call it a life. She hardly ever asked for anything. And now he couldn't even get the one thing she did want. It wasn't as if he could go off and buy another one. This was the best chocolate Easter egg ever made. And anyway he didn't have any money.

Pockets stared at the ground. Cactus made a despairing search for mushrooms. 'Give up,' said Pockets. 'It's too late.'

Cactus didn't reply. He was peering at something on the ground 'Look at this,' he yelled. 'Whopping big mushrooms.'

'They're brown,' said Pockets. 'They're no good. They're toadstools. Probably poisonous. Don't touch 'em.'

'I'm taking 'em anyway,' said Cactus. 'They might be valuable.' He dropped the three toadstools into the sack. 'Wonder what they're called?' he said.

'Yuggles,' said Pockets.

Pockets was always making up names for things. It was just a strange habit he had.

'Okay,' said Cactus. 'Yuggles it is.'

'It's getting light,' said Pockets. 'We'd better get home before our parents wake up. I'll meet you at eight-thirty at my place.' They ran off in different directions. Pockets took the sack with him. Inside, the yuggles jiggled, quietly. They didn't make a sound.

5

Pockets sneaked home to bed. After a bit he got up and had breakfast. Then he met Cactus at the gate and they walked to school together. 'What did you bring them for?' said Cactus pointing to the sack.

Pockets took out one of the brown toadstools. He gave it a sniff. 'It smells awful,' he said. 'Yuck.'

They stopped outside a shop. It was Took's Real Estate agency. On the window someone had sprayed brown graffiti. It said TOOK IS A ROOKER.

Suddenly the door of the shop burst open. Mr Took rushed out and grabbed Pockets by the scruff of the neck. 'Got you,' he screamed. 'You little devil. I'll teach you to write on my window.'

'I didn't,' babbled Pockets.

'Don't give me that,' yelled Took. His eyes bugged out in his head like jelly marbles. 'Look at your fingers, they're covered in brown paint.'

Pockets stared at his hands. They were brown. 'It's the toadstool,' he said, holding it up in front of Took's face. 'It's not paint. It's toadstool.'

Took was furious. He smacked the toadstool out of Pockets' hand. It bounced across the footpath and stopped near a dustbin.

'It's true,' said Cactus. He walked towards the yuggle. Then he stopped. Something was happening. The toadstool moved. It wobbled. Then it began to change shape. It grew and lost its toadstool shape. It turned into a large brown blob like a lump of clay.

And then, just as if it was being formed by invisible hands, it changed into a rubbish bin. It turned into a bin. Exactly the same as the one on the footpath. It even had the same broken handle and large dent on the top. Twin bins, standing silently together.

Mr Took screamed. He rubbed his eyes. He blubbered and blabbered. 'What? How? Quick, help, run. No, no, no.' He seemed to want to run. But like Pockets and Cactus he couldn't tear himself away.

The next bit is hard to believe. But it really happened. The new bin seemed to have a problem. It is hard to explain. It was sort of like it was holding its breath. As if it was going to explode with the effort of staying together. Nothing happened for about two or three minutes. The bin just kind of stood there. Perhaps it gave a wobble. But mostly it just put all its effort into staying a bin.

6

Mr Took took a step forward. Carefully, mind you. Not in a brave way. But like someone who sees a hundred dollar note in a snake's mouth. He just had to get a bit closer.

Then it happened. The new bin gave three little squeaks. And erupted. Like a volcano. It bubbled and burst into a horrible brown sludge. A mountain of muck. It was putrid. Mr Took screamed and fell back onto the footpath.

Cactus and Pockets stared in horror.

'Aaaagh,' bellowed Pockets.

'Uugh ...' yelled Cactus.

The revolting brown goo blistered and plopped like a hot mud pool. 'Disgusting,' gasped Cactus. 'It looks like brown vomit.'

'Foul,' said Pockets.

Mr Took crawled back into his shop and locked the door. The two boys were alone with the pile of rotting brown gunk.

'What is it?' groaned Cactus. He stared at the horrible lumps that festered and swam in the remains of the melted bin.

Pocket scratched his head. 'It's brommit,' he said. 'We'll call it brommit.'

Mr Took burst out of his door carrying a broom and a shovel. He stared nervously at the brommit. He didn't want to get too close. He shouted angrily. 'You two can clean that stuff ...'

He never finished the sentence. Pockets and Cactus were already running down the street as fast as they could go. The sack with the mushroom and the last two yuggles in the bottom bumped against Pockets' knee.

Finally they stopped on a corner. They puffed and panted. Cactus had a pain in his side. Pockets stared nervously behind him. 'There's no one there,' he gasped. 'We're safe.'

7

'I can't believe what happened,' said Cactus. 'That yuggle turned into a bin.'

'Then it squeaked three times,' said Pockets.

'And melted into brown vomit,' added Cactus.

'You mean brommit,' said Pockets.

They grinned at each other. But not for long.

'Get them,' screeched a voice. 'Get 'em, boy.'

A fierce growl made them turn. An enormous dog snarled and salivated. It snapped at their ankles with teeth like steel. Its red eyes bulged with hate. It darted in and out, looking for a chance to tear and rip at their unprotected legs.

'Go, boy. Get 'em, get 'em,' shouted a woman from behind a hedge. Pockets looked at the woman. Her eyes were as fierce and angry as the dog's. 'I've told you not to stand on my grass,' she shrieked. 'Go, Bandit, go.'

Pockets and Cactus wanted to turn and run. But they

were too scared. 'Keep your eyes on him,' whispered Cactus. 'Don't move.'

The dog's growl grew even more terrible. It pulled back its lips like a curtain to reveal green and jagged teeth. It circled, waiting for its chance.

Pockets looked for a weapon. A stick. A stone. Anything. But the grass was bare. Without really knowing why, he put his hand in the sack and pulled out a yuggle.

He felt a tingle in his fingers. A small vibration. A sort of frightened quiver. He threw the yuggle at Bandit. It hit the dog on the head and dropped onto the nature strip. The dog renewed its attack. Barking and lunging forward.

Then it stopped. And sniffed.

The yuggle had begun to grow. It bubbled and fizzed like brown soapsuds pouring out of a washing machine. Then it began to take shape. A bulge formed at one end. Four muddy stick legs grew underneath it. It sprouted fur.

The yuggle turned into a dog. A frozen copy of the savage animal that snapped and snarled around it. Not a live dog. More like a stuffed dog. A replica of Bandit. It had fur. It had red swollen eyes. And its mouth was pulled back in a solid snarl. But it wasn't alive. It was only a statue. Of sorts.

Bandit growled and circled the new dog. It sniffed and snuffed. The woman peered over the fence in terrified silence. Pockets gave a nervous smile and stepped back.

Cactus followed him. Time seemed to stand still. The minutes ticked by. Nothing moved except Bandit who darted in and out, snapping at its silent twin.

The yuggle dog quivered, just for a second. It gave a tense little shiver. Then it squeaked three times.

'Oh no,' yelled Pockets. 'It's going to collapse.' He moved back. Bandit moved closer.

The copy of Bandit couldn't keep it up. A bulge like a boil grew on its head. It suddenly erupted and a brown river of brommit poured out. Bandit grabbed the decaying dog in its teeth. The yuggle dog burst and melted into a brown stinking mess on the grass.

Bandit's nose was covered it in. The poor animal yelped and wiped at its snout. It rolled over on the grass, rubbing its mouth on the ground in a pitiful effort to remove the smell. Then it gave a yelp and a squeal. And raced down the street at enormous speed. The woman took one last horrified look at the brommit. Then she ran after her dog. 'Bandit,' she called. 'Bandit, come back.'

8

Pockets and Cactus ran too. They didn't stop until they reached the school gate. They didn't even notice the kids milling around the gym waiting for the mushroom weigh-in.

'Boy,' said Pockets. 'These yuggles are dangerous.'

'Maybe we should get rid of it,' said Cactus slowly.

Pockets peered into the bag at the last yuggle and the

one lonely mushroom next to it. 'Nah,' he said. 'It might be useful. We can still win that Easter egg, you know. If we use our brains.'

'How?' asked Cactus.

'This yuggle might be able to help,' said Pockets. He reached into the bag and pulled out the last yuggle. He held it up and stared at it. Then he reached down and took out the little mushroom. 'Go on,' he said to the yuggle. 'Change.' He rubbed the yuggle and the mushroom together. Nothing happened.

'Something's missing,' said Cactus slowly. 'It's not going to change. You know what? I think it only changes when someone mean is around. Maybe when it's scared. Mr Took was real mean. And so was that woman with the dog. The yuggle only changes if someone nasty is around.'

Pockets was desperate. He thought of poor little Midge in hospital. He thought of that enormous Easter egg covered in chocolate angels. He thought of the bag of mushrooms that had been stolen. The prize should have been his. He watched sadly as kids walked into the gym carrying bags of mushrooms. None had a bag as big as the one that had been stolen. None except Smatter, that is.

9

Smatter and Johnson staggered up to the door carrying an enormous sack between them. They sneered at Pockets and his little mushroom and toadstool. Then they disappeared inside.

'That's it,' yelled Pockets. 'I can't take any more of this.' He was trying not to cry.

'What are you going to do?' asked Cactus in a worried voice.

'I'm going in,' said Pockets. 'With the last yuggle. If it won't do its thing, well I'll ...'

'You'll what?' said Cactus.

'I'll nick the Easter egg.'

'Steal it?' yelled Cactus.

'Yeah,' answered Pockets. 'It's in a fridge, out the back. I'll take it and escape out the back door. Everyone will be too busy watching the weigh-in. No one will know.'

'You can't,' said Cactus. 'It would be stealing.'

'No it won't,' yelled Pockets. 'It should be mine. We had the most mushrooms. Smatter stole them.'

Without another word Pockets rushed into the hall.

'I'm not coming,' shouted Cactus. 'Not if you're going to steal it.' Cactus stood there, looking at the gym and listening to the shouts and cheers coming from inside. He felt sorry for Midge. But stealing the egg wasn't the answer.

Minutes ticked by. Half an hour passed. Cactus waited and worried. Suddenly an enormous cheer went up inside the hall. Cactus wondered what had happened. It didn't take long to find out.

Smatter had won the competition. He burst out of the

door followed by dozens of cheering kids. He held the enormous Easter egg above his head like a trophy. Then he spotted Cactus standing there looking at his boots. Smatter smirked. 'Suffer,' he yelled at Cactus.

Cactus felt the anger boiling inside him. But he didn't say anything. Not a word. Smatter came over. He broke a chocolate angel off the egg and ate it. He stuffed it into his mouth. Then he started eating the egg. In front of everybody.

'Pig,' said Cactus.

'You think I'm a pig,' said Smatter. 'Just watch this then.' He broke off enormous chunks of chocolate and stuffed them into his mouth. No one had ever eaten so fast. Or so greedily.

Cactus felt his heart sink inside him. He thought of grabbing the remains of the egg and running for it. But it wouldn't be any good now. Little Midge wouldn't want a half-eaten egg. And anyway all the chocolate angels had already disappeared down Smatter's gullet.

Cactus took a step forward. He couldn't control himself. He wanted to punch Smatter on the nose. But before he could move, he noticed something. It was Pockets. He was waving through the gym window. Making signals. And shaking his head. Cactus stopped. And watched as Smatter scoffed down the whole Easter egg. What a guts. No one else even got a taste.

10

Smatter looked around at the crowd of kids outside the gym. They couldn't believe that anyone could scoff so much chocolate in so short a time.

Just as Smatter was wiping the last traces from his lips, Pockets burst out of the door. He was carrying another Easter egg. It was exactly the same as the one Smatter had just eaten. Even the little angels were identical.

Cactus couldn't take it in. He tried to work out what was going on. The yuggle must have copied itself into an Easter egg. And Pockets was carrying it. 'Drop it,' screamed Cactus. 'Run for it.'

Pockets just smiled. He wasn't scared at all.

Smatter stared at the egg in Pockets' hands. His mouth fell open. But he didn't say anything. Not a word. He just stood there sort of quivering. And then something strange happened. He gave three little squeaks. Or, to be more exact, three little squeaks came out of his mouth.

Cactus stared at Pockets. He pointed at Smatter with a question on his face. Pockets nodded. 'He's eaten the yuggle,' he yelled.

Well, it was horrible. Just horrible. You wouldn't want me to tell you how that brommit came pouring out of Smatter's mouth. You really wouldn't want to know how everyone screamed and jumped back from the foul flow. It was too terrible to tell. Too terrible.

But you probably won't be surprised to hear that

Smatter didn't want the real Easter egg. Neither did anyone else. Except Pockets.

It was something to see when he took it to the hospital. Little Midge's face lit up. She had the biggest smile. She just couldn't believe it when Pockets walked in the door with that egg all covered in chocolate angels.

Pubic Hare

Why couldn't I be called Peter Smith or Peter Jones? Or even Peter Rabbit? Why did it have to be Peter Hare? Why oh why oh why?

1

'Okay, boys,' says the Phys. Ed. teacher. 'Take off all your clothes and hang them on your peg. Then make your way to the showers.'

What? With nothing on? On the first day at a new school? In front of everyone? Waltz across the changing room in the nude? Just like walking down the street as if everything is normal? I can't do it. I just can't.

The other boys all start to undress. They don't seem to care about being in the nuddy. They just drop their pants and hang them up without a thought. Some of them have started to head towards the showers already.

'Right, boys,' says the Phys. Ed. teacher. 'There are five showers. All line up in front of the first one. When I blow the whistle you move to the next shower. Each shower is a little cooler than the one before it. The last shower has no hot water at all. That will freshen you up a bit.'

The kids all start to moan and groan. 'Torture,' says Simons, the first boy in line.

'No wimps here,' says the Phys. Ed. teacher. 'And hurry up, all you stragglers.'

The line waiting for the showers grows longer and longer. Nearly all the boys are standing there, as naked as the day they were born. But I can't do it. I just can't. I take off one shoe, slowly. Then I pull off the other. Now I am the only boy still dressed. The others are all lined up, laughing and joking. In the raw.

The Phys. Ed. teacher looks at me. 'Come on, Hare. Hurry up. What are you waiting for?' he says.

Everyone looks at me. Every single boy. I can feel my face burning.

'No need to be embarrassed,' says the Phys. Ed. teacher. 'We're all the same. No one has anything that the others don't.'

If only this was true. But it isn't. I am different to all of them. Slowly I take off my clothes. I am standing there in my jocks. All alone. I lower my underpants and try to hide my nakedness with my hand. But it doesn't work. Everyone can see my shame.

Not one other boy is like me. I am the only one with hair. No one else has it. Not where I do. I am not talking about hair on the head. We all have that. But hair in other places – if you know what I mean.

I hold my hands over my private parts. A couple of

boys are sniggering. They have seen. Oh, the shame of it. 'Pubic Hare,' says Simons. Everyone laughs. Even the teacher thinks it is funny although he tries to cover it up. Why did I have to be called Peter Hare?

'Check out the legs,' says someone else.

I have skinny, hairy legs. I have skinny arms. I have ribs that stick out. I am a total wreck. I am a physical wimp. An embarrassed bag of bones. The Phys. Ed. teacher blows the whistle and we all move forward.

How I wish I was hairless. And big and handsome. Like Simons and all the others. But I am just a little wimp. I am all alone. And the only boy in Year Seven with pubic hair. My face is so red you could warm your hands on it.

2

When I arrive home Mum gives me her usual lecture. 'Why don't you go out and play with the other children, dear?'

I give a smile. 'I have to go and concentrate,' I say.

'Concentrate,' she shouts. 'You just sit in your room staring at the wall. You will never get friends like that. Go out and play,' she says.

'Kids my age don't play,' I say.

'What do they do then?' she asks.

I think for a bit. 'Muck around,' I say.

Mum gets really cross at this point. 'Well, for heaven's sake go out and muck around.'

Mum will never understand. The other kids will just mock someone with pubic hair. Especially Simons. He will just give me heaps if I show my face. Or anything else for that matter. I head off to my room to stare at the wall.

Actually, staring at the wall is what I do best. But I also stare at other things. I have been staring at a leaf, a pin and a pen. Nothing has happened yet but I am sure it will. See, my idea is this. I reckon that it is possible to make things move by willpower. If you concentrate hard enough.

A wise man called Riah Devahs is teaching me this skill. He says that anyone can move things with their mind if they try hard enough. You just stare at something and think about it moving.

Riah Devahs can't actually show me how to do it. 'Everyone has to find their own path,' he says. He can do it himself. But he is not allowed to actually show me how.

'Mind over matter', it is called. You can do all sorts of things just by concentrating. Riah Devahs says that you should start with simple things. Like making a bit of hair float up into the air. Or moving pins. Then you can move on to bigger and better projects. I know that everyone will admire me if I can move things with my mind. Once I can do it I will be popular. You bet.

I stare at a pin on my desk. Then I start to think. 'Move pin. Move pin. Move pin.' That is all I am allowed to have in my mind. If any other thoughts creep into my brain then it won't work. 'Move pin. Move pin. Move pin. I wish I could stick this pin into Simons' bare backside. That would teach him to laugh at me for having pubic hair.' Oh no. I am thinking about Simons. I have let another thought creep in. I have to concentrate. Don't let other thoughts creep in.

I start again. 'Move pin. Move pin. Move pin.' My brain is just about busting. I have never concentrated so hard in my life. Not even the time when I subtracted four hundred and sixty-seven point five from seven hundred and two point one without even writing it down. Rats. I have done it again. I have stopped concentrating on the pin. I am thinking about sums. This will never work.

I will give it one more go. I close my eyes and screw up my eyelids. 'Move pin. Move pin. Move pin.'

I open my eyes and look at the pin. Look for the pin I should say. It has gone. It is not on the desk any more. It is on the floor. Did I move it with my mind? Or did I brush it with my arm? I am not quite sure. Nah, it was just my imagination.

Nothing is going right for me. Basically I am hopeless. I go and stare in the mirror. Look at me. Just look at me. Freckles everywhere. What a face. There should be somewhere you can go to get a new one. I would go down there and trade mine in. They probably wouldn't give me much for the old one, though. I can just hear the man in the face shop. 'Not much demand for turned-up noses, pointy ears and the first signs of a moustache,' he would say. 'I'll give you ten cents for it.'

I undo my belt and look down inside my underpants. The hair is still there. Ugly pubic hair. There seems to be more there every time I look.

I am looking down my pants. And Mum is looking at me. How embarrassing. 'What on earth are you doing?' she says with a funny look on her face.

'Just a bit of staring,' I say.

I stare into the mirror again to make things seem a bit more normal. 'I'm ugly,' I say as I look at my reflection.

'No you're not, dear,' says Mum. 'You look just like your father.'

'That's what I mean,' I mumble under my breath.

Dad is a great bloke, but let's face it – he's no oil painting.

Mum is slowly getting mad. 'If you're not going to go out and play you can come and do the washing-up,' she says.

3

I decide to go out for a walk. Mothers can be so sneaky sometimes.

I will go and see Riah Devahs. That's what I will do. I have been a bit busy lately. I haven't seen him for about six weeks. He will be thinking I have forgotten all about him. He is a great bloke, is Riah Devahs. He wears a long green robe. He has a bald head and fifteen earrings.

He never leaves his little hut in the forest. He just sits there on the dirt floor with his eyes closed and his legs crossed. 'Og,' he says to himself. 'Og. Og. Og.' Over and over, he says it in his mind. This is his mantra. His special word. It is how he makes things move. He just thinks about his special word and he can move mountains. That's what he says anyway.

I am not allowed to use his special word. Everyone has to have their own. One day I will get mine.

I walk on through the bush. There are probably birds singing but I don't hear anything. I wander along concentrating on something else. 'Pubic hair vanish. Pubic hair vanish.' I say it over and over and over. Then I stop for a check. I look inside my jeans but the hair has not disappeared. If anything there is more than before. What a life. Geeze, it is tough to be a person sometimes.

When I get my own mantra – my own special word – I will be able to move things. Riah Devahs says that he will give me a mantra one day. 'When the time is right.' For the time being I will have to make do with 'Pubic hair vanish'. Even though it doesn't work.

I hurry on through the bush. Maybe Riah Devahs will give me my mantra today. Maybe the time is right. Maybe I will get the word that will help me to move things with my mind. I grin. I feel very lucky all of a sudden.

Finally I reach the hut. But something is wrong. There is chanting coming from inside. There are a lot of voices. Riah Devahs is not alone. There has never been anyone else but him in the hut before. Except for me.

I tiptoe up to the open door and look inside. My eyes grow wide at what I see. There are five holy men sitting in a circle. They all wear green robes and fifteen earrings. They are all bald. They are staring at an urn in the middle of the circle and chanting in deep voices.

Riah Devahs is not there. But I remember what he taught me. I must not interrupt the chanting. I stand on my head in the doorway. This is to show that I come in peace.

The chanting goes on and on. No one looks at me standing there on my head. The blood starts to run to my brain. To be perfectly honest I am not very good at standing on my head. My ears start to throb. Then my nose. I feel as if all of my blood is inside my head. I am sure that my skull is going to explode at any minute.

I can't last any longer. Crash. I collapse in a heap on the dirt floor. No one looks up. The holy men just keep chanting.

'Sorry,' I say. Talk about embarrassing. All the blood is still in my head. My face is so red that you could warm your feet on it. The holy men go on chanting. Nothing can stop them.

Finally they are finished. Silence falls over the hut.

I say nothing. I just sit and wait.

Suddenly they all speak together as if in one voice. 'Welcome, brother Hare,' they say.

'Greetings, brothers,' I answer politely. 'Where is Riah Devahs?'

'He has moved on,' says one of the holy men.

My heart sinks inside me. 'Is he coming back?' I ask.

They all shake their heads.

Oh no. Now I will never get my mantra. I will never achieve mind over matter. Riah Devahs will not be there to give me the word I need.

Suddenly I have a thought. Maybe he has left a message. Maybe he left a message with my own special word written on it.

'This is for you,' says one of the holy men. He hands me the urn from the centre of the circle. I know that this is a present from Riah Devahs because his name is written on the side of the urn.

He has not forgotten me. 'Is my mantra inside?' I say excitedly.

'Each foot must find its own path to wisdom,' says a different holy man.

This means that I must go. This means that I cannot say another word. Riah Devahs always finished our sessions with those words. Once those words are uttered I must leave at once. No arguments. I take the urn and walk outside. I walk for a bit without looking back. Then I turn around. The holy men are filing off into the forest.

I wonder if I will ever see them again. Their bald heads shine in the sun.

After a bit I sit down and look at the urn. I am excited. I just know that Riah Devahs has written my mantra and placed it in the urn. With trembling hands I pull off the lid.

My heart falls. Dust. It is filled with dust. Maybe something is buried in it. I rummage around in the dust with my fingers. It gets all over me. 'Achoo.' It makes me sneeze but that is all. There is no mantra. No paper. No words at all.

I put the lid back on and try to get the dust off my hands. Why did Riah give me this urn of dust? Why didn't he give me my word?

I look at his name written on the side. *Riah Devahs*. An idea starts to form in my mind. This is a puzzle. Each foot must find its own path to wisdom. There is an answer. Yes. Yes, yes, yes. My mantra is here somewhere. If only I can find it.

Where is it? Where, where, where?

Suddenly it hits me. It is there. On the side of the urn. Right in front of my eyes. *Riah Devahs*. They are the magic words. What could be better? My mantra is the name of my wise and holy teacher. I have solved the puzzle that he set for me. Riah Devahs has not let me down.

I stare at an ant that is crawling towards me. I concentrate very hard. I will make the ant turn around.

'Riah Devahs. Riah Devahs,' I chant to myself. I am concentrating so hard that my eyeballs bulge out.

The ant turns around and crawls off the other way.

Coincidence. I mean, it probably didn't like the look of me. And I wouldn't blame it either. Still, I might as well try something else. But before I have time to think I feel a sneeze coming. The dust is getting up my nose. 'Ah, ah, ah, choo.' Rats, I hate sneezing. So does Mum.

Mum. That reminds me. She said to be home by five-thirty. It is already five-forty. I clutch the urn to my chest and rush off as fast as I can go. It is best not to be too late. Especially when Mum is in a bad mood.

4

On the way home I pass the cemetery. There is a late evening funeral going on. The priest is reading from a book as the coffin lowers into the ground. 'Ashes to ashes. Dust to dust,' he says.

For some reason his words stick in my mind. They make me feel a bit uncomfortable but I don't know why. A sort of cold feeling crawls all over me. I clutch my urn to my chest and hurry on.

I push the words out of my mind and think of something else. Phys. Ed. Tomorrow we will have to go to Phys. Ed. and all the boys will line up at the showers. I will get the Peter Hare, pubic hair treatment again. The boys will laugh and mock. I can't stand it. I just can't stand it. I am blushing just at the thought of it.

Maybe I can save myself with my mantra. Maybe the magic words will save me.

I still have some of the dust on my hands. I wipe it off and look around for something to concentrate on. There is a brick on the footpath. I will move it by strength of mind. 'Riah Devahs,' I say to myself. 'Riah Devahs.' I concentrate and concentrate on moving the brick while chanting my mantra to myself. Nothing happens. I try harder. 'Riah Devahs. Riah Devahs.'

It happens. It really happens. The brick starts to slide slowly along the path. It moves along as if pulled by an invisible magnet. This is incredible. Fantastic. I can make things move by thinking about it. As long as I am closing my eyes and saying my mantra.

I wonder if the magic words can help me with my pubic hair. I mean, if I concentrate and chant my mantra I might be able to get rid of it.

I close my eyes and start to concentrate on losing my pubic hair. 'Riah Devahs. Riah Devahs,' I say. After a bit I open my eyes and take a look down my jeans. But then I stop. I can feel someone looking at me. Someone is looking at me looking at my pubic hair.

It is Simons. And his mates. Now I am in for it. 'Still there?' says Simons. The others all hoot with laughter.

'Please,' I say. 'I have to get home. Mum is ... '

'Mummy's boy,' says Simons. 'Mummy's hairy little boy.' He looks at the urn. He looks at it with a great deal of interest. 'What has little Pubic Hare got there?'

He starts to walk towards me. He is big and tough and I am skinny and weak. He is going to take my urn. I can't let that happen. I just can't. I grip the urn firmly in my hands. Then I close my eyes.

The gang start to laugh. 'No need to close your eyes, darling,' hoots Simons. 'We won't harm a hair on your ... '

I don't listen. I concentrate as hard as I can. I will get rid of them. I will say my mantra and get rid of them. I close my eyes. 'Riah Devahs,' I say to myself. 'Riah Devahs. They will steal my urn. They will take it away. I just know they will.' Rats, I am letting other thoughts into my mind. I must concentrate harder. 'Riah Devahs.' I say the words and think about getting rid of Simons and his gang. It is a real strain on my brain but I keep going with it.

There is a long silence. Then there is a shuffling noise. I still have the urn in my hands. I open my eyes. 'Hey,' says Simons. 'Hey, what's going on?' He rolls over on the ground waving his legs and arms up in the air. He looks just like a dog begging to be scratched on its tummy. The others do it too. They look ridiculous lying there on their backs on the ground. Their eyes are bulging out of their heads. They don't know what is going on. They don't know that it is me making them do it. I head off around the corner. Their angry voices fade off behind me. They will go back to normal once I am out of range.

I can't believe it. It works. It really works. I have made them lie on their backs and beg. Mind over matter. When I say the mantra and concentrate I can make things happen. I run for home as fast as I can.

Life is good. Well, at the moment it is anyway.

5

When I arrive home I cop it for being late for tea. But I don't care. I just smile and think about my new powers. I also think about Phys. Ed. in the morning and how I will be embarrassed in front of all the boys again.

After tea I go up to my bedroom and think about my problem. I check out my pubic hair.

What if I was to say my mantra and concentrate really hard? I might be able to make my pubic hair vanish by wishing it away. It is a good idea but it is filled with danger. What if something goes wrong? What if I made something else down there disappear by mistake? That would be terrible.

Or the wrong hair could vanish. Then I would be bald. No hair on top and too much down below. No, it is too risky. Much as I like the holy men I don't want to look like them. I will have to think of some other way of getting rid of the pubic hair. I am still not skilled enough with my mantra to risk changing my appearance.

There must be some other way of getting rid of the rotten hair.

An idea comes into my mind. Shaving. Dad shaves

his face every day. I could shave my pubic hair off. Why didn't I think of it before? Simple.

I sneak off to Dad and Mum's bedroom and borrow Dad's electric razor. That will do the trick. I plug in the razor and it starts to buzz away like a hive of bees. I drop my pants and start to shave.

'Ow, ouch, ooh, ooh, ooh.' The pain is terrible. The long black hairs are caught in the razor. It is pulling and nipping at me. My eyes water. I scream out like crazy and dive for the switch. Click, it is off. The pain stops. Wonderful. But I still have a problem. The electric razor is stuck to me. Hairs are all fuzzled up into it. The electric razor clings on like a dog biting a shoe.

Just then Dad bursts into the room. His eyes grow wide when he sees the electric razor stuck to my private parts. 'Peter,' he yells. 'What on earth are you doing, boy?'

'Er, shaving,' I say.

'Shaving. You don't shave down there, lad.'

He comes into the room to remove the razor. He pulls and twists. 'Ouch,' I scream. Suddenly it comes away with bits of hair still sticking out. My eyes start to water with the pain. It hurts like crazy but I decide not to say anything. Not under the circumstances.

Finally, Dad sits down on the side of my bed. He gives me a talk. A long, long talk. About the birds and the bees and all that. It is all stuff I have heard before. But I nod and try to look interested. My mind is just not on it. I am thinking about Phys. Ed. and the showers. And how everyone will laugh at my pubic hair.

6

Finally Dad finishes his lecture and gets up to go. But his eye falls upon something. The urn. He picks it up and looks inside. 'What's this?' he says.

'Dust,' I say.

Dad stares for a long time. His mind is ticking over. 'This is not dust,' he says.

'No?' I say. 'What is it then?'

He utters the dreadful word. 'Ashes,' says Dad.

This word rings a bell in my mind. It takes a few seconds but finally I remember. The funeral. 'Ashes to ashes. Dust to dust.'

'Aargh,' I scream. 'It is human ashes. It is the final remains of . . . ' I look at the urn in horror. 'Riah Devahs.'

Tears rush down my face. My friend is gone for ever. He has moved on to a better place. All I have left of him is his ashes. And my mantra.

I tell Dad the whole story. Well, not the whole story. I don't tell him about concentrating. About how I can change things by willpower. I leave that bit out. But I tell him all the rest about how the holy men gave me the urn.

Dad nods and listens to my tale. He puts an arm around my shoulder. 'I am sorry you have lost your friend,' he says. 'But they should have known better.

Giving human ashes to a boy. That's not right. We have to return these ashes to nature,' he says. 'You can't keep someone's remains in your bedroom.'

I think for a bit. What Dad says is true. Riah Devahs left me his urn and ashes as a puzzle. I had to find my own way. Work out the mantra. But now I have it I can return his ashes to nature like Dad says. 'What about the urn?' I ask. 'Can I keep that?'

Dad thinks for a bit. 'Okay,' he says. 'I guess that will be okay.'

Dad drives us out into a lonely part of the forest. We stop at a high cliff overlooking black gum trees far below. Stars twinkle in the sky. A faint breeze is blowing. Dad tips the urn upside down and the ashes scatter in the breeze.

'Look,' says Dad. 'The breeze is carrying the ashes into the outstretched limbs of the trees below. The forest is welcoming the holy man back to the earth from which he came.'

I didn't know Dad was a poet. It is all rather beautiful actually. I know that Riah Devahs would be pleased at what we have done.

'Ashes to ashes. Dust to dust,' I say.

Dad hands me a tissue. 'Wipe out the inside of the urn,' he says. 'I don't want any human ashes coming back to the house.'

I take the tissue and do what he says. Then I throw it away.

Dad frowns. 'Don't litter the forest,' he says. 'Put it in the bin at home.'

He is right. Riah Devahs would not like tissues floating around the bush. I pick it up and we head for home.

7

That night I have a peaceful sleep. Normally I would stay awake worrying about the Phys. Ed. class in the morning. But I have my mantra to help me. I will use my magic words to save myself from embarrassment. Riah Devahs is gone for ever but his words are fixed firmly in my mind.

How will I use my magic words? What will I do? I think again about making my pubic hair vanish. Nah, it's still too risky. But there are plenty of other things I can do. I can use my powers to jam the lock on the shower room door. Then none of the boys or the Phys. Ed. teacher will be able to get in. Or I could turn the water to the showers off. Or maybe freeze the water in the pipes. Or, better still, I could make the Phys. Ed. teacher take a long walk in the bush. No, there is nothing to worry about any more. I sleep the sleep of a boy who knows what it is to be happy.

The next day we have Phys. Ed. We throw the shotput. We run laps of the oval. We kick the football. The usual stuff. Then, after it is all over, we head off for the showers. We file inside.

'Okay, boys,' says the Phys. Ed. teacher. 'Strip off

and line up for the showers.'

I shut my eyes and start to concentrate. What will I do?

At the last minute I decide to get rid of my pubic hair after all. I don't want to be different. I want to be like everyone else. No, it is the best answer to my problem. I think about losing my pubic hair and start to chant my mantra. 'Riah Devahs. Riah Devahs.' I say to myself, all the time thinking about making my pubic hair vanish. I am nervous but I concentrate really hard. 'Riah Devahs.' I open my eyes and look down inside my shorts. Oh no. The hair is still there. It didn't work. Why didn't it work? Something is wrong.

The mind over matter didn't work. I still have a healthy stand of pubic hair. What is different? Why won't the words work now? Maybe it wasn't the words giving me the power. But what else could it be?

I decide to try it on something easy. I pull a hair out of my head. I take it out and put it on the bench. I concentrate on moving it. 'Riah Devahs. Riah Devahs,' I think to myself. My brain is nearly boiling with the effort but nothing happens. I have lost my power.

Now nothing can save me. I am about to be called Pubic Hare all over again. My private parts will be a public joke. I am history.

The other boys all start to undress. They don't seem to care about being in the nuddy. They just drop their pants and hang them up without a thought. Some of them have started to head towards the showers already. They don't have a pubic hair between them.

I can feel a sneeze coming on. I pull a tissue out of my pocket. A used tissue. I notice that it still has a few flakes of ashes clinging to it. It is the same tissue I used to clean out the urn. I tap the ashes onto my palm. It is all that is left of Riah Devahs. Ashes to ashes. Dust to dust.

I remember the first time I had ashes on my hand. And the time after that. Suddenly it hits me. Like a bolt of lightning. It wasn't the mantra giving me the power. It was the ashes. The power was coming from the last remains of Riah Devahs. Every time I concentrated I had ashes on my hand. And I still do. Only a few but it might work. You never know. It is worth a try. It is worth giving Riah one last try.

I think about my pubic hair. And how I am different from everyone else. I get an idea. I will risk it. I close my eyes and concentrate. Boy, do I concentrate. I have never thought about anything so much in all my life. Talk about mind over matter. All I think about is pubic hair.

A sneeze is coming. I try to stop it. The last thing I need is a sneeze, especially when I have ashes on my palm. 'Ah, ah, tishoo.'

Did it work? I open my eyes and look. The ashes have gone. Sneezed away into oblivion. I will never be able to work my magic again. But it doesn't matter. Not if it worked. Not if my one last effort was successful.

I make a quick check inside my pants. It is still there. But I am not worried. Not one bit. Because it worked. Yes it worked. I am the same as everyone else. Yes, yes, yes.

No, that's not right. I am not the same as everyone else. They are all the same as me. Simons and all the other boys start to scream and cover up. They yell and shout and wrap towels around themselves. Each of them has a thick forest of pubic hair. It is long and curly and wonderful. They are shocked out of their brains. Their faces are so red you could warm your hands on them. None of the boys know where in the heck all the hair has come from.

But I do.

Moonies

I, Adam Hill, agree to stand
on the Wollaston Bridge at four
o'clock and pull down my pants.
I will then flash a moonie at
Mr Bellow, the school Principal.

Who would be mad enough to sign such a thing? Suicide – flashing a bare bottom at Mr Bellow.

1

I'm going to explain what happened on the Wollaston Bridge. Then you will know the worst thing that has ever happened to me.

Normally I would never have agreed to sign the contract. Not in a million years. But I did. And do you know why? Well, I'll tell you, even though it's embarrassing. Even though it is something I'd rather not talk about.

The truth of the matter is: I couldn't read. I didn't know what I was signing.

I couldn't write. I couldn't spell. And I couldn't tell anyone.

Not being able to read was a big problem. I used to get into that much hot water over it.

Like, for example, when I ordered food in the hamburger shop. I would look up at the prices but didn't know what to order. Did it say, 'Hamburger with the lot'? Or did it say, 'No cheques accepted'?

Once I pointed at the sign and said, 'One of those, please, with sauce.'

The woman who was serving stared at me for quite a while. Then she said, 'You'll find the ladies toilet is a bit tough, love. Especially with sauce.' Everyone in the shop laughed. I ran out with tears in my eyes. It was no joke, I can tell you.

After that I worked out a new approach. I would listen to what the person in front of me asked for. If they said, 'One piece of grilled fish with chips,' I would say, 'Same again.'

Or they might ask for 'A dollar of chips and two potato cakes.'

When it was my turn I would pipe up, 'Same again.'

That worked well because I always knew what I was going to get.

The only trouble was that I wasn't listening properly one day. I didn't hear what the guy in front of me ordered. 'Same again,' I said.

The girl handed me fifteen cheeseburgers. And I had

to take them. It cost me a month's pocket money. I still can't look at a cheeseburger. You don't feel too good after eating fifteen of them.

Anyway, not being able to read and write was the pits. Especially when I started a new school.

'I'll write a note to the teachers,' said Dad. 'Then they'll give you special help with your reading. There's nothing wrong with that.'

'No,' I said. 'I don't want anyone at this school to know.'

Dad looked sad. 'Adam,' he said. 'You have to face up to it, not hide it. You're no good at reading but you can do other things. You're about the best drawer I've ever seen. Most people can't draw for nuts. Everybody's good at different things. You're good at painting and drawing.'

'Give me a week,' I said. 'Just one week at the new school before you tell them I can't read.'

He didn't want to do it. But in the end he agreed. My Dad is the greatest bloke out. The best. 'Okay,' he said. 'But look, why don't you take one of your paintings? On the first day. Show them how good you are. Take that one of the wallaby.'

2

So there I was on the first day at the new school. Shaking at the knees.

Straight away I found out two things – one good and one bad.

I'll give you the bad first.

There was a bully at the school. Isn't there always? His name was Kevin Grunt but everyone just called him Grunt. He was big and tough and had a long nose.

It was almost as if he had been waiting for me. He took one look at me and then marched across the classroom. He whacked this piece of paper down on the desk. 'New kids have to prove themselves,' he said. 'Sign here. It's a contract.'

I went red in the face. Not because I didn't want to prove myself. No, not that. But because I didn't want anyone to know that I couldn't read. I had no idea what was written on that bit of paper.

I gave a little grin and held up my bandaged arm. 'Can't write,' I said.

I always used to put my left arm in a sling when there was going to be writing to do. That way no one would be able to know I couldn't spell. Easy. It never failed.

Except this time.

'Just write your name with your right hand, idiot,' said Grunt. 'Put a cross if you like.'

I looked at the piece of paper. Then I stared up at the faces that surrounded me. The whole class was waiting to see what I would do. I wanted to say, 'Will someone read it out, please?'

But of course I couldn't say that. They would all know my terrible secret. So I picked up the pen and scribbled my name with my right hand.

A kid with red hair and freckles pushed through to the front. 'I think it's mean,' he said. 'He's only a new kid. Give him a break, Grunt.'

'Shut up, Blue,' said Grunt. 'Unless you want to take his place.'

That's how I became friends with Blue.

'You're mad,' he said. 'You have to go out on Wollaston Bridge. At four o'clock. And flash your behind at Mr Bellow. There's nowhere for you to run or hide. You'll be in the middle of the bridge all alone. You'll get caught for sure.'

I smiled weakly. 'I could just go home,' I said.

Blue shook his head. 'Grunt and his mates will never leave you alone if you break your contract. Not now that you've signed. You have to do it.'

And the good thing? What was the good thing that happened?

Well, they were having this competition in Melbourne at the National Gallery. An exhibition. One person from each school could put in a piece of art.

Before the first period was over I found myself in Mr Bellow's office. He stood there looking at my painting of the wallaby. He shook his head. 'Fantastic,' he said. 'I can't believe that you are only thirteen. The Gallery director is coming tomorrow. I'm sure that she will pick this. It's terrific. We're very glad to have such a talent at our school.'

I was rapt. Maybe I would become famous. More

than anything in the world I wanted to be a painter. I was never happier than when I had a brush in my hand.

I would have been the happiest person in the world – if I didn't have to go onto the Wollaston Bridge after school. And flash my bare behind at Mr Bellow.

To be honest, I am a shy person. I didn't want anyone to see my bottom. Oh, oh, oh. What a terrible thing. I just couldn't do it. But I couldn't not do it either. Could I? Not after I had signed a contract.

3

The whole school turned out to see the sight. Girls. Boys. Little kids. Big kids. The lot. They hid in the grass. Climbed trees. Every hiding place was taken. No one wanted to be seen by Mr Bellow.

So there I was. In the middle of the bridge. Kevin Grunt was clever. He had made sure that there was no hiding place for me. Mr Bellow would see my lonely bottom. Then he would see my face. And I would be dead meat.

Oh, the shame. Oh, the misery. The bushes were filled with giggling and laughing. What could I do? How could I get out of it? I didn't want anyone to see my behind. Bottoms are very personal things.

My knees were knocking. I felt like crying. I couldn't chicken out. Not with the whole school watching.

I looked along the road. A car was coming. It was

Mr Bellow's Falcon. Oh no. Help. Please. Please. I can't do it.

I undid my belt. I fumbled with my top button.

The car was coming closer. My fingers were like jelly. I couldn't get my zip down.

Mr Bellow was so close that I could see his bushy eyebrows.

I pulled down my jeans. And my underpants. I was undone. My skinny backside was there for all to see.

With gritted teeth and closed eyes I turned and stuck my bare bottom up into the air.

There was a squeal of brakes. The car stopped. There was dead silence on the bridge. I dared not breathe. I tried to pull up my pants. But I was frozen with fear. I just stood there like a man before a firing squad.

Hopeless. Jeansless. Defenceless.

Mr Bellow stood there shaking. He was snorting through his nostrils like a horse. I have never seen anyone so angry in all my life.

He only said two words. But they were terrible words. They were words that spelled doom.

'Adam Hill,' he spat out.

Mr Bellow jumped back into the car and drove off. I knew that tomorrow would be the end of the world. Mr Bellow knew who I was. There was no doubt about that.

4

The funny thing is that the kids didn't laugh much. I pulled up my pants and started to walk off the bridge.

Blue rushed up and put his arm around me.

'Good on ya, Adam,' yelled out a girl with black hair.

'Good one, Hill,' someone else called out.

Quite a few kids came up and patted me on the back. They were all glad that it wasn't them who'd had to do it.

Kevin Grunt didn't like all this. Not one little bit.

'Pathetic,' was all he said. Then he and his mates headed off down the road.

I was glad that it was over.

Except that it wasn't all over. Not by a long way. In the morning I would have to go to the office for sure. Mr Bellow might kick me out of the school. What if he called the police? Baring your behind could even be against the law.

When all the kids had gone I took off my bandage and headed home.

'How did your first day go?' asked Dad.

I smiled weakly. I couldn't tell him what I had done. He would be so ashamed. 'Er, I think my painting of the wallaby is going to be shown in the National Gallery,' I said.

'Wonderful,' yelled Dad. 'Well done, Adam. I am so proud of you.'

That night I couldn't sleep. I just worried and worried.

What if it got in the newspaper? What if the whole world found out what I had done? What was Mr Bellow going to do?

I tried to think of the worst punishment. Saturday morning detention. Expelled. Told off in front of the whole school. Mr Bellow complaining to Dad. The police brought into it.

But it was none of those. It was something worse.

I stood in Mr Bellow's office and stared at the carpet.

'This afternoon,' said Mr Bellow, 'the director of the National Gallery will be coming to see if we have a painting for the exhibition. We won't. We are not going to be represented by a boy who disgraces the school by revealing his private parts.'

He handed me back the painting of the wallaby.

My heart sank. Oh no. This was the very worst. I wanted everyone to see my painting. I wanted Dad to be proud. I wanted to be good at something. Before all the kids found out that I couldn't read.

I trudged back to class. Tears were running down my cheeks. I tried to wipe them off but I didn't have a tissue. I hoped that the kids wouldn't see I had been bawling.

5

When I got back to class there was no teacher there.

'The poor little wimp has been crying,' jeered Kevin Grunt.

I looked at him. I couldn't stand it any more. From somewhere deep inside I found a little speck of courage. 'You're a coward,' I yelled. 'You wouldn't have the guts to do what I did.'

Grunt looked around the class with a fierce expression. 'Yeah,' said Blue. 'You wouldn't do it.'

A few other kids joined in. 'Yeah,' they said. 'Let's see you flash a moonie, Grunt.'

'Okay,' said Kevin Grunt. 'Just watch me.'

He grabbed a bit of paper and started to scribble on it. 'This is another contract,' he said. 'I'll flash a moonie myself. See if I don't.'

I looked at it. I could make out a few words but most of it was just scribble to me. I pulled out the first contract and compared them. This one looked just the same. But I couldn't be sure.

'We'll both sign it,' he said. He put his name on the bottom and held it out for me. I was in a spot. I couldn't very well ask him to read it out. But I had to do something.

'I have one extra requirement,' I said.

Everyone looked at me. I tried to think of something. Anything.

'I get to paint a picture on your behind first.'

A great howl of laughter went up. 'No way,' yelled Kevin Grunt.

'Chicken,' said Blue.

I thought that Grunt's face was going to fall off. He

just couldn't take being called a chicken. He grabbed the paper and wrote an extra bit on the bottom. Then we both signed it. 'See ya after school, wimp,' said Grunt.

Just then the teacher came in and everyone scurried back to their seats.

At recess I told Blue that I couldn't read. He was good about it really. He didn't care at all and promised to keep my secret. He read the contract out to me.

'One word is different,' I said.

Blue nodded. 'It says Wollaston *Road*, not Wollaston *Bridge*. He's going to hide in the bushes and stick his behind out. Then he will run off into the trees and Mr Bellow won't know who did it. He might even think it is you doing it again.'

'Oh no,' I groaned. 'I didn't think of that. I'll get the blame and Kevin Grunt will get off scot free.'

Blue was really glum. I could see that he thought I had been sucked in. 'And why did you say you wanted to paint his behind? What are you going to paint?'

'A wallaby,' I said. 'I'm good at wallabies.'

Blue looked at me as if I was crazy. 'If you paint a wallaby Mr Bellow will be sure it's your bum. He's already seen your painting.'

My heart sank. I sure was dumb. I was in trouble with Mr Bellow. Dad would find out for sure. And I had missed out on my chance to have my painting in the National Gallery. And now Mr Bellow would see Grunt's painted bottom and think I was flashing a moonie again.

I felt like screaming. But there was nothing I could do.

6

Everything happened just like I hoped it wouldn't.

There was Grunt. On Wollaston Road. He had picked out a nice little hole in some bushes. He was going to poke his bare behind out through it. Then he was going to run away unseen. And I was going to get the blame because one of my paintings would be there for Mr Bellow to see.

'Er, it's all right about the painting. I don't need to do it,' I said.

But Grunt was too smart for me. He had already figured out that I would get the blame. He even brought his own box of paints with him. 'Get on with it, Hill,' he said. 'It's in the contract.'

Well, all the kids were there. I had no choice.

Grunt dropped his daks and I started to paint away with my left hand. I couldn't think of what to do. 'Hurry up,' growled Kevin Grunt. 'He'll be here soon.' Grunt was having the time of his life. He knew that he'd tricked me again.

I had just finished putting the last dab of paint on when a car approached. Mr Bellow's Falcon.

We all ran and hid. Kevin Grunt stuck his behind out through the hole in the bushes. I closed my eyes and held my breath.

There was a squeal of brakes. A car door opened. Mr

Bellow jumped out. So did someone else. There was a passenger in the car.

Grunt ran for it. He pulled up his daks and shot off into the scrub. There was no way that Mr Bellow would have seen who it was.

Mr Bellow stood there shaking. He was snorting through his nostrils like a horse. I have never seen anyone so angry in all my life.

He only said two words. But they were terrible words. They were words that spelled doom.

'Kevin Grunt,' he spat out.

Mr Bellow jumped back into the car and drove off. I knew that tomorrow would be the end of the world. For Kevin Grunt. Mr Bellow knew who he was. There was no doubt about that.

7

Well, Grunt really copped it. He was given three Saturday morning detentions. And no one was sorry. Not one single person.

Still and all, his punishment wasn't as bad as mine. I had missed out on having a painting in the National Gallery.

That night I was pretty miserable. Until the phone rang. 'For you,' said Dad.

'Yes?' I said into the phone.

I listened. I listened real good. It was the director of the National Gallery.

'I was travelling home with Mr Bellow today,' she said. 'And a painting stared out at me from the bushes. An unusual painting. I believe you were the artist. A left-hander they tell me.'

'Yes,' I mumbled.

'It was wonderful,' said the director. 'I want you to give us something to put in the Gallery.'

Well, talk about rapt. Dad was so proud. He went out and bought me a book about this painter Van Gogh who cut his own ear off. The words were hard to read. But it was so interesting that I started to get the hang of it. I just had to find out what happened in the end.

Blue was proud of me too. 'You're a genius, Adam,' he said. 'But you're lucky. How did Mr Bellow know that it was Grunt's bare bottom? And what did you paint on it anyway?'

Blue laughed when he heard my answer.

'I painted a face,' I said. 'One with a long nose. I think Mr Bellow recognised who it was straight away.'

Smelly Feat

'No,' screamed Dad. 'Please don't. No, no, no. Have mercy. Please, Berin, don't do it.' He dropped down on his knees and started begging.

'Very funny,' I said as I pulled off one running shoe.

Dad rolled around on the floor. 'I'm dying,' he yelled. 'I can't stand it.' He held his nose and watched me untie the other shoe.

Talk about embarrassing. He was supposed to be a grown-up man. My father. And here he was acting like a little kid in Grade Three. He always carried on like this when I came back from tennis.

My feelings were hurt. 'I can't smell anything,' I said.

'You need a nose job then,' he snorted.

My little sister Libby put her bit in. 'The fox never smells its own,' she said through a crinkled nose.

Talk about mean. I was sick of them picking on me every time I took off my shoes. I shoved my socks into my runners and stomped off to my bedroom. I threw myself down on the bed and looked around the room. Garlic was running around in her cage. I tapped the wire with my toe.

Garlic was my pet mouse. 'At least you like me,' I said.

The little mouse didn't say anything. Not so much as a squeak. In fact something strange happened. Garlic sniffed the air. Then she closed her eyes and fell fast asleep.

I jumped up and tapped the cage. Nothing. Not a movement. At first I thought she was dead but then I noticed her ribs going in and out. She was breathing.

I ran across the room to fetch Dad. But just as I reached the door I noticed Garlic sit up and sniff. She was all right. I ran back over to her. She started to totter as if she was drunk. Then she fell over and settled down into a deep sleep. I walked away and waited on the other side of the room. Garlic sat up and scampered around happily.

Something strange was going on. Every time I went near the cage, Garlic would fall asleep. When I left she woke up. My mouse was allergic to me.

I looked down at my feet. It couldn't be. Could it? No. They weren't that bad. I put on my slippers and approached the cage. Garlic was happy. I slowly took off one slipper and held a bare foot in front of the wire.

Garlic dropped like a stone. She didn't even have time to wrinkle her nose. I put the slipper back on. Garlic sat up and sniffed happily.

This was crazy. My feet smelt so bad they could put a mouse to sleep. Just like chloroform. I had to face up to it. Even though I couldn't smell a thing, I had the strongest smelling feet in the world.

2

I went out into the back yard to look for our cat. She was licking herself in the sun 'Here, Fluffer,' I said. She looked up as I pushed a bare foot into her face.

Her eyes turned to glass and she fell to the ground. Fast asleep. I put the slipper back on my foot and Fluffer sprang to life. With a loud 'meow', she hurtled off over the fence.

This was crazy. My feet worked on a cat.

A loud noise filled the air. Barking. It was that rotten dog down the street. Its name was Ohda and it barked all night. 'Ruff, ruff, ruff.' On and on and on. Most nights you couldn't get to sleep for it barking.

I smiled to myself. This was my big chance. I left my slippers on the porch and set off down the street. Ohda was a huge dog. An Alsatian. She growled and snapped and tore at the wire gate with her teeth. I was glad she couldn't get out. I approached the gate carefully and held out a foot. Ohda stopped barking and sniffed. Her eyes watered. She held her feet up to her nose and rubbed at it furiously with her paws. Then she rolled over on her back and whimpered.

The poor dog was suffering terribly. It was just like Dad rolling around on the floor and pretending he was dying. Suddenly Ohda yelped and squealed. The huge dog bolted off into the far corner of the yard and sat staring at me as if I was a monster. Ohda was terrified.

3

I walked home slowly and thoughtfully. My feet could put a mouse to sleep. And a cat. But not a dog. They weren't powerful enough for dogs. 'Dogs must be too big,' I said to myself.

Dad sat on the sofa watching the TV. As soon as I entered the room he screwed up his nose. 'Oh, Berin,' he groaned. 'Those feet are foul. Go and have a shower.'

I couldn't take any more. The world was against me. Dad was picking on me again. Garlic had fallen asleep. Fluffer had collapsed into a coma. Ohda had been reduced to a whimper. Even the animals didn't like me.

I rushed out of the house and slammed the door. I headed down the street without caring where I was going. Tears pricked behind my eyes. I loved animals. It wasn't fair. I was born with smelly feet. I couldn't help it.

After a bit I found myself at the beach. The tide was in and a little river of sea water cut Turtle Island off from the shore. I felt a little better. Turtle Island. My favourite spot. And in three months time, in November, my favourite thing was going to happen.

Old Shelly, one of the last of the South Pacific sea turtles, would haul herself up the beach to lay her eggs. If you were lucky and knew where to look you might be there when she arrived. Every year, on the twentieth of November, she came to lay her eggs.

Once there had been hundreds of turtles crawling up the beach every summer. But people caught them for soup. And stole the eggs. Now there were hardly any turtles left. I knew where she would come ashore. But I didn't tell anybody. Not a soul. Old Shelly was two hundred years old. I couldn't stand it if anything happened to her. Or her eggs.

Seagulls swooped down and formed a swarming flock on the sand. I walked towards them. As I went they started to collapse. One after another they fell over and littered the beach like feathery corpses.

Even the seagulls were passing out when they smelt my feet. The smile fell from my face. I had to clean my feet. I strode into the salty water and headed for Turtle Island. The sand swirled between my toes. The water was cold and fresh.

I looked behind me and saw the gulls waking. They flew and squawked, alive and wide awake. Some of them followed me to the other side. They scuttled along the sand and approached me as I left the water. Nothing happened. The gulls didn't fall asleep. The sea had washed away the smell. The animals of the world were safe again.

4

I looked along the beach and frowned. Footsteps in the sand. They walked off along the shore into the distance. I always felt as if Turtle Island was my own special place. I didn't like anyone else going there. There are some cruel people in the world and the fewer that knew about Old Shelly the better.

I followed the footsteps along for about a kilometre. They finally led into a huge sea cave. I silently made my way inside and edged around the deep pools that sank into the rocky floor. It was a favourite crayfishing spot.

Three kids were lowering a craypot into the water. It was Horse and his gang. They didn't see me at first. 'Empty,' said Horse. 'Not one rotten cray. I bet someone's been here and nicked 'em.'

Horse was a real big kid. All the members of his gang were big. Greg Baker was his closest mate. 'Just wait till November the twentieth,' he said. 'Turtle soup.' They all laughed.

'And turtle omelette,' said Horse.

I couldn't believe what I was hearing. They planned to catch Old Shelly. After two hundred years of swimming free in the sea the grand old creature would end up as soup. It wasn't right. My head swam. I jumped out from behind the rock.

'You can't do it,' I screamed. 'There's hardly any turtles left. She might even be the last one.'

They all turned and looked at me. 'A spy,' said Horse.

'Berin Jackson,' said his mate Greg Baker. 'The little turtle lover. What a dag.'

The other kid there was nicknamed Thistle. I didn't notice him edging his way behind me. I was too mad to notice anything.

'You can't hurt that turtle,' I screamed. 'It's protected.'

'Who's going to stop us?' sneered Greg Baker.

'Me,' I yelled. 'I'll tell my Dad.'

They thought about that for a bit. 'We wouldn't hurt the turtle, would we?' sneered Horse.

'Nah,' said the other two.

I knew they were lying. And they knew that I knew they were lying. But there was nothing I could do. You can't dob someone in for something they might do.

'Get him,' yelled Horse.

Thistle grabbed me from behind. The other two held one leg each. They lifted me into the air.

'Let me go, you scumbags,' I shouted. There were tears in my eyes. I tried to blink them back as they swung me higher and higher. I struggled and kicked but they were too strong for me.

Suddenly they let go. I flew through the air and splashed into the deep water. I sank down, down, down and then spluttered up to the surface. I spat out salt water and headed for the rocky shore. The gang were already leaving. They laughed and shouted smart comments back at me.

5

It was the worst day of my life. Animals fainting at my feet. Tossed into the water by a bunch of bullies. And now, Horse's gang were going to try and catch Old Shelly.

I walked home along the beach, shivering and wet. I thought about that turtle. Two hundred years ago she hatched out on this very beach. Her mother would have laid scores of eggs. When the tide was right the babies would have hatched and struggled towards the water. Seagulls would have pounced and eaten most of them. In the sea, fish would have gobbled others.

Old Shelly might have been the only one to live. And for the last two hundred years she had swum and survived. And now Horse and his rotten gang were going to catch her.

There was nothing I could do. If I told Dad about the gang they would just lie and say I made it up. I knew those kids. They were in my class at school. I had tangled with them before. They were too strong for me. I couldn't handle them on my own.

Or could I?

I suddenly had an idea. Three months. I had three months to get ready before Old Shelly began to lumber ashore and dig a hole for her eggs. Three months should be enough. It might work. It just might work. I might just be able to save the turtle if I used my brains.

And my feet.

6

That night I emptied out my sock drawer. I had six pairs of blue socks. Mum bought them at a sale. I slipped one pair on my feet. Then I put on my running shoes. After that I struggled into my pyjamas. I could just get my feet through the legs without taking off my shoes.

I hopped into bed. But I felt guilty. I pulled back the blankets and looked at the sheets. The runners were making the sheets dirty. I jumped out of bed and crept down to the kitchen. I found two clear plastic bags. Just right. I pulled them over my shoes and fastened them around my ankles with elastic bands. Terrific. I pulled up the covers and fell asleep.

I had a wonderful dream.

In the morning I faced my next problem. The shower. As soon as the coast was clear I nipped into the bathroom and locked the door. I didn't want my little sister Libby to see me. She would dob for sure.

The shower was on the wall over the bath. I put in the plug and turned on the shower. When the bath was full I took off my pyjamas and lowered myself in. But I left my feet hanging out over the edge. I couldn't let my running shoes get wet. And I couldn't take them off. Otherwise my plan would fail.

That night before bed I took a pair of clean blue socks out of the cupboard. I went outside and rubbed them in the dirt. Then I threw them in the wash basket. That way Mum would think I had worn the socks that day and she wouldn't get suspicious.

Every morning and every night I did the same thing. I wondered if it would work. I planned to go for three months without taking off my shoes.

It was a diabolical plan. I wouldn't have done it normally. Not for anything. But this was different. I had to save Old Shelly from the gang. And smelly feet were my only weapon.

If my feet could send a cat to sleep after only one day, imagine what they could do after three months. Three months in the same socks and the same shoes. Three months without taking off my running shoes. What an idea. It was magnificent. I smiled to myself. I really hoped it would work.

7

Well, it was difficult. You can imagine what Mum would have said if she'd known I was wearing my shoes to bed.

And I had to stop Libby from finding out too.

Every night for three months I went to bed with my runners on. And every night I dirtied a pair of socks outside and put them in the wash. Mum and Dad didn't suspect anything. Although I did have a couple of close calls.

One day Mum said, 'Your socks don't smell like they used to, Berin. You must be washing your feet a lot more.' I just smiled politely and didn't say anything.

I also had problems at school with the Phys. Ed. teacher. I had to forge a note to get out of football and gym. 'These corns are taking a long time to heal,' he said to me one day. I just smiled and limped off slowly.

Three months passed and still I hadn't taken off my shoes or socks once. I hoped and hoped that my plan would work. I knew that Horse's gang were planning to catch Old Shelly. They sniggered every time I walked past them at school.

Finally the day came. November the twentieth. High tide was at half past four. After school. Old Shelly wouldn't arrive until the top of the tide. And the gang wouldn't be able to do anything while they were in school.

All went well in the morning. But after lunch it was different. I walked into the class and sat down in my seat. The day was hot. Blowflies buzzed in the sticky air. Mr Lovell sat at his desk and wiped his brow. I looked around. There were three empty seats.

Horse and his mates weren't there.

They were wagging school. And I knew where they were. Down the beach. Waiting for Old Shelly.

I went cold all over. What if Old Shelly came in early? What if I was wrong about the tides? Turtle soup. I couldn't bear to think about it.

'Mr Lovell,' I yelled. 'I have to go home. I forgot something. Horse is after Old Shelly.'

All the kids looked at me. They thought I was crazy. Mr Lovell frowned. He didn't like anyone calling out without putting up their hand.

'Don't be silly, Berin,' he growled. 'We aren't allowed to let students go home without their parents' permission.'

'But I have to go,' I yelled. 'Old Shelly is ...'

Mr Lovell interrupted. He was angry. 'Sit down, boy, and behave yourself.'

'You don't understand ...' I began.

'I understand that you'll be waiting outside the principal's office if you don't be quiet,' he said.

I sat down. It was useless. Kids don't have any power. They just have to do what they're told.

Or do they?

8

I looked at my feet. I looked at the running shoes and socks that hadn't been changed for three months. I bent down and undid the laces. Then I pulled off my shoes and socks.

I stepped out into the aisle. In bare feet.

The room suddenly grew silent. The hairs stood up on the back of my neck. I looked at my feet. Long black nails curled out of my putrid toes. Slimy, furry skin was coated with blue sock fuzz. Swollen veins ran like choked rivers under the rancid flesh. The air seemed to ripple and shimmer with an invisible stench.

I sniffed. Nothing. I couldn't smell a thing. But the others could.

The blowflies were first to go. They fell from the ceiling like rain. They dropped to the floor without so much as a buzz.

Mr Lovell jumped as if a pin had been stuck into him. Then he slumped on his desk. Asleep. A crumpled heap of dreams. The class collapsed together. They just keeled over as if they had breathed a deadly gas.

They were alive. But they slept and snored. Victims of my fetid feet.

I wish I could say that there were smiles on their lips. But there weren't. Their faces were screwed up like sour cabbages.

9

I ran out of the room and across the school yard. The caretaker was emptying a rubbish bin into the burner. He dropped the bin and flopped unconscious to the ground as I passed.

My three month smell was powerful. It could work in the open at a distance of ten metres. Horse and his gang wouldn't have a chance. They wouldn't even get near me.

But I had to hurry. If Old Shelly came early ... I couldn't bear to think about it.

The beach bus was pulling up at the kerb. I had one dollar with me. Just enough. I jumped onto the bus steps.

'Turtle Island, please,' I said to the driver.

He didn't answer. He was fast asleep in his seat with the engine still ticking over. I looked along the row of seats. All the passengers were snoring their heads off. I had gassed the whole bus.

'Oh no,' I said. I jumped off the bus and headed for the beach. The quickest way was straight through the shopping mall.

I didn't really want to run barefooted through the town but this was an emergency. I passed a lady on a bike. She fell straight asleep, still rolling along the road. The bike tottered and then crashed into a bush.

This was terrible. No one could come near me without falling asleep. I ran over to help her but her eyes were firmly closed. The best thing I could do was to get away from her as quickly as possible.

10

I jogged into the shopping mall. People fell to the ground in slumbering waves as I approached. I stopped and stared around.

The street was silent. Hundreds of people slept on the footpaths and in the shops. A policeman snored in the middle of the road. I felt as if I was the only person in the world who was awake.

Suddenly I felt lonely. And sad.

But then I thought of Old Shelly. That poor, helpless

turtle dragging its ancient shell up the beach. To the waiting Horse and his cooking pot.

I ran on. My heart hammered. My knees knocked. My feet fumed. 'Old Shelly,' I said. 'I'm coming, I'm coming, I'm coming.'

I pounded on and on, not stopping for the people around me as they fell to the ground like leaves tumbling in autumn.

At last I reached the beach. The tide was in. A strong current cut me off from Turtle Island. A flock of sea-gulls flew overhead. They plummeted to the ground, reminding me of planes that had lost their pilots.

My feet still worked. They were as powerful as ever.

I gazed at the swiftly running water. I peered along the beach for a boat. There was none. I looked at my foul feet. If only I could fly. On the wind I thought I heard wicked laughter. 'Old Shelly,' I mumbled. 'I'm coming.' I plunged into the sea and waded towards the island.

My toes sank into the sand. I could feel the grains scouring my skin. Washing away at three months of muck. The water was clear and cold and salty. On and on I struggled through the cleansing stream. Splashing. Jumping. Crying. Until I reached the other side.

The seagulls scampered around my feet. They were awake. They didn't even yawn.

11

I looked down at my lily-white toes. They were spotless. The water had stolen their strength. Three months of saving my smell. Gone. Scrubbed away by the salt and the sand.

There was no sign of the three bullies. But I knew where to find them. I staggered up to the top of a huge sand dune and stared along the beach. There they were. And there in the clear blue water was a moving shadow. Old Shelly.

Horse and his mates hadn't seen her. There was still a chance. I plunged down the dune towards them, yelling and screaming. Trying to distract them from their search.

It worked. They turned around and watched me approach. I had to draw them off. Once they saw the turtle they would know which part of the beach she was on. Even if Old Shelly escaped they would dig around and find the eggs.

I knew it was no use arguing with them. They wouldn't listen. I had to say something mean.

'Bird brain,' I said weakly to Horse. I felt silly. It didn't come out right. It wasn't tough. I bunched up my fists. 'Get off this island,' I ordered.

'Who's going to make us?' jeered Horse.

'Me,' I said.

I felt very small. They were real big kids. They walked towards me with snarling faces.

I turned and ran.

'Get him.' They pelted after me. I scrambled up the sand dune and along the top. I felt them panting behind me. The sandy ground turned to rock. It cut my bare feet. They hurt like crazy. I slowed down to a hobble. My toes were bleeding. It was no use. The gang had me trapped.

I turned and faced the gang. Behind them, way below, I could see Old Shelly hauling herself over the sand. They hadn't seen her. Yet.

Thistle circled around me. They closed in. I tried to find something to defend myself. There was nothing. I put my hands in my pocket in a desperate search. My fingers found something useful.

'Get back,' I yelled. 'Or I'll use these.'

Horse laughed out loud. 'We're not scared of a pair of ...'

He never finished. He crashed to the ground like a tree falling. The others followed. They were fast asleep on the sand. I held my putrid socks in the air. Boy, were they powerful.

12

I put the socks near the sleeping bullies. Then I walked down to the beach.

Old Shelly was digging a hole with her flippers. Slowly, painfully, she dug and dug and dug. She was helpless. 'Don't worry, girl,' I said. 'I won't hurt you.'

I sat a little way off and watched the miracle. I watched the eggs drop like beads from a broken necklace. The sun sank into the sea, lighting the old turtle with gold.

I watched as Old Shelly covered the eggs and then crawled back towards the shore. Just as she reached the edge she turned. And nodded her head as if to thank me.

'Think nothing of it,' I said. 'Your eggs are safe now. I'll see you next year.'

I have to admit there was a tear in my eye as I watched her sink under the water and swim out beneath the silvery arms of the rippling moonbeams.

I went back and fetched the socks. I threw them in the sea and waited. In no time at all, Horse and his mates started to stir. They sat up and peered into the darkness. They couldn't work it out. It was light when they had fallen asleep. They didn't know where the sun had gone.

Suddenly Horse gave an enormous scream. He ran for it. The others followed him, belting along the sand as if a demon was after them. They thought I had strange powers. I guess if you think about it, they were right in a funny sort of way.

I walked slowly home.

A nasty thought entered my mind. What if Horse found more members for his gang? What if they came back to wait for Old Shelly next November?

I was worried. Then I chuckled and spoke to myself. 'If I start going to bed with my shoes on tonight,' I said, 'my feet ought to be pretty strong by this time next year.'

Sniffex

Remember that kid Boffin I told you about?* The one who made his own lie-detector and embarrassed the heck out of me? Well, this is about another of his wacky inventions. It's called Sniffex. It is a smell-detector of sorts.

See, I am hanging out down the street when Boffin saunters up.

'How's it going?' I say.

'Sniffingly,' says Boffin. He grins at my questioning glance and hands over a little glass test tube with a cork in it.

'What is it?' I ask innocently.

'Take a whiff,' says Boffin.

I pull off the cork top and sniff. 'Can't smell a thing,' I say.

'You will,' says Boffin.

We start to walk down the street towards Kermond's hamburger joint. On the way we pass a little cottage with a rose garden out front. Suddenly I race into the garden and start sniffing the roses. I don't know why but I just seem to have a need to smell roses.

An old lady of about forty or so comes out. 'How

* Boffin first appeared in 'Ex-Poser', *Unmentionable!*, 1991. *Ed.*

wonderful to see a boy who loves flowers,' she says. She picks a bright red rose and hands it to me.

I go as red as the rose. Talk about embarrassing.

'What happened?' I say.

'Try again,' says Boffin.

'No thanks,' I say.

'Trust me,' says Boffin. 'It's for a good cause.'

I take another sniff and wait. Boffin has a strained look on his face. Like he is trying to lift up a heavy weight. Suddenly he lets off a loud fart.

And suddenly I drop down onto my knees and start sniffing around his backside. Shame, shame, shame. People are looking. And the stink is terrible. Boffin starts cackling away like a crazy chook.

To be perfectly honest I have never been into farting. I think it is foul. People get a cheap laugh by doing it in public places. Not me, though. I don't think it is funny.

Once my big sister's boyfriend pinned her to the floor. Then he sat on her face and let off a really bad one. They both laughed like crazy. And they are eighteen. Can you believe that? I will tell the police if he ever does it to me.

Don't get me wrong. I have let one or two foul smells fly myself. But never in the movies or anywhere like that. I go out under the starry sky and release the surplus energy into the clean, fresh air.

Once or twice I've done it in bed. But I always flap the sheets so that the odour doesn't linger long.

Anyway, to get back to Boffin.

'This stuff makes you sniff out the source of each new smell you come across,' he says. 'We can find the Phantom Farter of 6B with it.'

'Yes,' I yell. 'Way to go.'

Someone in our class lets fly with a foul one every day. It is disgusting. No one knows who it is. Everyone calls him the Phantom Farter of 6B.

'What if it's poor old Freddie Fungle?' I say. 'We wouldn't want to make life any tougher for him.'

Freddie Fungle is the main suspect. He bites his fingernails and won't brush his teeth. He just doesn't know any better.

'I think it's that mean Herb Hackling,' says Boffin. 'He is a rat. He is just trying to get poor old Freddie Fungle into trouble.'

'Could be,' I say. 'They sit close to each other.'

'If Ms Gap ever catches the culprit,' says Boffin, 'she will really give it to them.'

This is true. Ms Gap is the strictest teacher in the school. Two kids have already been expelled from her class. And she hates the Phantom Farter. Whoever he is.

'If I catch the person making that dreadful smell,' she said, 'they will be out of this school for ever.' She looked straight at poor old Freddie Fungle when she said this. She might as well have pronounced him guilty on the spot. He went bright red.

Herb Hackling gave a snort of laughter and held his

nose. He pointed straight at Freddie Fungle. A lot of the kids laughed. Freddie hung his head in shame.

'Look,' I say to Boffin. 'What if it is Freddie? If we sniff him out with the Sniffex his life will be misery.'

'No,' says Boffin. 'We won't tell anyone about it. If you sniff Freddie we say nothing. People will laugh at you but they won't know what's going on.'

'And if it's that rat, Herb Hackling,' I say. 'We expose him.'

We smack hands and exchange a bunch of fives. It is a great idea.

Later that morning things go exactly as Boffin predicted. Ms Gap is writing on the board when the Phantom Farter lets off a silent but deadly one.

'Phwar,' says Herb Hackling. 'What a stink.'

Ms Gap spins around quicker than a tiger snake. 'Someone has done another dreadful smell,' she shouts. 'And I'm going to find out who it is.'

Freddie Fungle is going red in the face. He is the main suspect. And he knows it. I feel so sorry for him.

Boffin hands me the test tube. It is time to get to the bottom of the mystery.

'Why me?' I say.

To be honest, I do not really want to sniff anyone's backside.

'I told you before,' says Boffin. 'I've got a cold. Can't smell a thing.'

'Bulldust,' I say. 'I'm not doing it.'

'Not doing what?' says a voice.

Oh no, it is Herb Hackling. The mean kid. He snatches the test tube from Boffin's hand, whips out the cork and takes a sniff. This is terrible. It has all gone wrong. Now Herb Hackling will sniff out poor Freddie Fungle and get him expelled from the class. But no. Hang on a bit. Things are taking a different turn.

I didn't ask Boffin what would happen if the Phantom Farter himself took a whiff of Sniffex. He would probably try and smell his own backside like a dog chasing its tail.

But no. Herb Hackling is not doing this. It must be Freddie then. What have we done? Exposed the very person we wanted to help?

For a second Herb Hackling's eyes glaze over. Then he races out the front and starts sniffing at Ms Gap's backside. He drops down on all fours and sniffs like crazy. He reminds me of a cat sniffing at another cat. The kids all pack up with laughter. I have never seen anything like it before.

Well, to cut a long story short we are all hauled down to the Principal's office. He doesn't believe about the Sniffex but after taking a snort from it and sniffing at the perfume on his secretary Mrs Jones' neck, he changes his mind.

Ms Gap is exposed as the Phantom Farter. She leaves the school.

And Freddie Fungle never gets teased by Herb Hackling again.

Funny that.

Ringing Wet

The man next door buried his wife in the backyard.

That's what I reckon, anyway. Dad says I have a vivid imagination. And my rotten, horrible, worst-ever big brother says I am nuts.

But I am not nuts. No way. See, it starts like this. I am reading a book where five kids go on a holiday. They discover smugglers in some underground caves but the adults won't believe them. Everyone thinks they are crazy. But in the end they catch the smugglers and become heroes. All the parents and police have to say sorry.

Since I read that book I have been on the lookout. To be honest there are not many smugglers around our way. I have looked and looked. There are not even any underground tunnels.

But there is Mr Grunge next door. He moved in two months ago. He acts in a very suspicious way. Consider these facts:

1. Mr Grunge has a crabby face.
2. He never comes out in the daytime.
3. He shouts at his wife in a loud, horrible voice.

4. His wife does all of the shopping and washing-up and cooking.

5. Mr Grunge just sits there all day watching TV.

6. Two days ago Mrs Grunge disappears.

   Yes, DISAPPEARS.

7. The night that his wife disappears Mr Grunge digs in the backyard.

   Yes, DIGS IN THE GARDEN *AT NIGHT*.

I know all this because I have been spying on them through a chink in their curtains.

Yes, it all fits in. They have an argument. He hits her with the frying-pan or something. Then he drags her out into the backyard. He takes off her diamond bracelet and buries her. I do not actually see this happen. But I put two and two together. It is the only explanation.

'Don't be crazy, Misty,' says Dad. 'She's probably gone on a holiday.'

'In the middle of winter?' I say.

'She could have gone to Queensland to get a bit of sun,' says Dad.

'Without her best diamond bracelet?' I say.

Dad looks at me through narrow eyes. 'How do you know she hasn't taken her bracelet?' he says.

'She's been peeping through the window,' says Simon, my rotten worst-ever brother.

Dad bangs down his paper on the table. He is as mad as a hatter. 'Misty,' he yells. 'That is a terrible thing to do. Spying and going into someone else's garden.'

Simon is such a dobber. He always spoils things. He is a real wet blanket. I decide to pay him back. 'Well, *he* got a detention at school yesterday,' I yell. 'For not doing his homework.'

Dad is really mad now. He rolls his eyes. 'What a way to start the school holidays,' he roars. 'Go to your rooms at once. Both of you.'

I stomp off to my bedroom and almost slam the door. There is an exact amount of noise you can make when you are almost slamming the door. If you do it too loud your parents will stop your pocket money for a month. If you get it right they cannot be quite sure that you actually slammed the door and they won't do anything. But it still annoys them.

My Dad is so stubborn. So is Simon. They won't believe that Mr Grunge has buried his wife in the garden. There is only one thing for me to do. One night, when there is no moon. When it is very dark. I will go and dig her up. Yes, DIG HER UP.

2

I am lying there in bed thinking about how I will dig up the body when Simon bursts into the room. He has his fingers held out like claws. 'Ticky, ticky, ticky,' he says with a nasty look on his face.

'No, Simon. No, no, no,' I scream. 'Not that. Don't. Please, please. I'm sorry I dobbed.'

'Ticky, ticky, ticky,' says Simon. Oh, he is so awful. He is bigger than me. Almost as big as Dad. I just can't stand up to him. I curl up in a ball on the bed. It is my only defence.

Simon gets his horrible fingers in under my armpits and starts to tickle. I hate it. I just hate it. I start to scream and kick and yell. 'Don't,' I yell. 'You pain. Dad, Dad, Dad.' I stop yelling. I am laughing. I don't want to laugh. I want to scream. But his fingers are digging in and I just can't help it.

I squirm and kick. And then I do it. I knew I would do it. And so did Simon. It is why he is tickling me. I always do it when someone tickles me.

I wet my pants. Yes, WET MY PANTS. Warm wet wee runs down my legs and onto the bed. Oh, it is terrible.

Simon sees. 'What's that?' he mocks. 'Where did that come from?' He laughs wickedly and then runs out the door.

I throw a pillow after him. 'You wait,' I say. 'You just wait.'

I hang my head in my hands. I am so ashamed. I always wet myself when someone tickles me. Even if I just get excited I do it. The doctor says I will grow out of it. Probably I will. By the time I am fifty.

There is something else, too. Even worse. Every night I wet the bed. It is awful. Just awful. In the mornings I wake up and everything is wet. I hate it.

I hate it. I hate it. I hate it.

Last year I couldn't go on the school camp. I was just too embarrassed.

I have a shower and change my clothes. Then I go into the lounge to see Dad. 'Something has to be done,' I say. 'Can't you do something to stop this bed-wetting? It is ruining my life.'

Dad nods his head. 'There is one more thing to try,' he says. 'I have been hoping we wouldn't need it. But I guess we have to give it a go.'

'Anything,' I say. 'I will try anything.'

3

That night Dad comes home with a rubber blanket. 'We put this under your sheet,' says Dad. 'When you wee it makes the blanket wet and it will ring a bell. You wake up and we change the sheets. After a couple of weeks your brain knows what is going to happen and it stops you wetting. Bingo – you are cured.'

I don't like the sound of it. Not one bit. But I am desperate. I will try anything. I snuggle down under the covers. Outside the moon is shining bright. It is not dark enough to go and dig in the neighbour's garden. So I close my eyes and drop off to sleep.

'Ding, ding, ding, ding.' Good grief. What is it? That terrible noise. I sit bolt upright in bed. It is like sirens from the police, the ambulance and the fire brigade all put together. My head is spinning. Is the house on fire or what?

I know. I know. I bet the police have come to arrest Mr Grunge. They will charge him with murder.

Dad bursts into the room with a smile. 'It works,' he says. 'Out you hop, sweetheart. You go and change your pyjamas and I'll put on fresh sheets.'

My heart sinks. It is not the police. I have wet the bed. The terrible noise comes from the bell attached to the rubber blanket. It works all right. It is the worst noise in the world.

Dad makes the bed while I put on dry pyjamas. 'See, that wasn't so bad,' says Dad as he walks out. He is quite chirpy really.

I snuggle down under the clean, crisp sheets. I am so tired. This getting up in the middle of the night takes it out of you. I have no sooner closed my eyes than 'ding, ding, ding, ding'. Oh no. I've wet the bed again. I look at the clock. Two hours. Have two hours really passed already?

Dad staggers into the room. This time he is not so chirpy. 'Geeze,' he says. 'I'd just dropped off to sleep. Okay, up you get. I'll get some dry sheets.' Dad is not exactly cross. Well, he is trying not to be cross. But I can tell that he does not like getting up in the middle of the night. And he is not the only one – that's for sure.

The next day is Saturday. It is Mum's weekend. Mum and Dad split up a couple of years ago and we live with Dad. Every second Saturday we go off with Mum. It is grouse because she takes us to lots of good places. To be honest, though, I wish she still lived at home.

Dad looks out of the window. 'Here's your mother,' he says. He never calls her Mum any more. He always calls her *your mother*. Funny that. Anyway, Simon and I race out and hop into Mum's car.

'Where are we going?' says Simon.

'Luna Park,' says Mum.

'Unreal,' we both yell.

We wander through the great big mouth that is the entrance to Luna Park and look around. We have a ride on the Big Dipper, the Water Caves and go into the Giggle Palace. They are all great.

'Let's go on the Rotor,' says Simon.

'What's that?' says Mum.

'It's this round room,' I say. 'You stick to the wall. I am not going on it. No way.'

'Neither am I,' says Mum.

'Wimps,' says Simon. 'I'm going on it. You can watch if you like. You can go upstairs and look down on the brave ones.' He bends one arm and bulges out his muscle. He thinks he is so tough.

4

We all get in the line, pay our money and file inside. The line splits into two. One line is for the people who are going to stick to the wall. The other is for those who want to watch. There is a lot of pushing and shoving and Mum is not sure where we are. 'You go in there,' says Simon.

Mum and I file through a door while Simon heads up some stairs. The door slams behind us. We look around. We are in a big, round room with about ten others. There are a whole lot of people up above looking down on us. It is sort of like a round squash court with spectators sitting around upstairs.

What is going on here? What has happened?

Simon has tricked us. That's what. I see his grinning face peering down from the spectators' seats. He thinks he is so smart. He has sent us into the wrong place. We are inside the Rotor. Yes, INSIDE.

I start to panic. I have to get out of here. I just have to. But where is the door? I can't even see it. There is no handle. And the walls are covered in rubber.

A loud voice comes over the microphone. 'All riders stand against the wall, please,' it says. Riders? I am not meant to be a rider. I am meant to be a watcher. 'Let me out,' I yell.

But it is too late. Mum drags me back to the wall and the room starts to spin. Faster and faster. The faces up above are just a blur. We are whirling around like a crazy spinning top. Suddenly the floor drops away. And we are stuck to the wall. Right up in the air.

This is terrible. Horrible. I am scared. I'm embarrassed. Everyone is looking at us. We are like flies on the wall.

Mum starts to squirm. She has turned sideways. If she

is not careful she will soon be upside down. Some of the people on the wall are groaning. Others are screaming. Some are laughing and having fun.

But I am not having fun. I am excited. When I am excited something terrible always happens.

And it does happen. Oh, horror of horrors. It happens. I wet my pants.

There on the wall with everyone looking – I wet my pants.

A river of warm wet wee runs along the wall. It snakes its way towards Mum. My shame scribbles its hateful way across the round, spinning room.

I close my eyes and try to pretend that this is not happening. But it is.

After ages and ages the walls start to slow. Gradually the floor comes up to meet us. Finally the Rotor stops and I am standing on the floor in front of a wet, smeared wall. My legs and dress are all wet. Mum and I stagger outside and blink in the sunlight.

Simon is going to die. Simon is history. I will get him for this.

Before I can reach Simon to strangle him, Mum grabs him by the shoulders and shakes him until his head just about drops off. 'You have ruined the day,' she yells. 'Now I will have to take you back to your father's so that Misty can change.'

We all drive home without talking. I am so angry. 'I will get you for this, Simon,' I think to myself.

'I will get you for this. If it is the last thing I do, I will pay you back.'

5

Mum drops us at the gate and drives off. As we walk up the drive I see Dad's startled face staring out of the window. I also see Mr Grunge in his backyard. He has a shovel in his hand. He stares at me as I go by. It is almost like he can read my mind. I shiver and hurry indoors.

Dad is surprised to see us. 'What are you doing back so soon?' he says. He is annoyed. And I know why. In the lounge-room is his girlfriend, Brook. She only ever comes over when we are out. Her hair is all ruffled and she looks embarrassed. Dad's shirt is hanging out. They have been cuddling. Yes, CUDDLING. And we have broken it up.

I am annoyed too. He should be pleased to see us back. Not annoyed.

'Simon made me wet my pants,' I yell.

'I did not,' he says.

'Liar, liar, liar,' I shout.

Dad rolls his eyeballs at Brook. Then he does something strange. He takes out his wallet. He bangs a fifty-dollar note down on the table. 'See this?' he says. 'This is for the person who keeps quiet the longest.'

Simon and I stop yelling. We are both very interested.

'The first one to speak,' says Dad, 'does not get the

fifty-dollar note. As soon as one of you speaks, the other one gets this. Do you understand?'

I open my mouth to say 'yes'. But I don't. No way. I just nod my head in silence. So does Simon.

'Not one word,' says Dad. 'Not a shout, not a scream, not a giggle. Total silence. That is the deal. Get it?'

We both nod our heads again.

Dad looks smug. 'Now maybe we will get some peace at last,' he says.

I grin an evil grin. Now I will get Simon back. I will win the fifty dollars and he will be really cut. It is perfect. He might be bigger than me. He might be stronger. He might even be smarter. But I am stubborn. I will not say a word to anyone. Even if it takes ten years.

That night I get into bed and wriggle down under the blankets. I turn off the lights and my mind starts to wander. Mr Grunge was giving me a funny look this afternoon. What was he thinking about? Suddenly I feel cold all over.

He knows.

He knows that I know that he has buried his wife in the backyard.

What if I am next?

I can't sleep. I toss and turn. Finally I drift off when … 'crash'. My bedroom door flies open. Someone bursts into the room. My brain freezes with fear. It is a person wearing a devil's mask. A horrible, horrible mask. The figure dances around at the end of my bed.

Suddenly I am not scared any more. I have seen that mask before. Simon bought it at the Show. He is trying to make me scream. He wants me to yell out. So that he can get the money. But it won't work. I turn on the light and take out a pencil and paper. 'Buzz off, Simon,' I write in large letters.

Simon pulls off the mask and pulls a face at me. Then he leaves.

6

It takes me ages and ages but finally I fall off to sleep.

'Ding, ding, ding, ding.' What, what, what? Rats. It is the bed-wetting alarm again. Already. What a racket. It's enough to wake the dead.

Dad comes in and turns on the light. He holds a finger up to his lips. 'Don't say a word,' he says. 'Remember the fifty dollars.' He sure is taking this seriously.

I put on a clean pair of pyjamas and Dad changes the sheets. Then he goes off to bed. Brook must have gone home.

An hour ticks by. And then another. I just can't get off to sleep. Too much has happened. I have wet my pants on the Rotor. Dad was cross because we came home early. Simon is a horrible worst-ever brother. Mr Grunge knows that I am on to him. My life is a total mess.

If only I was rich or beautiful or famous.

Outside it is dark. There is no moon.

Famous.

That's it. Tonight is the night. I will sneak out into Mr Grunge's garden. I will dig up his wife before he can come and get me. I will be famous. I bet there will be a reward. And it will be worth at least fifty dollars. Maybe more.

I get dressed, push up the window and sneak out into the night. Down to the shed for a shovel. Up over the fence. This is easy. It is dark. Very dark.

The garden is as silent as a graveyard. A little shiver runs up my spine. This is not easy. This is scary. Where is the grave? Where is the spot where Mr Grunge has buried Mrs Grunge? Where is Mr Grunge?

I feel my way around. Gradually my eyes grow used to the dark. There it is. Over there. Crafty. What a crafty devil. He has planted tomato plants on top of the grave. And tied them up to stakes. He is trying to make everyone think it is just a vegetable garden. But he can't fool me. I know it is a grave.

Graves are spooky things. Maybe this is not such a good idea. What if Mr Grunge is nearby? Watching. Waiting. I peep over my shoulder. What was that? Nothing. Terrible thoughts enter my mind. If Mr Grunge catches me I will be history. What will he plant on my grave?

Run, run, run for it. No, stay. You will never sleep at night until this mystery is solved. I lean over the vegetable garden. I take a deep breath and rip out the little seedlings and the stakes. Then I start to dig.

It is slow, hard work. As I dig I start to think. What will I find? What if I suddenly uncover a horrible white hand? What if I hit a nose? What if there are staring, dead eyes down there? With dirt in them.

I dig more and more slowly. I don't want to find Mrs Grunge. But I do, too. I am so scared. There is a rustle in the bushes. What was that?

'Aargh,' I scream. Eyes. Someone's eyes. Staring at me from the bushes.

I drop my shovel and run. I scream and scream and scream. I am up and over that fence before you can blink. I am through that window and back into bed before you can snap your fingers.

I have my eyes closed. I want to fall asleep. And quickly. There is going to be big trouble. I can feel it in my bones.

7

There is a knock on the front door. I hear footsteps. I hear the front door open. I hear voices. Oh no. This is terrible. I have had it.

Footsteps approach my bedroom. Someone comes into the room and turns on the light. I pretend to be asleep but through my closed eyelashes I see Dad. He is carrying a shovel. He is looking at the open window. 'I know you're awake, Misty,' he says. 'Come with me.'

Dad pulls me out of bed towards the lounge-room. 'Mr Grunge is here,' he says. 'Someone has gone and ruined his tomato patch. A vandal has dug it up.'

I pull my hand away from Dad and tear back to the bedroom. I grab a bit of paper and a pencil. 'He murdered his wife,' I write. 'I was digging her up.'

Dad reads the note and throws it onto the floor. Then he drags me into the lounge. 'This is Mr Grunge,' says Dad. Mr Grunge is sitting there on the sofa. He is not saying anything. He is staring at me with evil eyes. Why can't Dad see it? Anyone would know that Mr Grunge was a murderer just by looking at him.

I open my mouth to speak. I open my mouth to tell Dad to call the police. That will prove it once and for all. They can dig up the vegetable patch.

But I do not get a chance to say anything. Dad goes on and on and on. Talk about trouble. Boy, do I cop it. I am a vandal. I am hopeless. I am mean. I am ungrateful. I will have to plant out a new garden. Just when Dad is starting to get some happiness in his life, I ruin everything. It seems like the lecture will never end. I start to cry. Silent tears run down my cheeks. In the end Dad feels sorry for me and sends me off to bed.

I hear Dad and Mr Grunge talking in the lounge. The front door slams. I look out of the window and see Mr Grunge walking down the front path. 'Murderer,' I think to myself. I just know that Mrs Grunge is dead and buried in the vegetable patch.

But no one will believe me.

Why doesn't anything nice ever happen to me? Why

does everything have to go wrong?

There is only one good thing about the whole episode.

I didn't say a word. I didn't even cry out loud. I am still in the running for the fifty dollars. I will get that fifty dollars and pay Simon back if it kills me.

Once again I try to fall off to sleep. More hours tick by but sleep won't come. My mind is too full of misery.

Suddenly I hear something. A rustle outside. There is someone in the garden.

And my window is still open. Yes, MY WINDOW IS STILL OPEN.

The skin seems to crawl over my bones. I am shivering with fear. What is outside? Who is outside?

It is him. I just know it is him. It is Mr Grunge. My throat is dry. I am petrified with fear. He is coming. He is coming. He is coming.

A dark figure appears at the window. A figure wearing a balaclava. The intruder puts a leg through the window. I open my mouth to scream out, 'Dad, Dad, Dad.'

But I don't call out. I don't say a word.

My heart is beating like a million hammers. I am so scared. But I am not stupid. My mind is working overtime. Because of the balaclava I don't really know who it is. This could be Simon again. It could be him trying to make me call out for Dad. So that he can get the fifty dollars.

Oh, what will I do? If it is Mr Grunge I will end up in the vegetable patch. But if it is Simon I will lose the bet when I call out. And he will get the money.

What will I do? What, what what?

I know. Suddenly it comes to me. I know what to do. And I do it. Yes, I do it.

ON PURPOSE.

I wet my pants. Wonderful warm wee runs down between my legs.

'Ding, ding, ding, ding.' What a racket. It is like sirens from the police, the ambulance and the fire brigade all put together.

The intruder straightens up with a jerk, bangs into the window and slumps to the ground – out like a light.

Dad bursts into the room. 'What in the . . . ?' he says. Then he sees the figure on the floor. We stare down. Who is under that balaclava? Is it Simon? Or is it Mr Grunge? Is it a man or is it a boy?

Dad bends down and pulls up the balaclava. We both stare with wide open eyes. It is not a man. And it is not a boy.

Just then Simon bursts into the room and looks at the burglar.

'Mrs Grunge,' he yells.

Yes, MRS GRUNGE. She is not dead. She is not buried. She is out like a light on the floor. Her diamond bracelet glints in the moonlight.

I am still sitting up in my wet bed. Okay, I was wrong. Mrs Grunge is not buried in the garden. She is not dead. I made a mistake. But I grin. Something good has happened.

'You spoke first,' I say to my rotten worst-ever, wet-blanket brother.

Simon looks as if his face is going to fall off. He is so cut.

Well, after that everything is fantastic. The police come and arrest Mr and Mrs Grunge. Then they dig up their backyard. They find lots of jewellery and watches and video recorders. 'We have been looking for these thieves for a long time,' says the police chief. 'There is a big reward. Two thousand dollars.'

Yes, TWO THOUSAND.

So I get the reward. And the fifty dollars as well. And my picture is in the paper and I am on television. Dad and Brook and Mum are so proud of me.

And just to top it all off, I never wet the bed again.

Yes, NEVER.

Little Squirt

Inside the toilet five boys are peeing in the air to see how high they can get. They are having a competition before the athletics start. My big brother Sam is winning as usual. No one can pee as high as he can. I go red in the face when I see them. 'Come on, Weesle,' he says to me. 'Have a go.'

I don't want to have a go really. It is embarrassing and I am not very good at it. He is asking me on purpose. He wants me to make a fool of myself again. 'Yeah,' say all the others. 'Come on, Weesle. Don't be a wimp.'

Oh, it is awful. They are all jeering at me. I will have to be in it. I undo my fly and have a try. I am so nervous that only a little dribble comes out. They all laugh and mock. 'Weak,' they yell. My brother Sam is the worst of the lot. 'Poor Weesle is a little squirt,' he says. They all crack up and laugh like mad.

We go out to athletics practice. I am in the hundred metres and so is Sam. Next week it will be the big run-off to see who is the fastest boy in the school. Today is just a try-out. How I wish I could win. I would do anything to beat my brother Sam.

But my heart is heavy inside me. He is better than me at everything. He is smarter than me. He is better-looking than me. He is taller than me. He is tougher than me. He can beat me at anything you care to name.

We crouch down at the starting line. 'I'll wait for you at the end, wimp,' jeers Sam. 'That is if you get there at all.'

The other boys are looking on. Oh, how I would love to beat Sam. I don't even care if I am not the winner. Just so long as I beat Sam. He is always showing off. He is always making me feel like a wimp.

Mr Hendrix has the starter's gun in his hand. My knees are starting to wobble I am so nervous. And this is not even the real race when the whole school will be watching. This is just a practice.

'Bang.' We are off. I get away to a good start. I am ahead by a couple of metres. Suddenly everything seems to go right. My legs whirr. I romp along easily. My breathing is steady. I look behind and Sam seems to be in trouble. I am in front and he is second. I am nearly up to the finishing line. For the first time in my life I am going to beat him at something.

I grin as I approach the string. But I grin too soon. Sam flashes by me so quickly that I can't believe it. He has beaten me again. I feel terrible. I try not to let tears show in my eyes.

Sam is jumping around and showing off. He holds his hands over his head like a boxer. 'I hung back on purpose,' he jeers. 'Thought you had me, didn't you, wimp?' he says. He gloats and shows off all the way home.

The other boys join in and tease me too.

I walk sadly along behind them. I try not to listen. Next Tuesday is the real race. I will never be able to beat Sam in that. I will be too nervous. I am just not good enough.

Sam goes off with the others to explore the big forest. They won't let me go with them. 'You'd only get lost,' says Sam.

2

Tears are in my eyes as I reach home. I try to dry them before Mum notices but once again I fail. 'What's the matter, Weesle?' says Mum.

'It's Sam,' I yell. 'He always wins at everything. Every time he beats me. He can even tie his shoelaces faster than me. I would love to beat him at something – just once. Today it was running. He won the hundred metres again. He always wins. Next Tuesday is the grand final.'

Mum bends down and puts her arm around me. 'Listen, Weesle,' she says. 'There is one way you can win at anything. I used to be a champion runner and I know.'

This is the first time that I hear about Mum being a champion runner. I look at her, waiting to learn the secret.

'You train,' she says. 'You practise. Every minute. Every day. Sam never trains. He is lazy. If you train every day you can beat him. He just wins because he is bigger than you.'

Mum could be right. I decide to give it a go.

I get up early in the morning and I train. I train at recess. I train at lunchtime. I train after school. I train in the hot weather and I train when it is cold. I get better and better, especially on the cold days. It is hard work. It is not easy. But I am determined to beat Sam. No one has ever trained as hard as I do.

Mum would be proud of me if she could see how hard I train. But I do it in secret. I am going to surprise Sam. No one is going to expect me to win. I can't wait to see the look on his face.

Tuesday comes at last. This is it. This is my big chance. All my training is going to pay off. It is cold so I wear my thick jumper to school.

I walk into the toilet where Sam and the boys are having the grand final. They are seeing which boy in the school will be the Grand Champion at peeing in the air. 'Give me a go,' I say. They laugh and jeer and call me squirt. But I don't care. I have been training for this all week.

Boy, do I squirt. I pee higher than anyone in the world has ever done. Higher than my head. The kids' eyes bug out with admiration. 'Wow,' they yell.

Sam, however, does not admire me. He is as mad as a hatter. He blows his top. He hits the roof.

But not in the same way that I do.

Piddler on the Roof

Dad and I were having a pee in the garden. Dad stood there staring at the moon and listening to the soft splash of wee on the grass. 'Poetry,' he said. 'It's the only word for taking a leak in your own backyard.'

I unzipped my fly. 'Magic,' I said.

Mum thought it was disgusting but there was nothing she could do about it. Dad said that Man had been standing in the forest peeing on the plants since the dawn of time. He had a speech all worked out about nature and Ancient Man sitting around the campfire.

'It's only natural,' he would say, 'for a man to get out and watch the stars ...'

'Twinkle,' I would yell.

Then we would both start to laugh like crazy. Every time it was the same old joke about the stars twinkling but we always thought it was funny. My dad was a great bloke. And we were great mates.

So there we were, standing side by side. Watering the lawn.

'Swordfight,' I yelled.

'You're on, sport,' said Dad.

Our two streams of pee crossed each other in the darkness like two watery blades fighting it out in times of old. Usually I ran out of ammo first and Dad would win. But tonight I beat him easily.

'Well done, Weesle,' said Dad. 'You're amazing. You could beat a horse.'

I blushed with pride and grinned as we walked back to the house. I remembered the time when the kids at school treated me like a little squirt. But that was long ago, before I proved myself in the great peeing competition.

Now life was really good.

But not for long.

2

'Look at this,' said Mum. Her eyes were glued to the television as she spoke. 'The tap water has got bugs in it. It's been contaminated. No one in the whole of Sydney can drink our water.'

'We'll have to drink Coke,' I said hopefully.

'Bottled water,' said Mum. 'They're selling it in all the shops.'

'We won't be able to have a shower,' I said even more hopefully.

'You can wash in it,' said Mum. 'But not drink it. It's disgraceful.'

We stood there listening to the man on the news saying how it was dangerous to drink the water. Especially for old people.

And children.

When he said the last two words I sort of felt funny inside. Mum and Dad were staring at me with a strange look in their eyes.

'Oh, no,' I yelled. 'No you don't. I'm not leaving. I'm not going back to the Outlaws.'

'You know what the doctor told you,' said Dad. 'One more infection and you're gone.'

I smacked my fist into my palm angrily. It was true. I had a problem with my lungs. If I got infected it was serious.

'Not the Outlaws,' I said. 'Please.'

'I wish you wouldn't call my sister and Ralph "the Outlaws",' said Mum.

'Dad does,' I started to say. He was shaking his head at me. He didn't want me to dob him in. He was the one who started calling Aunty Sue and Ralph the Outlaws. He couldn't stand them either.

'Sorry, mate,' said Dad. 'But you'll have to go to Dingle until the scare is over.'

I stared hopelessly at them both. I decided to save my breath. When they both lined up against me there was no way I could win.

3

The next morning I stepped off the train at Dingle. Horrible Aunty Sue and her even more horrible son, Ralph, were there to meet me.

'Hello, Weesle,' said Ralph in a sickly sweet voice. 'I'm looking forward to this.'

He was too, and I knew why.

'Get in the car, Weesle,' said Aunty Sue. 'We're running late. This visit really is inconvenient. You couldn't have come at a worse time. You'll have to look after yourself. I'm too busy with the hospital fete.'

'I'll look after him again,' said Ralph with a sneer.

Aunty Sue smiled at him. 'You are a kind boy,' she said. She picked up my bag and frowned.

'What have you got in here?' she said.

'Bottled water,' I told her.

'You don't need that here, droob,' said Ralph. 'Our water is pure. Not like the stinky stuff in the city.'

'The doctor said I have to,' I told him. 'Just to be on the safe side. But I'm allowed to drink lemonade.'

'No soft drinks,' snapped Aunty Sue. 'Bad for your teeth.'

I secretly felt the ten dollars in my pocket. I could buy my own Coke.

4

Aunty Sue and Ralph lived in a small cottage in the middle of Dingle. My room was up in the roof.

I plonked down my bags and sat on the bed. Ralph closed the door so Aunty Sue couldn't hear. He held out his hand. 'Pay up, Weesle,' he said. 'A dollar a day. Pay the rent.'

Ralph was much bigger than me. And he was a bully. But I shook my head.

'No way,' I said. 'Not this time. You can sneak on me all you like. Last time I stayed ten days. Ten dollars. All my pocket money. I need it to buy Coke. I can't just drink water the whole time.'

Ralph stood up and left. He didn't say a word. He didn't have to. We both knew what he was going to do.

Dob. Rat on me. Tell tales.

Call it what you like. It is the same thing. He was going to tell Aunty Sue every time I did the slightest thing wrong.

And he did. Right away.

Aunty Sue held out her hand. 'Give me the ten dollars, Weesle,' she said. 'Soft drinks are bad for your teeth.'

I handed over the ten dollars with a big sigh. This was going to be a long ten days.

The way it turned out it was a long ten hours. Ralph dobbed me in for the smallest little thing.

'Mum, Weesle didn't wipe his feet.'

'Inconsiderate child,' said Aunty Sue.

'Mum, Weesle didn't clean his teeth.'

'Unhealthy child,' said Aunty Sue.

'Mum, Weesle stole some ice-cream.'

'Thief,' yelled Aunty Sue.

'Mum, Weesle picked his nose.'

'Disgusting child,' sniffed Aunty Sue.

'Mum, Weesle didn't wash his hands before the meal.'

'Filthy boy,' yelled Aunty Sue.

This went on all afternoon. Aunty Sue had a thing about health. You had to have clean fingernails. You had to wipe your mouth with a napkin after a meal. You had to spray stuff that smelled of flowers around in the toilet. You had to search the plug-hole in the shower for hairs after you had used it.

Aunty Sue was a health freak of the worst sort. And every time I broke a rule Ralph would dob on me.

5

By the time night came I just couldn't take any more. I looked out of my little attic window on the roof and blinked back tears. I wanted to go home. I wanted to see Mum again. I wanted Dad. I wanted my own messy room.

I looked up at the stars.

I wanted a twinkle.

I was really busting by the time I got outside. Oh, it was lovely to be out there in the backyard at night. It reminded me of Dad and our sword fights. And our conversations about the meaning of life.

I quickly pulled down my fly and let fly.

'Filthy, disgusting, despicable child.' The words broke the peaceful night like a stone thrown through a window. It was Aunty Sue. And Ralph. He had dobbed on me. He knew I liked to take a leak in the garden. And he had told Aunty Sue.

'Get back inside,' she shrieked. 'Get back to your room. And don't leave it. Stay in that room and don't come out. Weesle, you are disgusting. You're going home first thing in the morning.'

I couldn't see Ralph's face. But I knew it had a smirk plastered all over it.

It was agony trying to stop the pee. Trying to stop in mid-piddle is really bad for your health. It is just torture. But I used all of my strength and managed to stop the flow. I pulled up my zip, raced back up to my room and slammed the door.

There was good news and bad news.

The good news was that they were sending me home in the morning. Terrific.

The bad news was that I couldn't leave the room to go to the loo. And I was busting to finish my leak.

There is really nothing worse than needing to have a pee and not being able to.

I knew that if I left the room Ralph would dob.

The minutes ticked by. Then the hours. The pressure built up. The pain was terrible. Unbearable. I rolled around on the bed. I staggered around the room with my knees held together. Finally, I couldn't stand it any longer. I ran to the little attic window and threw it open.

Oh, wonderful, wonderful, wonderful. The yellow stream fizzled out into the night like a burst water main. A beautiful melody. Magic. Music to the ear. Wee on a tin roof is not as good as wee on the grass. But it is still a lovely sound. I smiled as it splashed on the metal and trickled down into the spouting.

6

The next morning Aunty Sue pushed me onto the train. 'Go back to the filthy city and its filthy water,' she said.

'Yeah,' said Ralph. 'Our tank water is pure.'

'Is it?' I said.

Little Black Balls

'What are these little black balls?' said Mum in a loud voice.

She was standing there holding a pair of my jeans in one hand and the little black balls in the other. I wasn't sure what to say. She wasn't going to like it. Mum usually checks the pockets before she puts my jeans in the wash. I should have emptied them. But I forgot. Now the jeans were all stained. 'Well ...' I began.

'Come on, Sally' said Mum. She thrust the little black balls under my nose. 'Out with it.'

I just looked at my toes for a bit. Then I took a deep breath. It was no good stalling. 'Goat poo,' I said.

'Goat poo,' shrieked Mum. She threw the droppings on the floor and scrubbed at her hands with a towel. Then she turned on me with flaming eyes. I could tell that she was just about to do something silly. Like ground me for a month. Or stop my pocket money.

'I can explain,' I said. 'You won't be mad when I tell you what happened. Just give me a chance.' I took another deep breath and launched into my explanation.

2

See, I've got this friend. Everyone calls him the Paper Man. He doesn't dress in clothes. He dresses in newspapers. He wraps them around his arms and legs and ties them up with string. In the winter he wears lots of papers and in the summer he takes some of them off.

The Paper Man doesn't believe in money. He's not into buying things. He thinks everybody should get by with a lot less. 'I don't need a car,' he told me. 'Or a house. Or a washing machine. I've got the stars. And the cool wind off the sea. I've got the birds. And the fish. I don't need television. Not when I can watch the clouds tell a different story every day.'

This is how the Paper Man goes on. He doesn't care what other people think. He has a mind of his own. He lives in a bark hut on the edge of a cliff overlooking the sea. His carpet is paper. His bedcovers are paper. And his friends are the wild creatures that live on the cliffside.

The kids at school think he's crazy. When they see him wandering around in his paper clothes they call out names. From a safe distance of course. They pretend they want to buy a paper. Or ask him for fish and chips. But really they're scared of him. No one goes near his hut except me. I'm his friend.

I help him to care for the animals. He has a blind possum that he feeds every day. And a hawk that sits on his bed. It's a pet. A black hawk with a yellow beak. The hawk can fly off whenever it wants to. But it never does.

Anyway, yesterday I went to see him after school. He was sitting on a rock in the sun. On his lap he had a bag made out of old newspapers. I could see straight away that there was something moving inside.

'What have you got?' I said.

The Paper Man looked up with a sad smile. 'A friend,' he told me. 'A sick friend.'

I pulled back the paper and looked. It was a beautiful little kangaroo. She stared up at me with soft, moist eyes. She felt safe in the arms of the Paper Man. He was strong and gentle. Animals knew that he would never harm them.

'Can you fix it?' I asked him. I thought I knew what his answer was going to be. The Paper Man had healed hundreds of animals. None of them had ever died.

He shook his head slowly. 'This one has bad trouble,' he said. 'It has a lump inside. It needs to go to a vet. For an operation.'

I knew he didn't like to go into town where people laughed at his newspaper clothes. 'No worries,' I said. 'I'll take her in for you.'

He looked up at me. 'That's really nice of you, Sally,' he said. 'But vets cost money. It's two hundred dollars for an operation. We have to get two hundred dollars.'

'I'll take up a collection,' I said.

He shook his head. 'It wouldn't be right. Not begging

for money.' He walked into the hut and brought out a rusty old tin. He reached inside and took out something. It was a jewel. Small and lovely. It was smooth with blue and purple swirls running deep inside.

'An opal,' he said. 'My last one. From the old days. When I was a miner.'

I looked at the opal as it rolled around like an egg on his cracked, brown palm. Suddenly he took my hand. He opened my fingers and gave me the opal.

'Take it into town,' said the Paper Man. 'And sell it at the jeweller's. It's worth two hundred dollars. Cash it in for me. I know I can trust you, Sally.'

I went red in the face. No one else would have ever trusted me with two hundred dollars. People always say I lose things. That I'm a scatterbrain living in a dream world.

I stood up tall. 'I'll do it,' I said. 'But I won't be able to go to the jeweller's until after school tomorrow. The shops will be shut by now. And I can't wag school.'

The Paper Man's face crinkled up with a smile. 'That's the girl,' he said.

3

I walked back along the clifftop. The sun was setting into the sea like an ingot in a blazing furnace. A soft wind ruffled my hair. I looked at the opal and knew that it had cost the Paper Man a lot to part with it. I would never let him down.

Suddenly I heard something strange. At first I thought it was someone playing a joke. A sort of sad, bleating call. Then I heard it again. A baaing noise, like a sheep makes. It was coming from the cliff face.

I looked over the edge but couldn't see anything. There it was again. A loud baa. A cry for help?

The cliff fell dangerously into the sea. The water swelled and crashed below. The edge was rocky and crumbling but there was a narrow track down. I clasped the opal firmly and started to edge my way along, sitting on my bottom because I was too scared to walk.

I managed to inch my way around a clump of rocks and there he was. A large billy goat. He had a piece of chain around his neck which was tangled in a bush.

It was the dirtiest billy goat I had ever seen. Its long hair was matted with dung and dirt. It was covered in burrs and twigs. Its teeth were green and horrible. It baaed at me crossly.

'Okay, okay, Billy,' I said. 'I'll get you out.'

I was still sitting down on the little ledge, too scared to stand. I pulled myself towards the goat carefully. The sea was a long way down. There were sharp rocks in the water. I hung on to tufts of grass with one hand. My other hand still clasped the opal. I was too scared to jam it into my pocket.

Finally I reached the goat. It wasn't a bit scared. The silly thing didn't even seem to know it was trapped. It started to nibble at my socks.

'Stop it,' I yelled. 'Stop it, you stupid goat.'

Billy kept on nibbling. He took a whole chunk out of my sock and swallowed it.

With my left hand I propped myself up so that I didn't fall. I tried to untangle the chain with my other hand. It was hard work because I was trying to hold the opal at the same time.

I felt the opal fall. It just slipped out of my fingers. It seemed to take for ever to hit the ground. It was as if it was in slow motion. I made a wild grab but the opal fell onto the track and rolled towards the edge.

Quick as a flash, the goat bent down and licked it up.

'No,' I screamed.

But I was too late. The goat gave a little swallow and had the opal for dessert. It was gone. Buried deep in the blackness of Billy's bowels.

The goat had swallowed the Paper Man's opal.

4

The chain came away from the bush and Billy tried to escape. He shoved between me and the cliff. I tottered on the edge. If it hadn't been for the root of a dead tree I would have tumbled to my death. I hung on like crazy.

The ungrateful goat pushed past and bolted up the track. With the opal still in its belly.

I managed to crawl back up the cliff on my knees. I stood up and looked around. Just in time to see Billy clip clopping off in the distance.

I felt cold all over. I began to shake as I realised what had happened. The opal was gone. The goat was going. And the poor little kangaroo would miss out on its operation. It would die. And it was all my fault. I couldn't go back and face the Paper Man. I couldn't look into his trusting brown eyes and tell him that I'd lost his opal. The opal I was supposed to have sold for two hundred dollars.

The goat. I had to catch him. I belted after Billy as fast as I could go. I tore along the clifftop. Billy was heading for town. Flat out. You might not think it but goats can run fast. I tried to keep up but I couldn't. My sides ached. I had a stitch. My lungs hurt.

I slowed to a fast walk. It was the best I could do. As I went I thought about the opal. How could I get it back?

I could take Billy to the vet's. I could offer him half the opal to operate and take it out. Or I could say, 'Operate on the goat and get the opal back. Then you can fix the little kangaroo and keep the opal. Two operations for one opal.'

But in my heart I knew he would just laugh. I was just a kid. And what if the opal had gone? Moved on, so to speak.

No, I had to catch that goat and get the opal back myself. But how? What goes up must come down. What goes in must come out. All I had to do was catch Billy and collect the droppings. Sooner or later the opal would appear in a little ball of poo. And everything would be all right.

Then I started to worry. How long would the opal take to complete its journey? Goats eat quickly. Maybe the opal would pass through before I could catch up with Billy. Slow motions wouldn't be Billy's style. I had to hurry.

5

I started to run again. I could see Billy munching some flowers in a garden just outside of town. This was my chance.

Boy, was I tired. But I kept running. Even with a stitch. Billy looked up just as I reached him. He broke into a trot along the footpath into town. He went past the shops. People stopped and laughed as he passed.

'Stop that goat,' I yelled at the top of my voice.

But no one did. Everyone thought it was a great joke. Billy ran across the road against a red traffic light. Then he stopped outside the chemist's shop. And did something.

'Oh no,' I groaned.

Billy ran on. I looked at the little black balls on the footpath. There was nothing else I could do. I couldn't risk leaving them there. One of them might have the opal inside. I picked up the pellets of poo and shoved them into my pockets.

You can imagine how I felt. There I was. On my hands

and knees in the middle of the main street. Picking up goat droppings in my bare hands. With everyone looking. I went red in the face. Then I jumped up and tore after the goat. How embarrassing.

Well, it was a terrible chase. Every time I caught up to Billy he dropped a few more pellets. I had to stop and pick them up. By the time I finally grabbed him my pockets were bulging with poo. And the people in the street thought I was crazy.

I walked slowly down the road, stopping every now and then to pick up Billy's latest offerings. Finally I reached home. I took Billy into the back yard and tied him up behind the garage where Dad wouldn't see him. 'Don't make any noise,' I said. 'This is a secret between you, me, and the little black balls.'

'Baaa,' said Billy.

6

That night I found it hard to sleep. I snuck out twice and searched around in the night with a torch. But no opal. Just more of the same.

In the morning I dressed for school. I found a small cardboard box and borrowed a cheese knife from the kitchen. Then I went to check on Billy. He was gone. 'Oh no,' I groaned. I scooped up the new droppings near the fence and put them in a box. Then I followed the trail. Out through the hole in the hedge and down the lane. The pile in the box grew bigger. Finally

I found him. His chain was tangled around a letter-box. The silly goat was munching away on someone's roses.

I didn't know what to do. If I tied Billy up he might get away again. And if the opal made an appearance someone else could find it. I thought of the little kangaroo. And my friend the Paper Man. I had to make the supreme sacrifice.

'Billy,' I said. 'You're coming to school.'

Well, talk about terrible. The first class was music. I sat there looking out of the window hardly singing at all. I could see Billy outside where I had left him. Chained up to a post on the school oval. He was straining on the chain. Looking towards me.

I had the box of goat poo under the desk. I hadn't had time to examine it carefully for the opal. I slipped up the lid and started cutting open the little black balls with the cheese knife. My hands were shaking with excitement. I didn't notice that the class had stopped singing. The silence was deafening.

Suddenly I realised. Everyone was looking at me. Shame. I tried to close the lid but my shaking hands let me down. The box fell onto the floor. The contents of Billy's belly scattered everywhere.

The kids laughed and jeered. They looked at me with disgust. I felt like a creep.

While all of this was happening, Billy had been busy. Goats are stupid things. It was lonely. It wanted to find me. It had broken free and was looking for me. Billy wandered through the front door and straight into the classroom.

'Who owns this goat?' yelled Ms Quaver.

Everyone looked at me.

'Sally Sampson,' she said. 'I might have known. What on earth have you brought a goat to school for? And what's that filthy stuff on the floor?'

I didn't know what to say. My head seemed as if it was going to explode. The kids were all giggling and laughing. 'I've got asthma,' I blurted out. 'I have to drink fresh goat's milk every hour.'

There was a long silence. 'You're not going to get much milk from a billy goat,' said Ms Quaver in a sarcastic voice.

The kids packed up. Talk about laugh. They rolled around on the floor, helpless with mad mirth. Some kids held their sides as they hooted and cackled. I felt stupid. Caught out in a silly lie.

7

Ms Quaver pointed outside with a quivering finger. I grabbed Billy and took him back to the oval. 'Stay there,' I ordered. 'And don't let that opal drop until I come back.'

The class was singing some song about pennies from heaven when I returned. I had to clean up the mess in front of everyone. As I worked, I stared out of the window at Billy. He was eating and doing his business at the same time.

A feeling came over me. It was sort of like when you know that someone is looking at you. Like the time I threw an orange in the air just for fun. As soon as it left my hand I knew it was going to fall next door and hit our neighbour on the head. I just knew it was going to and it did. Well, I had another feeling like that.

I knew that Billy had finally dropped the opal. It was lying there on the grass. I just knew it.

A football team jogged out onto the field. One of the boys untied Billy because he was in the way. Another boy with a large 2 on his jumper kicked at the goat droppings. Then he stopped and looked down. He bent over and picked something up.

I forgot all about the music class. And Ms Quaver. I rushed out the door and over to the oval. 'Hand that over,' I shrieked at Number Two.

'No way,' he said. 'Buzz off, little girl.'

Little girl. He called me little girl. I saw red. And I saw the blue opal in his hand. There was no time for talking. I grabbed Number Two's arm. The opal flew into the air. Up, up, up.

Then it started to fall. Way over the other side of the oval. It landed right between the goal posts. My opal almost landed on a bird that was searching for worms. A black bird with a yellow beak.

You might not believe what happened next. I could

hardly believe it myself. The bird picked up the opal and flew off with it. It flapped right over our heads. I could see the opal clearly in its beak.

'Come back,' I screamed. 'Drop that opal.'

But it was no good. The bird flapped off towards the sea. I ran after it as fast as I could go. Billy trotted along behind. He stopped every now and then to nibble at a gate or some flowers.

What a day. Everything was going wrong. I puffed after the bird and finally caught up. It stopped for a rest by the beach and perched on top of a swing in the playground. 'Good bird,' I said. 'Good birdy. Drop it, birdy.' I tiptoed towards it.

Deep in my heart I knew it was hopeless. Birds don't come to you when you call. But I hoped that it might throw the opal away if I came close. I mean, why would a bird want an opal?

I could see the bird watching me with one beady eye. I crept closer. I reached up.

And the bird flew off. I watched as it flew out to sea, higher and higher. Then it opened its mouth and dropped the opal. It seemed to take for ever falling. A small speck plunging down. I didn't hear it hit the water but I saw it disappear. Way out deep. Where no one would ever find it. The opal was gone. Lost at sea.

'Rotten blackbird,' I shouted at the bird.

8

I turned and started walking towards the Paper Man's hut. What was he going to say? I had no opal. And no two hundred dollars. And the poor little kangaroo was dying and needed an operation.

Soon I was on top of the cliff, walking along a twisting track. I walked slowly. I didn't really want to get there. It was the worst day of my life. 'Baa,' said Billy. He was still following me.

'It's all your fault,' I said. 'Stupid goat.' I grabbed his chain and looked around for somewhere to tie him up. I'd had enough of goats for one day.

I found a tree by a small pond and this time fixed the chain very carefully. 'There's enough for you to eat here until I come back,' I said to Billy.

He stared back without saying anything. Trying to make me feel guilty. The way dogs do when you won't take them for a walk.

I trudged along the cliff with my head down. The poor little kangaroo. Now it couldn't have the operation because we didn't have the two hundred dollars. What if it died?

I had ninety-five cents in the bank. That was no good. I could ask for my pocket money in advance. I tried it out in my mind. 'Dad,' I could say. 'Will you let me have the next one hundred weeks' pocket money right now?'

The answer would be 'no' with a long lecture to follow.

By now I could see the Paper Man's shack in the distance. I stopped. I just couldn't tell him. My feet refused to move.

'Excuse me,' said a voice.

I just about jumped through the roof. Except there wasn't any roof.

I turned around and saw a man with a worried look and a bald head. 'Have you seen a goat?' he asked.

'A goat?' I replied.

'Yes, a Kashmir goat. With long hair. I brought it out from India. But it's run off. It's worth fifteen thousand dollars.' He hung his head and shook it in despair.

Then he looked up and said something that was music to my ears. 'There's a two hundred dollar reward for whoever finds it.' He took out two one hundred dollar notes and waved them in the air.

I gave an enormous smile. Then I grabbed the money. 'Follow me,' I said.

Well, that's just about the end of the story. I took the bald-headed man to Billy and the little kangaroo to the vet's for the operation. The Paper Man was rapt. I've never seen anyone as happy as he was when the kangaroo came back. She made a complete recovery.

9

Mum was standing there, still holding the jeans with goat-poo stains on the pockets. She had a soppy smile on her face. The sort of smile people have when they see someone's new baby. It was the type of smile that Mum rarely gave me any more.

'Why, Sally,' she said. 'What a lovely story. How sad. You kind girl. What a terrible time you've had.' She looked at the little black balls on the floor and the dirty jeans. 'Don't worry about the stains. Just clean up the mess and we won't say any more about it.'

I gave her a big smile and ran up to the kitchen to get a brush and dustpan. Dad was there. He was just going to open the fridge and get a beer. 'Don't,' I screamed.

But it was too late. He opened the fridge door. There on the top shelf was a little mouse. Sitting up on a saucer, begging. A dead mouse all covered in mould. It looked lovely. As if it was a polar bear wearing a long white coat.

Dad didn't think it was lovely. He stood there quite still. He didn't even turn around. He spoke slowly with a really mean voice. 'Sally, did you put this disgusting thing in the fridge?'

He turned on me with flaming eyes. 'Come on, Sally,' said Dad. He thrust the saucer under my nose. 'Out with it.'

I could tell that he was just about to do something silly. Like ground me for a month. Or stop my pocket money.

I took a deep breath and tried to think of another good story. Fast.

Too Many Rabbits

Sex is not talked about in our place. No one has told me anything. I have worked out quite a few things myself though. I keep my ears open and my eyes to the ground.

I know the main bits. I see things. Like when Sky's dog had pups. One day Sandy was fat and there were no puppies and the next day she was thin and there they were. You don't have to be too smart to work out where they came from.

How they got in there, I even know that too.

Sandy is a great dog. And the puppies are beautiful. I would like one of them more than anything in the world. But I just can't talk Dad around. He will not have any pets at all.

'Can I have a pet, Dad?' I asked him.

'What sort of pet?' he said.

'A dog?'

'Nah, they bark too much. And they dig holes and annoy the neighbours.'

'A cat?' I said.

'Nah, they leave fur everywhere.'

'A bird?'

'Nah, it's cruel to keep them in cages.'

'A mouse?' I begged.

'Nah, they breed like rabbits.'

'An elephant,' I yelled.

Dad grinned at this. 'If you can find one you can have it,' he said.

I raced out and grabbed Saturday's paper. Before he changed his mind. You have to strike while the lion is hot. I looked and looked but there were no elephants for sale. Not one. I bet that Dad knew this all along. Parents can be so sneaky sometimes.

After this I was sent to my room for throwing the paper on the floor and yelling.

We live in a bookshop in the main street. Upstairs is Mum and Dad's room. Under that is the shop. Down the bottom is the storeroom and my bedroom. There are no windows in my room. It's like a jail. I am always getting sent to my room. It's not fair.

If I was to dig a hole in the wall I could make a tunnel. I could escape. Like prisoners of war do.

It would be great to have an escape tunnel. Even if it took me twenty years to dig, I would have a way out when I was sent to my room. It would be worth it in the long run.

Anyway, there I was lying on my bed and not allowed out. I just stared at the wall. It was made out of wooden panels. There was nothing else to do so I decided to pull a panel off and start to dig into the wall behind it. I started pushing at the wood with an old screwdriver. I put the blade in a crack and levered.

Bingo. Kerpow. Wow. The panel just swung open. Just like that. It was a door. A secret door. I couldn't believe it. I didn't have to dig a tunnel. There was already something there.

I stared into the hole but I couldn't see a thing. It was dark. And musty. It smelled all stale. I wanted to go straight in and explore. But I didn't have a torch. It might be dangerous.

No, this would take a bit of thinking about. I wouldn't go in until I could get a torch. There could be horrible things lying around. I could hurt myself in the dark. It's important to look before you weep.

I shut the door and waited for my time in solitary confinement to be over.

2

The following day I went next door to see Sky. She owned a junk shop and I knew she would have an old torch somewhere. You could find wonderful things in that shop.

Sky grinned when I asked her. 'A torch? I don't know, love. There might be one in the corner over there.'

I rummaged around for ages. Beads, candles, bits of broken bikes, one thong, hats, a cracked toilet seat, a knife with no handle, a rabbit in a cage.

A rabbit in a cage.

A beautiful, lovely, pink-eyed rabbit with a black patch on its white back. 'Wow,' I said. 'This is the most beautiful rabbit in the world. I wish it was mine.' I pressed its warm fur up to my face.

'Ten dollars,' said Sky. 'You can have it for ten dollars. That's what I paid for it.'

I shook my head. 'Dad will never let me have it,' I said. 'Anyway, I haven't got ten dollars.'

Sky smiled at me kindly. 'You can have it for eight,' she said. 'That's pretty generous. But you'll have to be quick. I had six yesterday and this is the last one left.'

I spent ages stroking the rabbit. 'Pinky,' I said. 'Her name is Pinky and she loves me.'

'I've only got ten cents on me,' I said. 'But I've got eight dollars at home.' I knew that Dad wouldn't let me keep the rabbit but I had an idea. I would hide Pinky. Dad would never know.

But where? Where could I hide her?

Of course. The space behind the wall. You could keep a rabbit in there and no one would know. But first I would need a torch.

'What about this?' said Sky. She had a torch in her hand. Not a bad one either. And it had batteries that worked.

'How much?' I asked.

Sky was wearing about a hundred strings of bright beads around her neck. She always fiddled with them when she was with a customer. 'Ten cents,' she said.

'Gee thanks,' I said. I put Pinky down and ran back into our bookshop. I was in such a hurry that I bumped straight into Dad. Oh no, he was going to ask me what I wanted a torch for.

'Where'd you get that?' said Dad. 'It's a nice-looking torch.'

'I bought it from Sky,' I said. 'Ten cents.'

'Ten cents,' said Dad. 'It's worth at least ten dollars. No wonder she's going broke.'

'What?' I said.

'She's got no money. She's behind with the rent. She feels sorry for people and sells everything for less than she bought it for. They'll kick her out soon for sure.'

'Who will?' I said.

'The bank. The bank owns all these shops along here.'

The bank was right next door. 'They can't kick her out,' I yelled. 'She's my friend.'

'We're not doing so well ourselves,' said Dad.

I ran down to my room and slammed the door. I was very upset about Sky. I looked at the torch. The torch. The tunnel. I had forgotten all about them.

I switched on the torch and stepped through the wall.

3

It was a big, dark cellar. The floor and three of the walls were concrete. The wall at the back was just dirt and stones. There was nothing there except cobwebs, dust and an old bookshelf with two ancient bird books in it.

Books. My heart sank. I had been hoping for treasure or jewels. I snooped around for a bit but there was nothing to be found. There was a light switch and I turned it on. No, there was nothing to see. Just a cold, gloomy cellar. Still, it would be great for a rabbit. I wouldn't even have to build a cage.

I looked up. Over the top was our shop. On one side was Sky's junk shop. And on the other was the bank. I just stood there thinking. That's when I got the idea. That's when it popped into my head. I could dig a tunnel.

And rob the bank.

Like Robbing Hood. You take from the rich and give to the poor. The bank was rich. Sky was poor. I would take some money and give it to Sky. I wouldn't keep any for myself. Not even eight dollars for a rabbit. I would give it all to Sky. Then she could give it back to the bank and they wouldn't kick her out of her shop. They would get their money back and everybody would be happy.

I smuggled Pinky in and she sniffed around her new home. I could tell that she liked it.

It was a good plan and I made a start straight away. I borrowed Dad's spade and started to dig at the wall. The spade was heavy and the wall was hard. All rocks and stones. After about an hour I stopped. My hands were blistered and sore. I was sweaty and tired. And I had hardly made a scratch on the wall.

Digging tunnels is hard work.

I picked up Pinky and gave her a cuddle. She was very, very fat. She nibbled at my hand. 'She wants food,' I said to myself. I went upstairs and raided the fridge. Two carrots. Pinky finished them off in no time at all. Talk about hungry. And fat. 'Your thighs are bigger than your stomach,' I said.

4

The next day I took the eight dollars in to Sky. 'Thanks,' she said. 'It's my only sale for the day.' She was down in the dumps. Just sitting there munching on an apple.

'Don't worry,' I said. 'They won't kick you out. I've got a plan.'

'What's that, love?' said Sky.

'I'm digging a tunnel into the bank. I'm going to get you some money.'

Sky shook her head. 'No, no, no,' she said. 'You can't do that.'

'Why not? They've got plenty of money.'

'Yes, but it's not ours. It belongs to other people. It wouldn't be right. And anyway, tunnels are dangerous. It might fall in and kill you. If you dig a tunnel I'll have to tell your dad.'

I couldn't believe it. Sky didn't want me to dig a tunnel. I made up my mind not to tell her anything about the secret cellar. Just in case.

'It was a sweet idea, love,' she said. 'But don't worry. Something will turn up. You shouldn't worry yourself too much about money.' She took a big bite out of her apple.

'Yeah,' I said. 'Money is the fruit of all evil.'

I went home and got some straw and rags for Pinky. The floor of the cellar was cold. I also took her another three carrots. She gobbled them down like crazy. Rabbits sure do eat a lot. Especially big fat ones like Pinky.

That night Mum had a few words to say at tea-time. 'Nearly all the carrots have gone,' she said. 'Have you taken them, Philip?'

I nodded my head.

'I'm glad to see you eating vegetables,' she said. 'But please ask first. Yours isn't the only mouth around here.'

She was right about that. When I got down to the cellar there were another eight mouths. Pinky had given birth to eight of the cutest little bunnies you have ever seen. They were pink and hairless and blind and they sucked away at Pinky's teats like crazy. No wonder she was hungry.

I rushed upstairs and took a bunch of celery out of the fridge. Pinky finished it off in ten minutes flat.

There was one thing I knew for sure. Feeding my family was going to be a problem.

5

I named the new bunnies One, Two, Three, Four, Five, Six, Seven and Eight. I couldn't give them real names because I didn't know what sex they were. I found out after a bit that all of them except poor little Eight were females.

Days passed. Weeks passed. Months passed. My little bunnies became big bunnies.

I had four big problems:

1. Sky was going broke and the bank people were talking about tossing her out of her shop.
2. The rabbits were eating more and more and food was hard to find.
3. What goes in one end comes out the other.
4. One, Two, Three, Four, Five, Six and Seven were all getting very fat indeed.

'Times are hard,' said Sky. 'People aren't throwing out their old things. I just haven't got enough stock to sell. The rent costs more than I make.'

I nodded wisely. I was short of money myself. I was spending it all on vegetables for my rabbits. 'It's hard to make lends meet,' I said.

Mum was watching the fridge like a hawk. She counted every carrot. Every leaf of lettuce. She even knew how many peas were in there. 'I think he must have a lack of Vitamin C,' said Mum. 'All he does is eat vegetables and fruit.'

'At least he'll be regular,' said Dad.

Well, things went on like this for quite a bit. Every day I searched for grass, thistles, old cabbage leaves. Anything for my rabbits to eat.

Twice a day I would pull back the secret panel and feed my rabbits. Then I would sweep up the poo and put it out in our tiny backyard.

Dad was starting to get suspicious. 'This is crazy,' said Dad. 'Why are all these rabbits coming into our yard? There are droppings everywhere. Why our place? Why not next door's?'

That night he sat up all night waiting for rabbits. He sat out there in the yard shivering behind some old boxes, waiting and waiting for the rabbits. But none came. 'Something's going on,' he said. 'And I'm going to find out what it is.'

I knew that if he discovered my secret he would give the rabbits away. Or let them go. Or even worse.

Rabbit pie.

That night I found something else. More rabbits. Five had had six babies. Wonderful, hairless little babies. Still blind with their eyes closed. My little bunnies. It was up to me to look after them. Protect them. Stop Dad finding them.

Two nights later One gave birth. Then Two, Three, Four, Six and Seven followed. My family had grown to thirty-nine wonderful rabbits.

It was great having so many. But going in with the food and out with the poo left no time for anything else. It took over an hour to find grass and thistles and stuff. Mr Griggs from the greengrocer's gave me rotten vegetables but I couldn't take too much. He might tell Dad.

And the poo was becoming a big problem. There was nowhere to put it in the middle of the main street.

One night I watched this movie about prisoners of war digging an escape tunnel. They had to hide the dirt that they dug out. What they did was put the soil in old socks and hide them in their trouser legs. When they pulled on a string the soil would fall out while they were walking along. No one noticed it.

Brainwave. I rubbed my hands together. Truth is stranger than friction.

I filled up two socks with rabbit poo and walked into the street. As I went along the footpath I let a little poo fall to the ground. It worked like a charm. No one noticed.

Well, not at first. 'I can't believe it,' said Dad. 'The whole footpath is covered in rabbit droppings. But you never see a rabbit. Where are they coming from? I'm going to call a meeting of the other shop owners. Something has to be done.'

Two nights later Dad and five of the other shopkeepers sat up watching for the rabbits. Sky told me all about it. 'We waited and waited,' she said. 'In the freezing rain. But not so much as a single rabbit showed up.'

I smiled and shuffled out onto the street to spread

a bit more joy around. I was only a kid but I could make things happen. I liked pulling strings.

6

More months went by. My whole life was spent looking after the rabbits. Dirt and sand for the floor. Straw for them to sleep on. Old vegetables and grass for food. Then carting out the poo and dirt and sand and spreading it along the street. It took hours and hours. I had to sneak out at night. In out, in out. The responsibility was getting too much for me.

Then it happened. The next batch of babies. Before I knew it I had one hundred and fifteen rabbits. I couldn't remember their names. I was so tired from carting poo and grass that I could hardly keep my eyes open. The whole thing was turning into a nightmare.

I had to do something.

I sat down and had a good think about my situation. They were all pet rabbits. I couldn't let any go. Foxes and cats would eat them. They didn't know how to look after themselves in the wild. I tried to give a few away at school but the kids' mothers just sent them back. Dad would find out if I kept on with that. But I couldn't let them keep breeding.

How could I stop them?

There was only one way. Keep the males and females apart.

Sky had a second-hand roll of chicken wire. You can

have it for two dollars,' she said. 'It doesn't matter any more. The bank is closing me down.' Her lips were trembling and her voice was all croaky. I looked at the window. There was a big sign saying: CLOSING-DOWN SALE – EVERYTHING CHEAP.

'No,' I yelled. 'You can't leave, Sky. You're my best friend.'

She just shuffled off into the back of the shop so that I wouldn't see her crying.

That afternoon I went into the bank when they were busy and spread some rabbit poo around on the floor. Everyone started sniffing and saying how disgusting it was. As I left I thought I heard someone say something about making a deposit.

After tea I sneaked into the rabbit cellar and built a fence. I put all the males on one side and all the females and babies on the other. It was a good fence. Now there wouldn't be any more babies. 'You are a genius, Philip,' I said to myself.

That night, after feeding the rabbits, I lay down to sleep. All was quiet. For a little while. Then suddenly I heard a terrible squealing noise coming from behind the wall. It grew louder and louder. Squealing and thumping and rustling. It would wake Dad for sure.

'Quiet in there,' I whispered.

The noise grew louder. Oh no. If Dad came down – rabbit pie.

I opened the secret door. A terrible sight met my

eyes. The male rabbits were fighting each other. Others were flinging themselves at the fence. Some of the bigger ones were jumping up in the air trying to get over. 'Stop it,' I whispered. 'Stop it.'

But they didn't stop it. More and more male rabbits threw themselves against the fence. They were crazy. They were wild. The fence began to sag. Wham. Down it came. The rabbits poured across like water from a broken dam. Then they started jumping all over each other.

I shut the panel. 'Disgusting,' I said to myself. 'Sex sure is a powerful merge.'

More powerful than I thought. In no time at all I had about four hundred and fifty rabbits.

Things were getting out of hand. The smell was so bad that I could hardly bear to go into the cellar. And it was starting to seep through into my bedroom.

'What's that smell?' said Dad. He sniffed around trying to find something. He looked under the bed and in the cupboard but he didn't find the secret panel. My rabbits were safe. For the time being.

'Make sure you change your socks every day,' Dad said. 'This room smells terrible.'

7

Everything was going wrong. I was facing a mid-wife crisis. I sat down and had a little talk to myself. 'Philip,' I said. 'You can't keep this up. You can't get enough food for the rabbits. You can't keep up with the poo pile. You can't give the rabbits away and you can't keep them. You can't let them go or the foxes will get them. You can't tell Dad and he is going to discover them any day. Sky is getting kicked out of her shop. You are just a kid. You are out of your depth. The rabbits are too much for you. You are too big for your brutes.' My eyes started to water.

There was worse to come. Dad sat next to me on the bed. He saw that I was crying. He took my hand and smiled kindly. 'You've heard then?' he said.

'Heard what?'

'We have to leave the shop. It's not just Sky who can't afford the rent. We've been behind for months. The bank is throwing us out.'

'No,' I screamed. 'No, no, no.' My heart was in my shoes. I didn't want to leave. And I would have to show Dad the rabbits. I couldn't leave them there to starve.

Rabbit pie.

Dad started sniffing around. 'There must be a dead possum in the walls,' he said. 'That smell is disgusting.' He started to tap on the walls, listening and sniffing. He was going to find the rabbits. I just knew he was.

I couldn't bear to watch. I ran up the stairs and into the sunlight. I ran and ran and ran. In the end I was out of breath. I just dropped down onto the footpath and hung my head in my hands.

I couldn't say how long I stayed there. It was a long

time. Finally I was driven home by hunger.

When I arrived back I knew straight away that something was wrong. No one was in the shop. Mum and Dad were both downstairs. In my room.

I crept down the stairs. The panel was open. Mum and Dad were inside the cellar. And the rabbits were gone.

'Murderers,' I yelled.

'What?' said Dad.

'You've killed my rabbits.'

'No,' said Dad. He pulled the old bookshelf away. 'Look at this.'

I couldn't believe it. Amazing. A tunnel. The rabbits had made a break for freedom. They were all gone. Every last one.

'The foxes,' I screamed. 'The foxes will get them.'

I pelted up the stairs.

I looked up the street. I looked down the street. Nothing. Not a rabbit in sight.

Then I looked at Sky's window. The closing-down sign had gone. There was a new one in its place. It said: RABBITS FOR SALE – $15.00 EACH.

The junk shop was full of rabbits. Sky was smiling. There were rabbits everywhere. She even had one on her head. 'I told you something would turn up,' she said. 'They just came out of a hole in the floor. I've sold fifteen already. I'll make a fortune. And I won't have to leave.'

I didn't say anything. There wasn't anything to say. I was happy for Sky. And happy for the rabbits. I smiled and walked slowly back to my room.

'Don't look so gloomy,' said Dad.

'I don't want to leave,' I said. 'I like it here.'

Dad was waving one of the old books I had found.

'We don't have to go,' he yelped. 'You've saved the day, Philip.'

'What?' I mumbled.

'This book. It's a John Gould original. Worth a fortune. We can pay off the bank now, no worries.'

I grinned. I was so happy.

'There's more good news,' said Mum.

'I'm going to have a baby − babies. I'm having twins.'

Geeze, I was happy. Fancy that. Twins. I know why she's having them, too. Mum and Dad own a bookshop. Well, it's obvious, isn't it?

They read like rabbits.

Picked Bones

Uncle Sam's dead body.

I can sort of picture it in my mind.

He is stretched out on the desert sand. Wild animals have torn his clothes. Birds have pecked at him. There is nothing left except his skeleton.

And the box – clutched in the bones of one hand. And a rusty nail clasped in the other.

1

Poor Uncle Sam. It was a horrible way to die. All alone in the outback with no friends. And no one knowing what happened.

Uncle Sam was a birdwatcher. He loved native birds and he hated feral cats. 'They get out in the outback and breed,' he used to say. 'They don't belong in this country. The birds have no defences. One cat will eat over a hundred birds a year.'

Uncle Sam had done a lot for the native wildlife in Australia. But now he was gone. Dad arranged for the bones to be brought back and we had a funeral. I watched sadly as the coffin went down into the grave.

We were alike were Uncle Sam and I. Two greenies trying to save the world. And now he was gone. It was the saddest thing ever.

As we walked out of the cemetery Dad wiped his wet eyes and handed me the box. It was made of carved wood and on the top was scratched: FOR TERRY. KEEP AWAY FROM K … The writing trailed off. Uncle Sam must have died while he was scratching the message with the nail.

'What's in it?' I asked Dad.

'I don't know,' he said. 'It doesn't have a lid. Anyway, I wouldn't open a present with someone else's name on it. It was meant for you.'

That's the sort of guy Dad is. He wouldn't even read your diary if it was left open on the desk. Still, he looked worried. 'Uncle Sam was a bit weird,' he said. 'Heaven knows what's in that box. You be careful with it.'

After the funeral everyone came back to our house for the wake. There was lots of drinking and laughing. It didn't seem right to me. 'Why is everyone having a good time?' I said to Mum.

She looked at me and smiled. 'Uncle Sam would have wanted it,' she said. 'We've said goodbye to him at the graveyard. That was the time to cry. Now we have to get on with life. That's the way it is.'

I still didn't like it. I went up to my room and shut the door so I couldn't hear all the noise. I put the box on my bed and had a good look at it. The wood had steel bands around it. There was no lid and no keyhole. I would have to get a saw to cut it open. But I didn't want to do that. It was too good. And I might break what was in it.

It was sort of spooky to look at the scratched writing on the lid. The last words of Uncle Sam. Written to me – his best mate. He died at the very moment of scratching out these letters. I shivered and put the box under my bed. Then I went down to join the party.

By now everyone had had too much to drink. They were drowning their sorrows. Laughing and arguing and telling jokes and stories. Mum was even speaking to Aunt Marjory. I couldn't believe it.

They hadn't spoken to each other since Aunt Marjory gave me Knuckles for Christmas. Mum had to let me keep Knuckles seeing that he was a Christmas present. She said that Aunt Marjory only gave him to me because he was a horrible cat and she wanted to get rid of him. Pet cats are okay if you keep them away from the native animals. But Knuckles was mean and sneaky. He yowled and scowled. He spat and hissed. He scratched our sofa to pieces. He wouldn't let anyone touch him. He was the king of the neighbourhood. All the other cats disappeared when Knuckles was around. And I just couldn't keep him in at night. He would always manage to get out and go hunting for birds.

Knuckles was my only pet. I *used* to have guinea pigs – two cute little black and white ones. Until Knuckles got into their cage one night and ate them both for supper. Now I had no pets except Knuckles. Not that you could call Knuckles a pet. A crocodile would have been more fun.

That got me to thinking. Knuckles. Where was he? Nowhere to be seen. That was strange. Normally he would be up on the table licking the best food. Then no one would eat anything and I would be in trouble for letting him inside.

I prowled around the house hunting for Knuckles. I looked in the kitchen. Under the tables. Behind the fridge. In the laundry basket. All the usual places. But he was nowhere to be seen.

I went upstairs to my room and caught sight of something strange. Through the window. Outside. On the porch roof. Knuckles was standing there. And when I say standing that's what I mean. Standing on his two back legs. And flapping his front ones up and down like chicken wings. He was staring into my bedroom window and waving his front legs about like a crazy chook.

2

Something strange was going on. Something really weird. There was Knuckles. Outside. On the window ledge trying to get in. He was screeching and yowling something terrible. He clawed at the glass with vicious swipes. I tapped on the window. 'Buzz off,' I said. 'You're not getting in until dark. No way.'

Suddenly, as if a clever thought had just crossed his mind, Knuckles turned and jumped down to the ground.

I picked up the box and examined it. What was inside? And how could I open it?

I gave the box a gentle shake and held my ear up to it. Nothing. Not a murmur. This was driving me crazy. What could be inside? I read the scratched words again. KEEP AWAY FROM K ...

Something was wrong. I could feel it in my bones. I thought about that last word that Uncle Sam had been scratching on the lid. KEEP AWAY FROM K ... He had been about to scratch a word starting with 'k' when he died. There were lots of possibilities. Kangaroos. Kookaburras. Kids. I looked around the room. There was a bunch of keys on my shelf. It could even be them. Just to be on the safe side I picked them up and threw them into the hallway.

I made one final check and couldn't see anything else that started with 'k'. I wasn't too good at spelling but I thought I had found everything. There was nothing left starting with 'k'. All I needed now was a saw.

Suddenly I felt nervous. There could be something dangerous inside. Maybe I should go and ask Dad to saw the box open.

Downstairs the party was getting louder and louder. I looked out of the window. People were staggering around out on the back lawn. Uncle Russell was having a pee behind some bushes. Another group were arguing about whether the women should have been allowed to carry Uncle Sam's coffin. Mum was saying they should. 'Women are not strong enough,' I heard Aunt Marjory say.

'Don't be ridiculous,' said Mum. 'It's not as if he weighed much. He was only bones.'

They were all off their faces. No, none of the adults would help.

I stared at the box. So did Knuckles.

Knuckles.

He was inside the house. He was inside my room. He had sneaked in while the drunken mourners were going in and out. Knuckles had a strange look in his eyes. A wild but gentle look. He pounced over to the box and started purring. Purring, do you mind. Knuckles had never purred in his life. He looked like a cat that had just eaten the cream. Knuckles was purring at the box.

He was staring at the box and licking his lips. It almost looked as if he was reading the writing on the lid. Uncle Sam's last words so to speak. KEEP AWAY FROM K... Of course. That was it. Why didn't I see it before? KEEP AWAY FROM KNUCKLES.

I mustn't let Knuckles get near the box. Whatever was inside could be damaged by cats. Even now Knuckles' very presence could be ruining something valuable. It could be treasure of some sort. Melting away because a cat was in the room.

'Get out,' I yelled. 'Go on. Buzz off, Knuckles.' I had

to shoo him out before he ruined everything.

Knuckles turned around slowly. He crouched down and the fur on his neck stood up like a necklace made of poisoned needles. His eyes were filled with hate. His muscles quivered, ready to spring. I had never seen an animal with such a vicious look in its eyes. I don't mind telling you I was scared. Scared of a cat.

'Okay,' I said, 'okay. Take it easy, Knuckles.' I took a few steps backwards to show that I meant no harm. Knuckles relaxed and turned back to the box. Then he did something weird. He started licking the box. Licking and purring at the same time.

Amazing. A cat licking a wooden box. It was strange. But not as strange as what happened next.

Click. The lid of the box sprang open.

Imagine that. Knuckles' spit had released the catch. Crazy but true. Now I could find out what was inside. I was dying to know. I took a silent step forward.

Hiss, spit, hiss. Knuckles crouched low, hate in his eyes. I backed slowly away. 'All right, all right,' I said. 'Don't go off your brain.'

Knuckles relaxed. Then he suddenly leapt. Not at me. Not at anyone. He jumped onto the top of the open box and curled up. Straight away he began to purr. He reminded me of a dragon curled up on its pile of jewels and gold.

What was inside the box? What was it? I just had to know. I couldn't handle this on my own. Knuckles might ruin everything. KEEP AWAY FROM KNUCKLES. That's what Uncle Sam had been writing. It was time to bring in the big guns. I went off to get the adults.

3

Most of the guests had called taxis and gone home. Their cars were still parked in the drive. They would probably come back and get them in the morning. When they felt a little better, if you know what I mean. Anyway, Dad and Mum and Aunt Marjory were still there. So was Uncle Russell. They all stared into my bedroom. Knuckles was still curled up on the box. Purring.

'He's a lovely cat,' said Aunt Marjory. 'He just loves me, you know.'

'Why did you give him to Terry then?' said Mum.

'A sacrifice,' said Aunt Marjory. 'I had to make the sacrifice. All children need a pet.'

'He won't get off the box,' I said. 'Knuckles isn't allowed near the box. I can't get him off. He's the meanest cat in the world.'

'Nonsense,' said Aunt Marjory. 'He's as quiet as a lamb.' She walked over and bent down to pick up Knuckles.

Swish. Swipe. Snarl. Knuckles struck out. Quicker than a snake's tongue.

'Aargh.' Aunt Marjory fell back with a terrible scream. Thin red lines of blood ran across her face. Aunt Marjory scrambled to her feet and ran into the corridor. She rushed to the hall mirror. 'My face,' she yelled. 'My beautiful face.'

Uncle Russell tried not to laugh at that.

Aunt Marjory looked at me in fury. 'You've ruined that cat,' she yelled. 'He had a beautiful nature before.'

'Perhaps you'd like him back,' said Mum.

'Now, now girls,' said Uncle Russell. 'No need to argue. I'll get the cat. I'm good with animals.'

He was brave, was Uncle Russell. There's no doubt about that. Raw Australian courage. He had heaps of it. He just strode across the room and grabbed the cat. Just like that. Bent down and picked up Knuckles by the scruff of the neck.

And just like that Knuckles twisted out of his hands. And fixed himself to Uncle Russell's face. Knuckles was so quick you could hardly see him move. He wrapped his legs around Uncle Russell's head. Uncle Russell's face was buried in Knuckles' trembling body.

'Mmff, ggg, mnnff.' Uncle Russell fell onto the bed. We couldn't hear what he was trying to say. He couldn't speak. He couldn't breathe. He was suffocating. Knuckles was killing Uncle Russell. He pulled and pulled at Knuckles but the horrible animal had its claws sunk into his neck.

'Quick,' screamed Dad. 'Turn on the shower, Terry.'

The shower? This was no time for a shower.

Dad started to lead Uncle Russell out into the corridor. The cat still clung to his head.

Mum ran into the bathroom and turned on the shower.

'Oh,' said Aunt Marjory. 'Oh, oh, oh. What have you done to that cat?'

Dad took Uncle Russell into the bathroom. He looked like a man wearing a hairy blindfold. Dad pushed his head under the cold water. Knuckles dropped off, wet and bedraggled. Uncle Russell collapsed onto the floor, gasping for air.

Knuckles sped back towards the bedroom.

'Quick, Terry,' shouted Dad. 'Shut the door. Don't let him back in.'

I wanted to shut the door. I mean I meant to shut the door. I was just a bit slow that's all. I wanted to see what was in the box. I had to know. I just managed to get a glimpse. Then I ran for the door. Too late. Knuckles flashed by. Straight back onto the box.

Uncle Russell wiped the blood off his neck. 'Right,' he said. 'That cat is history.'

'I know what's in the box,' I said.

They all fell silent and looked at me.

'Well?' said Mum.

'Eggs,' I said. 'Two lovely bird's eggs.'

4

We all stared through the doorway at Knuckles. He was curled up on the box, purring and looking happy. In an evil sort of way.

'Isn't he sweet?' said Aunt Marjory. 'He thinks he's their mother. He's trying to hatch the eggs.'

She was right. And she was wrong. He was trying to hatch the eggs. But he didn't think he was their mother. I didn't think so anyway. Not for one minute. Knuckles licked his lips.

'He's going to eat them,' I screamed. 'Knuckles is going to hatch the eggs and then eat the birds. That's why Uncle Sam scratched "Keep Away From K ... " on the lid. Keep away from Knuckles. Uncle Sam knew I had a pet cat.'

I could just see it in my mind. Two lovely little birds. Helpless. Harmless. Newborn chicks. Knuckles would eat them alive.

'He's right,' said Dad. 'And we don't know what sort of birds they are. They could be very rare. We have to save them. That's what Sam would have wanted.'

'And me,' I said. 'That's what I want too.'

Uncle Russell nodded. 'Leave it to me. I'll fix the ruddy cat. No worries.'

'Don't hurt him,' said Aunt Marjory. 'He means well.'

'I'll do it, Russell,' said Dad. 'You can be a bit rash sometimes.'

Dad went out to the backyard and fetched our rubbish bin. You know – the sort with wheels that you get from the council. Dad tipped out the rubbish and cut a small hole in the side. Then he put on a raincoat and slipped a garden glove on one hand.

We took the bin upstairs and Dad hopped inside and closed the lid. He looked out of the hole. 'Wheel me in,' he said. 'Park me next to the box. I'll stick out my gloved hand and grab Knuckles. He won't be able to get at me because I'll be inside the bin. Then you wheel me outside and we dump Knuckles in a cage.'

It was a good plan.

Uncle Russell carefully wheeled the bin into my bedroom. Knuckles hissed and raised his fur but he stayed curled up on the eggs. Uncle Russell quickly walked back to us. He was in a hurry to get out of the way. And I didn't blame him. Not one bit.

We all held our breath and watched. The fingers of Dad's glove slowly moved out of the hole. Then the whole glove. Then Dad's arm, safely enclosed in the raincoat. The glove moved closer and closer to Knuckles. The cat didn't move. Well, only his eyes. Knuckles' eyes were glued to that glove. Dad opened his fingers just above Knuckles' neck. At any second he would have Knuckles firmly by the scruff of the neck.

Peow. Talk about fast. I've never seen anything like it. Knuckles moved like a flash. His teeth sank into the glove. Into Dad's fingers. 'Ouch,' came Dad's muffled voice from inside. He shook his arm around like a crazy windmill. Knuckles hung on for grim death. A ginger streak, whipping back and forth through the air. 'Et it off, et it off,' came a shrieking voice from inside the bin.

'What did he say?' asked Mum.

'Sounds like "Get it off",' said Uncle Russell.

Before anyone could move, Dad pulled his hand back inside the bin.

The only trouble was, he pulled Knuckles in with it.

There was dead silence for about two seconds. I snatched a look at where the eggs had been. 'Look,' I yelled.

But no one did. A terrible yowling, howling noise came from the bin. Was it Dad? Or was it Knuckles? You couldn't tell. The screeching and shaking went on and on and on. Something horrible was going on in there. The bin rocked and rolled. Hissed and heaved. There was a lot of pain inside that bin.

'Don't hurt Knuckles,' yelled Aunt Marjory. 'He means well.'

Suddenly a silence fell over the room. The bin stopped shaking. A bleeding and tattered glove pushed up the lid. 'I surrender,' came Dad's voice. With a quick yowl, Knuckles flashed out of the bin and sat back on his perch. He licked his lips and started to purr.

Slowly, slowly Dad emerged from the bin. Like a long-buried corpse rising from the grave. He was scratched, torn and bleeding. His clothes shredded to rags. It was a terrible sight. He didn't have enough strength to get out of the bin. Uncle Russell had to wheel him down the stairs into the kitchen.

5

Altogether Mum put thirty-five bandaids on Dad. He was scratched from head to toe.

'At at as oo go,' said Dad. He could hardly move his bleeding lips.

'What?' said Aunt Marjory.

'That cat has to go,' said Mum.

'It does too,' I said. 'The eggs have hatched.'

They all looked at me.

I took a deep breath. 'They're funny looking birds with no feathers and great big beaks. And ... '

'Yes?' said Uncle Russell.

'Nothing,' I said. I was too embarrassed to say. In case I was wrong. I mean I only had a quick look.

'I've got an idea,' said Mum. 'We'll put some cat food on a saucer outside the door. As soon as Knuckles comes out to get it, Russell can nip inside the room and lock him out.'

'I dunno,' said Uncle Russell. 'He moves pretty fast.'

'I'll do it,' I said. 'I have to save those birds. They could be the last of the species. Uncle Sam put his trust in me.'

'No,' said Uncle Russell. 'I'll do it.'

Mum put two lamb chops on a saucer and placed them on the floor outside my door. Knuckles looked up and sniffed. Quick as a whippet he flashed over to the saucer and grabbed the meat.

None of us moved. We forgot all about shutting the

door. We were too busy gawking at the birds. They had already grown feathers. Their beaks were enormous. They were squawking for food.

Knuckles grabbed the raw chops. But he didn't eat them. He turned round and gave one each to the birds. They gobbled them down like crazy. Knuckles just stood and watched. It was like he was in a trance. Or a spell. Soon only the chop bones were left. Picked clean.

'Isn't he kind?' said Aunt Marjory.

'He's fattening them up,' I said. 'To eat. Like in *Hansel and Gretel*.'

The birds screeched and chirped for more. They looked at Knuckles, standing there as if he was hypnotised.

We just stared at those birds. None of us had ever seen birds like them before. My eyes hadn't tricked me. I really had seen what I thought I'd seen. They had teeth. Birds with teeth. Can you imagine that?

Dad closed the door. We all felt uneasy. I pressed my ear to the wall.

A terrible screeching, squealing, chirping and burping came from inside. 'Oh no,' I yelled. 'Knuckles is eating the birds.'

We all rushed downstairs and out the door. Uncle Russell scrambled up a vine onto the porch roof and peered in the window. 'Horrible,' he mumbled. 'Just horrible.'

We all climbed up after him. There wasn't much

room on the porch roof by the time we were all perched up there. We stared inside. The birds sat on the end of my bed, wiping their teeth on my sheets. Knuckles was nowhere to be seen.

Suddenly it clicked. We all realised at the same time. KEEP AWAY FROM KNUCKLES. That was the message. But it wasn't to stop Knuckles eating the birds. It was to stop the ...

Knuckles lay stretched out on the floor. All that was left of him. There was nothing but bones. A skeleton, totally picked clean.

6

It was time for a council of war. Dad nailed up my bedroom door and we all sat around the kitchen table.

'Sam must have bred them,' said Dad, 'to even things up. To get rid of feral cats.'

'That's what the message was for,' I said. 'He knew I had a pet cat. He wanted to warn me.'

'It's not right,' yelled Aunt Marjory. 'Birds that eat cats. It's not right.'

'Why not?' I yelled back. 'Feral cats eat birds. What's the difference?'

'Sam hated feral cats,' said Dad. 'He must have bred these birds to give the native animals a chance.'

'To save the environment,' I said.

'What are we going to do with them?' asked Uncle Russell. 'They could be the only two in the world.'

'They're mine,' I said. 'Uncle Sam gave them to me. I'm keeping them.'

'Better call the zoo,' said Mum. 'They'll take them off our hands.'

I didn't want them to go. They were my birds. I loved them. They couldn't help it if they liked cats (so to speak). I wasn't going to let anyone take them away.

Suddenly Aunt Marjory jumped up. She ran outside and grabbed a shovel. 'I'll take them off your hands,' she yelled. 'Murdering mongrels.'

Oh no. She was going to kill the birds. She ran over to the vine and started climbing. I followed as quickly as I could. Aunt Marjory lifted up the shovel and smashed my window before I could stop her. Then she started to climb inside. I tried to pull her back but she was too strong. She clambered into my room. I went in after her.

Where were the birds? They were nowhere to be seen.

There were two lumps under my bed covers. The birds were snuggled down in my bed. Aunt Marjory rushed over and pulled back the covers. The birds were twice as big as before. I have never seen anything like it. They had hatched and become adults in less than a day. The birds looked up with funny smiles that showed their teeth.

No, they weren't smiling at Aunt Marjory. No one would want to eat her. They were smiling at the open window.

Before anyone could move they flapped their wings and flew out into the sunshine. They rose high in the air and circled over the house. Then they headed west into the sunset.

We never saw them again. I was so sad. Uncle Sam had left those birds in my care and now they were gone.

They were cute in their own way, were those birds. Even if they did have teeth.

'Probably gone back to the desert,' said Uncle Russell.

'They'll never make it,' said Aunt Marjory. 'It's a long way. Someone will shoot them.'

I looked at Aunt Marjory. 'You are so mean,' I said. I ran up to my room and shut the door. I was heart-broken.

I jumped into my bed.

I touched something with my toes.

I looked under the covers.

I smiled.

I decided not to tell anyone what I had found.

I put the two freshly laid eggs into Uncle Sam's box and gently closed the lid.

Then I went over to the window and looked out at the rising moon.

It was a lovely summer's evening. I could see a cat on the prowl. Someone had let it out at night. And it was hunting for birds. It turned and looked at the box in my hands. Then it started to walk towards me with a funny expression on its face.

Squawk Talk

Go for it. That's what you've got to do. Look after number one. No one else will, that's for sure. Everyone thinks of themselves first. Like that fool sitting opposite. He's only about my age. Look at him. Thinks he's good-looking. Thinks he's cool. What a nerd.

Or take that little kid walking on top of the railing out there. The train has stopped on the bridge, so I could jump off and save him if I wanted. But why should I? I might fall in myself. It's a long way down to the river. The water is deep. I could drown, or skin my knees getting out of the train.

Nah. It's his problem. He is showing off. He should know better. He's going to fall in and it will serve him right.

Or take this guy sitting next to the nerd. A real weirdo with purple hair, a nose ring and ... wait for it. Yes, really. A parrot sitting on his shoulder. He must think he's a pirate or something.

The stupid parrot can talk. Not much. Just a bit. One sentence is all it can say. The weirdo says crazy things back to the parrot. I can hardly believe it.

'Say it again, Sam,' screeches the parrot.

'I hate apple pies,' says the weirdo.

'Say it again, Sam,' screeches the parrot.

'This place stinks,' says the weirdo.

I look out of the window at the pathetic kid tottering along on the edge of the railway fence. Still showing off.

I lean out of the door. 'Stupid idiot,' I yell.

The little kid looks up with panic on his face. My voice has startled him. Suddenly he is scared. His knees start to wobble. He holds out his arms like a tightrope-walker but it only makes things worse. He flaps his arms like a crazy bird.

Oh no. Slowly, slowly, slowly, he starts to topple backwards.

Everyone in the train is looking now.

'Aaagggh.' Over he goes. Twisting and turning in the air. Down, down, down. *Kersplash*. He disappears beneath the surface of the muddy Yarra River.

We all jump out of the train and stare over the edge. Nothing. Nothing but bubbles. He has gone. For ever. No he hasn't. There he is. He's thrashing around. No, he's gone again. He can't swim. He's going to drown.

Everyone stands there frozen. Except the weirdo with the parrot. He runs over to a box on the railing. He opens it. He pulls out a lifebuoy. He throws it in.

What a shot. The lifebuoy lands right next to the drowning kid, who looks like he is going down for the last time. He grabs onto it and starts kicking. He kicks and kicks until he reaches the bank of the river.

The train driver and a few others scramble down to pull him out.

The crowd from the train goes wild. They cheer and yell. They pat the weirdo on the back. Then they lift him over their heads. He has this great big grin on his face. Anyone would think he had saved the world or something. The parrot flutters around over his head.

The train driver starts to carry the little kid up from the river. We all have to wait for them to get back.

When they arrive we gather around for a look. There is quite a racket. 'Quiet, everyone,' says the train driver. 'This guy here,' he says, pointing to the weirdo, 'should get a medal. His quick thinking saved the day. He grabbed the lifebuoy and threw it in.'

'Big deal,' I say.

Everyone falls quiet. They turn and look at me. Especially the train driver. He is really angry. He looks at me as if I am a load of dog poop. 'Some people,' he says, 'stood by and did nothing.'

An old lady pushes through to the front and puts her face close to mine. 'He caused it all,' she said. 'He yelled out and made the poor boy fall in the first place.'

'If you can't say something useful,' says the train driver, 'better to say nothing at all.'

The crowd all started to mumble and grumble and abuse me.

'Scum.'

'No-hoper.'

'Layabout.'

'Good for nothing.'

This makes my blood boil. 'I didn't do anything,' I spit out.

'Precisely,' says the stupid train driver. 'But this bloke did.' They all start patting the weirdo on the back again.

It is sickening. All that fuss over nothing.

Suddenly the parrot flies off into some trees and disappears. The weirdo watches it go with a smile. He doesn't seem to care that he has lost his stupid parrot.

And I don't care either. Good riddance to it.

2

In the end we all have to walk to the next station because they can't start the train. I hurry along in front so that I don't have to listen to everyone telling the weirdo how good he is.

Far off in the trees I hear the parrot screech. It is an awful noise. No one seems to notice it except me. It gives me the creeps. I have a nasty feeling I haven't seen the last of that parrot.

I get to the station before anyone else. The other passengers are all waiting for the old lady and helping to carry the little kid who fell in the river.

I am mad. I am angry. I decide to do a bit of damage. I go into the dunny and look for something to smash up.

I try to rip a dunny seat off but it won't come. I pull and pull but it is bolted on tight. My hands are hurting something awful. I let all my feelings out. I curse and I yell. I swear something terrible.

Then I give the dunny seat a kick but it won't budge. Suddenly I see something grouse. It is a dunny seat for little squirts. It is small and titchy, if you know what I mean. If you were a gnome or something it would be just the shot.

This ought to be easy. I grab the wooden seat and give it a yank. *Snap.* It is only held on with plastic bolts and they break just like that. No worries.

I hold the little dunny seat up in the air and am just about to smash it down on the ground when I see something. A pair of shoes. With feet in them. Someone is in the next cubicle.

It could be the law. I stand there with the dunny seat held up over my head. I am as still as a statue. Then I decide to run for it. But suddenly, *whomp.* I slip on some water and down I go.

And down comes the dunny seat. Straight over my head. Yow. Ouch, ooh. Geez, it hurts. And it won't come off. I pull and yank and everything but it won't move.

I jump up onto my feet and take a gawk in the mirror. I stare and stare. No, no no. My head is jammed inside the toilet seat. My eyes and ears and nose poke out of the hole. And the lid is flapping up above me. *Whump.*

The lid falls down and hits me fair on the back of my head. Ow. This is my unlucky day. My skull is killing me.

The shoes in the next cubicle are moving. It is time for me to leave. Just then, without warning, the door swings open. It is the train driver. How did he get here so quick?

'You're fast for an old guy,' I say.

'And you have a fast tongue,' he says. 'I've been listening to you cursing and swearing. And you made that little boy fall off the bridge.'

'Get lost, Pops,' I say.

'You should think before you speak,' he says. 'You have a mean tongue.'

The dunny seat is hurting my face. I have no time for his lectures. 'Get a life, Grandad,' I say.

The train driver goes red in the face. For a moment I think his head is about to explode but it doesn't. He stomps off out of the dunny. I sure fixed *him* up. If there's one thing I know how to do it's to make people feel small. I'm real good at it.

Then I notice something.

The parrot. It is sitting on the cubicle looking down at me.

Screech.

A little shiver runs down my spine. I don't like this parrot. I look around for something to throw at it but there is nothing about.

'Beat it, Feather Head,' I yell.

The parrot flies up into the air flapping its wings like crazy. And I run out of the dunny as quick as I can go. The toilet seat is starting to hurt my face. I have to hang on to the lid to stop it banging me on the nut every time I take a step.

I burst out onto the platform. The sun hurts my eyes but I squint and see that the train has arrived. And it is ready to go. Quick as a flash I jump onto the train. The toilet lid bangs down and hits me like a hammer. 'Ouch, ooh, ow.'

Things are bad. But they get worse. Everyone is looking at me. Sitting there on the train with a toilet seat jammed on my head. There is no sign of the weirdo. His parrot is gone. But the nerd is trying to smother a laugh. This is the worst day of my life.

The train is about to leave. The doors start to close. But before they do, a last-minute passenger steps onto the train. *Flies* onto the train I should say. It is the parrot. It seems to be staring at me. I don't like the look of it.

The parrot gives a bit of a jump and sits up on the seat next to me.

3

This is unbelievable. This is unreal. What is going on here? First I get a dunny seat stuck around my face and now this little parrot is following me around. I don't get it. And neither does anyone else. Every eye is looking at my face or this little parrot.

'What are you lot gawking at?' I say. 'Why don't you mind your own business?'

The parrot gives a squawk.

Okay. I know what to do with this parrot. I will chuck it out of the window. I make a dive for the parrot but it is too quick and it dodges away. I fall over and graze my knee. I make another lunge but again it is too quick for me and it flaps up onto the luggage rack. I slip onto the lap of an old lady.

'Careful,' she says crossly.

'Get lost, Grandma,' I say.

Squawk, goes the parrot, and everyone laughs.

Right. I'm going to fix them. They have embarrassed me. I will embarrass them back.

There is a blonde aged about sixteen sitting as far away from me as she can get. She is looking at my toilet seat out of the corner of her eye. I put my face up close to hers. I look straight at her. 'Give us a kiss, darling,' I say.

Squawk, says the parrot.

The girl does not like this suggestion. Her nose starts to twitch.

I put my face next to hers and make little kissing noises. 'You are a little sweetheart, aren't you?' I say.

Squawk, says the parrot.

'Leave her alone,' says the nerd.

'Yes,' says someone else. They all start to mumble and grumble at me.

'You are all wimps,' I say. 'I reckon I might have to teach you all a lesson.'

Squawk, shrieks the parrot. It is almost as if it doesn't approve of what I am doing. Like a nagging parent ticking me off.

I let go of the toilet lid and shake a finger at the parrot. *Whump*, my toilet lid falls down and dongs me on the head again.

Everyone in the carriage laughs. Everyone. Even the parrot seems to think it's funny. Okay. This is war. I will tell them what I think of them.

'You are all snobs,' I say. 'Stuck-up, snotty snobs.'

Squawk, says the parrot.

They all pretend not to hear me. They look at their papers or stare out of the window. A tall skinny guy is nibbling a sandwich. The filling looks like horse droppings. 'Hey, stupid,' I say. 'Can I have a bit of that horse manure?'

He tries to ignore me, so I bend over and take a bit of sandwich. I chew it quickly. Actually it's not too bad. 'That was lovely,' I say. 'Can I have some more?'

A woman with a baby in a pram does not like this. 'Leave him alone, you horrible boy,' she says.

'You're an ugly cow,' I say to her. 'Why don't you mind your own business?' That fixes her up. She goes as red as a beetroot.

Every time I say something the parrot squawks. It is starting to get on my nerves.

A very old codger is sitting in the corner with earplugs stuffed in his ears. He is trying not to look at me. I can hear the tune because he has it up so loud. I know this song. My old grandma sings it all the time when she is doing the dishes.

I start to sing and dance around in front of him, pulling funny faces. I know this rotten song backwards. I pull a leering face while I sing.

> *Her eyes they shone like the diamonds,*
> *You'd think she was Queen of the land,*
> *And her hair hung over her shoulder,*
> *Tied up with a black velvet band.*

I sing all of the verses, making the old boy as embarrassed as anything. All the time the parrot goes *squawk, squawk, squawk.* Finally I stop because the train pulls into the station. We have arrived. Flinders Street. The middle of the city. I wait until everyone has stepped off. The parrot waits too. It is just sitting there next to me with its little wings flapping every now and then. I have to lose it. And quick.

I wait until everyone is off the train. I wait until it is just about to pull out of the station. I hold down my toilet lid and leap off. But I am not quick enough. The parrot almost seems to read my mind. It hits the platform at the same time as me. There is no way it is going to let me shake it off.

The parrot follows me along the platform. I feel like a pirate out of some old movie. Ridiculous. That's how I feel. The stupid bird flaps up in the air and tries to land on my shoulder but I brush it off.

Talk about embarrassing. Travellers stop to look. A boy with a toilet seat stuck on his head, running away from a parrot. What a sight. Everyone starts to laugh. They think it is some sort of a show. Rats, rats, rats. I am a joke. I am pathetic. I have to get this stupid thing off my head. And I have to get rid of the parrot.

I kick out at the parrot with my foot. I kick hard enough to send it into orbit. But it is too fast. It flaps out of the way and my leg goes flying up over my head. I lose my balance and *bang*, down I go onto the platform. And *bang* goes the toilet lid onto my head.

Oh, agony, agony. I have to get this thing off my head. I will have to get to a hospital. It's the only way. Someone will have to cut the toilet seat away from my face.

The crowd stare down at me, laughing. I need help. I need someone to drive me to a hospital. A little old woman comes over to me and bends down. She smiles at me and helps me up. 'You poor boy,' she says. 'Can I help you?'

I go to say yes. But 'yes' does not come out.

Say it again, Sam, screeches the parrot.

'Get lost, Grandma,' I say.

The old woman lets go of my arm and *plonk*, I fall back down again.

'You have a bad mouth,' she says. She wags a finger at me and starts to hurry off through the crowd.

Oh no. This is no good. This is terrible. Why did I tell her to get lost? I will never get to hospital this way. People are staring down at me. Surely someone will have mercy on me. I look up at the staring faces. I will ask them for help.

Suddenly the parrot speaks. *Say it again, Sam.*

'What are you lot gawking at?' I say to the passers-by. 'Why don't you all mind your own business.'

The onlookers mumble and grumble. They say things like, 'What a rude kid' and 'The nerve of it'.

They are all going off and leaving me. No, no no. Don't go. I didn't mean to say that. I will call out to them and ask for help. 'You are all snobs,' I say. 'Stuck up, snotty snobs.'

The crowd hurry off. Soon the platform is empty.

Why did I say all those things? I didn't mean to be rude. Why am I insulting people? My mouth seems to work on its own. It won't say what I want it to. I look down at the parrot. It just sits there. Watching. Saying nothing. This has something to do with the parrot talking.

I pick myself up and head out of the station. I must get to hospital. I could catch a taxi but I only have two dollars. That won't get me far. I show my ticket and go out onto the street. There is a horse hitched up to a stagecoach. It's there to take tourists and little kids for rides around the town. Maybe the guy who drives it will help. He has a kind face. He is busy shovelling up horse manure and putting it into a bin.

He looks up when I approach. He stares at my toilet seat and smiles.

Say it again, Sam, screeches the parrot.

I open my mouth to speak. 'Hey, stupid,' I say. 'Can I have a bit of that horse manure?'

The smile falls from his face. He does not like being called stupid. 'Sure, toilet head,' he says. He looks down at his shovel and the pile of sloppy steaming manure. Then he throws it straight in my face.

Oh, yuck. The stinking stuff is in my eyes and ears and nose. I start clawing it away with my fingers. It is so foul that I think I'm going to faint.

The guy is picking up another shovelful. I must tell him to stop.

Say it again, Sam, screeches the parrot.

'That was lovely,' I say. 'Can I have some more?'

What? What? Why did I say that? Oh, no. *Sploosh.* He lets me have it again.

I stagger away as quickly as I can, before he has time to scoop up another shovelful.

The parrot follows after me.

4

People in the street make way for me. They avoid me like the plague. I don't blame them. A guy with a toilet seat on his head. Covered in stinking horse manure and followed by a stupid parrot that flaps around just over his head. They probably think I am a lunatic or something.

My mind is spinning. Why am I saying these things? Each time I have spoken, the parrot has said *Say it again, Sam.* What's going on? My own words start to buzz around in my head. I said, *Hey, stupid, can I have a bit of that horse manure?* I have heard that before.

Then it hits me. It's what I said on the train. To the tall skinny bloke with the sandwich. And, *Get lost, Grandma.* I said that on the train too. And, *What are you lot gawking at? Why don't you all mind your own business.* I also said that on the train.

The parrot is making me repeat myself. It has remembered every word I said. Like a tape recorder. And now it's making me say them all again. When I don't want to. Parrots can copy what people say. But this one is making me copy myself.

What else did I say? I can't remember. But one thing's certain. I have to get away from this parrot. And quick.

I look around. There must be someone who can take me to hospital. Someone who can save me. A police-woman. She is giving parking tickets to some bikies. They are great big blokes with beer bellies and beards. They do not like getting parking tickets.

I wouldn't normally talk to the police. But this is an emergency. The police are there to help. That is what they always say. I will give it a go and ask her to take me to the hospital. I will be very polite to her. Very polite indeed.

She looks up as I approach. She starts to grin when she sees my toilet seat. 'Yes?' she says.

I open my mouth to speak. But the parrot gets in first.

Say it again, Sam.

'You're an ugly cow,' I say to the policewoman. 'Why don't you mind your own business?'

Oh, no, no, no. The parrot has made me repeat my words. The policewoman steps towards me. 'You are under arrest,' she says.

'What for, ugly?' says the bikie with the biggest beer gut. 'Why don't you leave him alone? He doesn't need a licence to walk around with a toilet seat on his head. And there is no law against telling the truth, either.'

The gang members kick their bikes into action. Before I can blink Beer Gut has lifted me up and plonked me on the back of his bike. In a flash we are speeding down the street with the rest of the gang thundering after us. The policewoman is yelling at us. But we don't hear what she says because the motorbikes are roaring.

This is good. This is better. I am with my sort of people now. They are rough. They are tough. They speak their minds. They do not mind people who say what they think.

We weave in and out of the streets. People stare at me and Beer Gut. A big fat bikie and a guy with a toilet seat on his head.

Some of the bikies have their women on the back.
The sheilas wrap their arms around their blokes' waists
and hang on like crazy. One bikie has a little parrot
sitting on the back seat. Oh, no, the parrot again. It is
still with me. It will never let me go.

The bikies screech to a stop in a back alley filled with
rubbish bins.

The parrot hops down from its little perch on the seat
and stretches its wings. All of the bikies stare at the
parrot. 'I like your mate,' says Beer Gut. 'Can it fight?' He
tries to grab the parrot but it's too quick for him.

Beer Gut gives up on the parrot and looks at me. 'You
helped us,' he says. 'How can we help you?'

At last someone is going to help me. I smile at Beer
Gut just as the parrot starts to talk.

Say it again, Sam.

'Give us a kiss, darling,' I say to Beer Gut.

Beer Gut does not like this suggestion. His beard starts
to bristle. 'What?' he yells.

I put my face next to his and make little kissing noises.
'You are a little sweetheart, aren't you?' I say.

I try to stop my mouth talking but I can't. I hold my
mouth with my fingers but it is no good. My tongue
just keeps flapping away saying one mean thing after
another. Beer Gut is getting madder and madder. The
gang close in around me. 'You are all wimps,' I say.
'I reckon I might have to teach you all a lesson.'

'Wimps, are we?' says Beer Gut. He lifts up my toilet

seat and slams it down on my head. That is all I remember because I am knocked out by the blow. It's goodnight for me for quite a while.

5

When I wake up I am upside down. Things do not look too good. In fact things do not look anything at all because everything is black. And smelly. I am upside down and I stink of dead fish and rotting cabbages. I am in a rubbish bin. I can hardly breathe because of the terrible stench.

Somehow or other I wriggle out of the bin and crash down onto the ground. The toilet seat is still on my face but the lid bit has broken off. At least I won't have that banging me on the nut any more.

The parrot, however, is sitting on a window-ledge watching me. Saying nothing. I want to yell at it. But I can't to say anything because it will start talking and I might start saying something that I wish I hadn't.

I am covered in stinking rubbish and something yellow is dribbling down my face. I try to pull off the toilet seat but it hurts too much. I push and struggle but it is going to rip my ear off. There's only one thing left to do. I will go home. Grandma is a crabby old girl but she will help me. She's used to me saying mean things and probably won't even notice if the parrot makes me insult her.

I fish around in my pocket for my train ticket.

It is gone. So are my two dollars. Beer Gut has taken them both.

Oh, rats. Rats, rats, rats. What else can go wrong? Now I can't get home. I will have to try and talk the ticket collector into letting me on without a ticket. But then the parrot will screech, *Say it again, Sam*. And I will say something rude and they will chase me off.

I trudge back towards Flinders Street Station. People stare at me. People avoid me. They see a smelly boy with a toilet seat on his face and a parrot flapping along above his head.

Finally the parrot and I arrive at the station. I am tired. I am scared. I am sick of saying rude things to people. How am I going to get onto the train without a ticket? I look around at the crowd. People are staring at me. Suddenly something snaps in my mind. I will tell them all what I think of them. I will yell. I will swear. I don't care about anything any more.

I stand on the top step and open my mouth.

Say it again, Sam, screeches the parrot.

Oh no. What now?

I start to sing. That's what. A happy little song that Grandma sings. Please, parrot, please don't make me sing. I try to keep my mouth shut but it is no good. I sing at the top of my voice.

> *Her eyes they shone like the diamonds,*
> *You'd think she was Queen of the land,*
> *And her hair hung over her shoulder,*
> *Tied up with a black velvet band.*

The crowd stop and look. But they are not mad at me. And they do not think I am mad. They are smiling. They think it's a show. They think I'm a busker. They clap and laugh at me and the toilet seat and the parrot, which is doing a little dance on top of my head.

I keep singing. I sing the next verse. And the next one. Finally I finish the song. I give a little bow. I'm quite proud of myself actually.

People throw money on the ground. They liked the show. Twenty cents. One dollar. Two dollars. Not bad. Not bad at all. I scoop up all the coins and when the crowd has gone I count them. Fifteen dollars and forty-five cents. Just the ticket. Just enough for a ticket actually.

I go over to the ticket machine and buy a one-way ticket to Colac.

I jump onto the train and sit down just as it moves off. The parrot sits on my shoulder. The passengers stare at me but not in a mean way. I see some of the people who threw money to me. The ones who liked the show. I also see the nerd. He's there too.

Well, I'm not going to say anything. The parrot will only make me insult them. I stare out of the window and think about my troubles. If only I could get rid of this toilet seat without ripping my ears off. If only the parrot would give me a break and go away.

The train rumbles on for quite a while. Finally it stops on a bridge. It's the same bridge where the little kid was walking on top of the railing.

There he is again. I can't believe it. The same kid is walking on the railings in exactly the same spot. Oh, what? It can't be true. My mind freezes. I can't think what to do. I can't take it in.

The nerd isn't frozen though. Not him. He rushes over to the door and opens it. 'Be careful,' he yells at the top of his voice.

The little kid looks up with panic on his face. The nerd's voice has startled him. Suddenly he is scared. His knees start to wobble. He holds out his arms like a tightrope-walker but it only makes things worse. He flaps his arms like a crazy bird.

Oh, no. Slowly, slowly, slowly, he starts to topple backwards.

Everyone in the train is looking now.

'Aaagggh.' Over he goes. Twisting and turning in the air. Down, down, down. *Kersplash*. He disappears beneath the surface of the muddy Yarra River.

We all jump out of the train and stare over the edge. Nothing. Nothing but bubbles. He has gone. For ever. No he hasn't. There he is. He's thrashing around. No, he's gone again. He can't swim. He's going to drown.

Everyone stands there frozen. Except the nerd. The hero. He runs over to a box on the railing. He opens it. But there's nothing there. They have not replaced the lifebuoy. There's nothing to throw. We all look around for something that will float. Anything. But there is not so much as a matchstick on that bridge.

The nerd starts trying to pull at a railing from the bridge but it won't come off. The little kid sinks out of sight again. It's a long way down. Everyone is too scared to jump in and save him. And there's nothing to throw.

Except.

My toilet seat.

I push and push like mad. But I can't shift it. The toilet seat won't budge. And the pain is terrible. My ears are starting to bleed. Oh, oh, oh, it hurts, it hurts. But I can't stop. The kid is drowning. I have to get this toilet seat off my head. *Sploosh*. The toilet seat comes off. So does a piece of my ear. There is blood everywhere. The pain is terrible.

'He's going down again,' yells the nerd. 'He's going to drown. Someone do something.'

I rush to the railing and throw over the toilet seat. What a shot. The toilet seat lands right next to the drowning kid, who looks like he's going down for the last time. The kid grabs onto the toilet seat. It's just like a lifebuoy. He starts kicking. He kicks and kicks until he reaches the bank of the river.

The train driver and a few others scramble down to pull him out.

The crowd goes crazy. A nurse from the next carriage has picked up the piece of my ear and put it in a bottle. 'They can sew it back on,' she says. She ties a bandage around my head and although it hurts I can tell you that it feels a lot better than a toilet seat.

Everyone pats me on the back. They cheer and shout. They say they have never seen such courage. 'You are a real hero,' says an old lady. 'They should give you a medal.' She looks at all the others. 'He almost tore off his own ear to save that little boy.'

'It was nothing,' I say. 'Anyone would have done the same thing.'

Everyone smiles at me. I smile to myself. They like what I said. So do I.

I look around. The parrot has gone. No, there it is. It is flying over the river towards the road on the other side. It is heading for a bikie who has been pulled over by the police. He is a big guy with a beer gut. He is shaking a fist at the police. I wonder what he is saying.

I hope it is something nice. Because I bet that stupid ... er, lovely little parrot is squawking its head off every time he speaks.

Wunderpants

My dad is not a bad sort of bloke. There are plenty who are much worse. But he does rave on a bit, like if you get muddy when you are catching frogs, or rip your pants when you are building a tree hut. Stuff like that.

Mostly we understand each other and I can handle him. What he doesn't know doesn't hurt him. If he knew that I kept Snot, my pet rabbit, under the bed, he wouldn't like it; so I don't tell him. That way he is happy, I am happy and Snot is happy.

There are only problems when he finds out what has been going on. Like the time that I wanted to see *Mad Max II*. The old man said it was a bad movie – too much blood and guts.

'It's too violent,' he said.

'But, Dad, that's not fair. All the other kids are going. I'll be the only one in the school who hasn't seen it.' I went on and on like this. I kept nagging. In the end he gave in – he wasn't a bad old boy. He usually let me have what I wanted after a while. It was easy to get around him.

The trouble started the next morning. He was cleaning

his teeth in the bathroom, making noises, humming and gurgling – you know the sort of thing. Suddenly he stopped. Everything went quiet. Then he came into the kitchen. There was toothpaste all around his mouth; he looked like a mad tiger. He was frothing at the mouth.

'What's this?' he said. He was waving his toothbrush about. 'What's this on my toothbrush?' Little grey hairs were sticking out of it. 'How did these hairs get on my toothbrush? Did you have my toothbrush, David?'

He was starting to get mad. I didn't know whether to own up or not. Parents always tell you that if you own up they will let you off. They say that they won't do anything if you are honest – no punishment.

I decided to give it a try. 'Yes,' I said. 'I used it yesterday.'

He still had toothpaste on his mouth. He couldn't talk properly. 'What are these little grey hairs?' he asked.

'I used it to brush my pet mouse,' I answered.

'Your what?' he screamed.

'My mouse.'

He started jumping up and down and screaming. He ran around in circles holding his throat, then he ran into the bathroom and started washing his mouth out. There was a lot of splashing and gurgling. He was acting like a madman.

I didn't know what all the fuss was about. All that yelling just over a few mouse hairs.

After a while he came back into the kitchen. He kept opening and shutting his mouth as if he could taste something bad. He had a mean look in his eye – real mean.

'What are you thinking of?' he yelled at the top of his voice. 'Are you crazy or something? Are you trying to kill me? Don't you know that mice carry germs? They are filthy things. I'll probably die of some terrible disease.'

He went on and on like this for ages. Then he said, 'And don't think that you are going to see *Mad Max II*. You can sit at home and think how stupid it is to brush a mouse with someone else's toothbrush.'

2

I went back to my room to get dressed. Dad just didn't understand about that mouse. It was a special mouse, a very special mouse indeed. It was going to make me a lot of money: fifty dollars, in fact. Every year there was a mouse race in Smith's barn. The prize was fifty dollars. And my mouse, Swift Sam, had a good chance of winning. But I had to look after him. That's why I brushed him with a toothbrush.

I knew that Swift Sam could beat every other mouse except one. There was one mouse I wasn't sure about. It was called Mugger and it was owned by Scrag Murphy, the toughest kid in the town. I had never seen his mouse, but I knew it was fast. Scrag Murphy fed it on a special diet.

That is what I was thinking about as I dressed. I went

over to the cupboard to get a pair of underpants. There were none there. 'Hey, Mum,' I yelled out. 'I am out of underpants.'

Mum came into the room holding something terrible. Horrible. It was a pair of home-made underpants. 'I made these for you, David,' she laughed. 'I bought the material at the Op Shop. There was just the right amount of material for one pair of underpants.'

'I'm not wearing those,' I told her. 'No way. Never.'

'What's wrong with them?' said Mum. She sounded hurt.

'They're pink,' I said. 'And they've got little pictures of fairies on them. I couldn't wear them. Everyone would laugh. I would be the laughing stock of the school.'

Underpants with fairies on them and pink. I nearly freaked out. I thought about what Scrag Murphy would say if he ever heard about them. I went red just thinking about it.

Just then Dad poked his head into the room. He still had that mean look in his eye. He was remembering the toothbrush. 'What's going on now?' he asked in a black voice.

'Nothing,' I said. 'I was just thanking Mum for making me these nice underpants.' I pulled on the fairy pants and quickly covered them up with my jeans. At least no one else would know I had them on. That was one thing to be thankful for.

The underpants felt strange. They made me tingle all over. And my head felt light. There was something not quite right about those underpants – and I am not talking about the fairies.

3

I had breakfast and went out to the front gate. Pete was waiting for me. He is my best mate; we always walk to school together. 'Have you got your running shoes?' he asked.

'Oh, no,' I groaned. 'I forgot. It's the cross-country race today.' I went back and got my running shoes. I came back out walking very slowly. I was thinking about the race. I would have to go to the changing rooms and get changed in front of Scrag Murphy and all the other boys. They would all laugh their heads off when they saw my fairy underpants.

We walked through the park on the way to school. There was a big lake in the middle. 'Let's chuck some stones,' said Pete. 'See who can throw the furthest.' I didn't even answer. I was feeling sick in the stomach. 'What's the matter with you?' he asked. 'You look like death warmed up.'

I looked around. There was no one else in the park. 'Look at this,' I said. I undid my fly and showed Pete the underpants. His eyes bugged out like organ stops; then he started to laugh. He fell over on the grass and laughed his silly head off. Tears rolled down his cheeks.

He really thought it was funny. Some friend.

After a while Pete stopped laughing. 'You poor thing,' he said. 'What are you going to do? Scrag Murphy and the others will never let you forget it.'

We started throwing stones into the lake. I didn't try very hard. My heart wasn't in it. 'Hey,' said Pete. 'That was a good shot. It went right over to the other side.' He was right. The stone had reached the other side of the lake. No one had ever done that before; it was too far.

I picked up another stone. This time I threw as hard as I could. The stone went right over the lake and disappeared over some trees. 'Wow,' yelled Pete. 'That's the best shot I've ever seen. No one can throw that far.' He looked at me in a funny way.

My skin was all tingling. 'I feel strong,' I said. 'I feel as if I can do anything.' I went over to a park bench. It was a large concrete one. I lifted it up with one hand. I held it high over my head. I couldn't believe it.

Pete just stood there with his mouth hanging open. He couldn't believe it either. I felt great. I jumped for joy. I sailed high into the air. I went up three metres. 'What a jump,' yelled Pete.

My skin was still tingling. Especially under the underpants. 'It's the underpants,' I said. 'The underpants are giving me strength.' I grinned. 'They are not underpants. They are *wunderpants*.'

'Super Jocks,' said Pete. We both started cackling like a couple of hens. We laughed until our sides ached.

4

I told Pete not to tell anyone about the wunderpants. We decided to keep it a secret. Nothing much happened until the cross-country race that afternoon. All the boys went to the changing room to put on their running gear. Scrag Murphy was there. I tried to get into my shorts without him seeing my wunderpants, but it was no good. He noticed them as soon as I dropped my jeans.

'Ah ha,' he shouted. 'Look at baby britches. Look at his fairy pants.' Everyone looked. They all started to laugh. How embarrassing. They were all looking at the fairies on my wunderpants.

Scrag Murphy was a big, fat bloke. He was really tough. He came over and pulled the elastic on my wunderpants. Then he let it go. 'Ouch,' I said. 'Cut that out. That hurts.'

'What's the matter, little Diddums?' he said. 'Can't you take it?' He shoved me roughly against the wall. I wasn't going to let him get away with that, so I pushed him back – just a little push. He went flying across the room and crashed into the wall on the other side. I just didn't know my own strength. That little push had sent him all that way. It was the wunderpants.

Scrag Murphy looked at me with shock and surprise that soon turned to a look of hate. But he didn't say anything. No one said anything. They were all thinking I was going to get my block knocked off next time I saw Scrag Murphy.

About forty kids were running in the race. We had to run through the countryside, following markers that had been put out by the teachers. It was a hot day, so I decided to wear a pair of shorts but no top.

As soon as the starting gun went I was off like a flash. I had kept my wunderpants on and they were working really well. I went straight out to the front. I had never run so fast before. As I ran along the road I passed a man on a bike. He tried to keep up with me, but he couldn't. Then I passed a car. This was really something. This was great.

I looked behind. None of the others was in sight – I was miles ahead. The trail turned off the road and into the bush. I was running along a narrow track in the forest. After a while I came to a small creek. I was hot so I decided to have a dip. After all, the others were a long way behind; I had plenty of time. I took off my shorts and running shoes, but I left the wunderpants on. I wasn't going to part with them.

I dived into the cold water. It was refreshing. I lay on my back looking at the sky. Life was good. These wunderpants were terrific. I would never be scared of Scrag Murphy while I had them on.

Then something started to happen – something terrible. The wunderpants started to get tight. They hurt. They were shrinking. They were shrinking smaller and smaller. The pain was awful. I had to get them off. I struggled and wriggled; they were so tight they cut into my skin. In the end I got them off, and only just in time. They shrank so small that they would only just fit over my thumb. I had a narrow escape. I could have been killed by the shrinking wunderpants.

Just then I heard voices coming. It was the others in the race. I was trapped – I couldn't get out to put on my shorts. There were girls in the race. I had to stay in the middle of the creek in the nude.

5

It took quite a while for all the others to run by. They were all spread out along the track. Every time I went to get out of the pool, someone else would come. After a while Pete stopped at the pool. 'What are you doing?' he said. 'Even super jocks won't help you win from this far back.'

'Keep going,' I said. 'I'll tell you about it later.' I didn't want to tell him that I was in the nude. Some girls were with him.

Pete and the girls took off along the track. A bit later the last runner arrived. It was Scrag Murphy. He couldn't run fast – he was carrying too much weight. 'Well, look at this,' he said. 'It's little Fairy Pants. And what's this we have here?' He picked up my shorts and running shoes from the bank of the creek. Then he ran off with them.

'Come back,' I screamed. 'Bring those back here.' He didn't take any notice. He just laughed and kept running.

I didn't know what to do. I didn't have a stitch of

clothing. I didn't even have any shoes. I was starting to feel cold; the water was freezing. I was covered in goose pimples and my teeth were chattering. In the end I had to get out. I would have frozen to death if I stayed in the water any longer.

I went and sat on a rock in the sun and tried to think of a way to get home without being seen. It was all right in the bush. I could always hide behind a tree if someone came. But once I reached the road I would be in trouble; I couldn't just walk along the road in the nude.

Then I had an idea. I looked at the tiny underpants. I couldn't put them on, but they still might work. I put them over my thumb and jumped. It was no good. It was just an ordinary small jump. I picked up a stone and threw it. It only went a short way, not much of a throw at all. The pants were too small, and I was my weak old self again.

I lay down on the rock in the sun. Ants started to crawl over me. Then the sun went behind a cloud. I started to get cold, but I couldn't walk home – not in the raw. I felt miserable. I looked around for something to wear, but there was nothing. Just trees, bushes and grass.

I knew I would have to wait until dark. The others would all have gone home by now. Pete would think I had gone home, and my parents would think I was at his place. No one was going to come and help me.

I started to think about Scrag Murphy. He was going to pay for this. I would get him back somehow.

Time went slowly, but at last it started to grow dark. I made my way back along the track. I was in bare feet and I kept standing on stones. Branches reached out and scratched me in all sorts of painful places. Then I started to think about snakes. What if I stood on one?

There were all sorts of noises in the dark. The moon had gone in, and it was hard to see where I was going. I have to admit it: I was scared. Scared stiff. To cheer myself up I started to think about what I was going to do to Scrag Murphy. Boy, was he going to get it.

At last I came to the road. I was glad to be out of the bush. My feet were cut and bleeding and I hobbled along. Every time a car went by I had to dive into the bushes. I couldn't let myself get caught in the headlights of the cars.

I wondered what I was going to do when I reached the town. There might be people around. I broke off a branch from a bush and held it in front of my 'you know what'. It was prickly, but it was better than nothing.

By the time I reached the town it was late. There was no one around. But I had to be careful – someone might come out of a house at any minute. I ran from tree to tree and wall to wall, hiding in the shadows as I went. Lucky for me the moon was in and it was very dark.

Then I saw something that gave me an idea – a phone box. I opened the door and stepped inside. A dim light shone on my naked body. I hoped that no one was looking. I had no money, but Pete had told me that if you yell into the ear-piece they can hear you on the other end. It was worth a try. I dialled our home number. Dad answered. 'Yes,' he said.

'I'm in the nude,' I shouted. 'I've lost my clothes. Help. Help.'

'Hello, hello. Who's there?' said Dad.

I shouted at the top of my voice, but Dad just kept saying 'Hello'. He sounded cross. Then I heard him say to Mum, 'It's probably that boy up to his tricks again.' He hung up the phone.

I decided to make a run for it. It was the only way. I dropped my bush and started running. I went for my life. I reached our street without meeting a soul. I thought I was safe, but I was wrong. I crashed right into someone and sent them flying. It was old Mrs Jeeves from across the road.

'Sorry,' I said. 'Gee, I'm sorry.' I helped her stand up. She was a bit short sighted and it was dark. She hadn't noticed that I didn't have any clothes on. Then the moon came out – the blazing moon. I tried to cover my nakedness with my hands, but it was no good.

'Disgusting,' she screeched. 'Disgusting. I'll tell your father about this.'

I ran home as fast I could. I went in the back door and jumped into bed. I tried to pretend that I was asleep. Downstairs I could hear Mrs Jeeves yelling at

Dad; then the front door closed. I heard his footsteps coming up the stairs.

6

Well, I really copped it. I was in big trouble. Dad went on and on. 'What are you thinking of, lad? Running around in the nude. Losing all your clothes. What will the neighbours think?' He went on like that for about a week. I couldn't tell him the truth – he wouldn't believe it. No one would. The only ones who knew the whole story were Pete and I.

Dad grounded me for a month. I wasn't allowed out of the house except to go to school. No pictures, no swimming, nothing. And no pocket money either.

It was a bad month. Very bad indeed. At school Scrag Murphy gave me a hard time. He called me 'Fairy Pants'. Every one thought it was a great joke, and there was nothing I could do about it. He was just too big for me, and his mates were all tough guys.

'This is serious,' said Pete. 'We have to put Scrag Murphy back in his box. They are starting to call me "Friend Of Fairy Pants" now. We have to get even.'

We thought and thought but we couldn't come up with anything. Then I remembered the mouse race in Smith's barn. 'We will win the mouse race,' I shouted. 'It's in a month's time. We can use the next month to train my mouse.'

'That's it,' said Pete. 'The prize is fifty dollars. Scrag

Murphy thinks he is going to win. It will really get up his nose if we take off the prize.'

I went and fetched Swift Sam. 'He's small,' I said. 'But he's fast. I bet he can beat Murphy's mouse. It's called Mugger.'

We started to train Swift Sam. Every day after school we took him around a track in the back yard. We tied a piece of cheese on the end of a bit of string. Swift Sam chased after it as fast as he could. After six laps we gave him the piece of cheese to eat. At the start he could do six laps in ten minutes. By the end of the month he was down to three minutes.

'Scrag Murphy, look out,' said Pete with a grin. 'We are really going to beat the pants off you this time.'

7

The day of the big race came at last. There were about one hundred kids in Smith's barn. No adults knew about it – they would probably have stopped it if they knew. It cost fifty cents to get in. That's where the prize money came from. A kid called Tiger Gleeson took up the money and gave out the prize at the end. He was the organiser of the whole thing.

Scrag Murphy was there, of course. 'It's in the bag,' he swaggered. 'Mugger can't lose. I've fed him on a special diet. He is the fittest mouse in the country. He will eat Swift Sam, just you wait and see.'

I didn't say anything. But I was very keen to see his

mouse, Mugger. Scrag Murphy had it in a box. No one had seen it yet.

'Right,' said Tiger. 'Get out your mice.' I put Swift Sam down on the track. He looked very small. He started sniffing around. I hoped he would run as fast with the other mice there – he hadn't had any match practice before. Then the others put their mice on the track. Everyone except Scrag Murphy. He still had Mugger in the box.

Scrag Murphy put his hand in the box and took out Mugger. He was the biggest mouse I had ever seen. He was at least ten times as big as Swift Sam. 'Hey,' said Pete. 'That's not a mouse. That's a rat. You can't race a rat. It's not fair.'

'It's not a rat,' said Scrag Murphy in a threatening voice. 'It's just a big mouse. I've been feeding it up.' I looked at it again. It was a rat all right. It was starting to attack the mice.

'We will take a vote,' said Tiger. 'All those that think it is a rat, put your hands up,' He counted all the hands.

'Fifty,' he said. 'Now all those who say that Mugger is a mouse put your hands up.' He counted again.

'Fifty-two. Mugger is a mouse.'

Scrag Murphy and his gang started to cheer. He had brought all his mates with him. It was a put-up job.

'Right,' said Tiger Gleeson. 'Get ready to race.'

8

There were about ten mice in the race – or I should say nine mice and one rat. Two rats if you counted Scrag Murphy. All the owners took out their string and cheese. 'Go,' shouted Tiger Gleeson.

Mugger jumped straight on to a little mouse next to him and bit it on the neck. The poor thing fell over and lay still. 'Boo,' yelled some of the crowd.

Swift Sam ran to the front straight away. He was going really well. Then Mugger started to catch up. It was neck and neck for five laps. First Mugger would get in front, then Swift Sam. Everyone in the barn went crazy. They were yelling their heads off.

By the sixth lap Mugger started to fall behind. All the other mice were not in the race. They had been lapped twice by Mugger and Swift Sam. But Mugger couldn't keep up with Swift Sam; he was about a tail behind. Suddenly something terrible happened. Mugger jumped onto Swift Sam's tail and grabbed it in his teeth. The crowd started to boo. Even Scrag Murphy's mates were booing.

But Swift Sam kept going. He didn't stop for a second. He just pulled that great rat along after him. It rolled over and over behind the little mouse. Mugger held on for grim death, but he couldn't stop Swift Sam. 'What a mouse,' screamed the crowd as Swift Sam crossed the finish line still towing Mugger behind him.

Scrag Murphy stormed off out of the barn. He didn't

even take Mugger with him. Tiger handed me the fifty dollars. Then he held up Swift Sam. 'Swift Sam is the winner,' he said. 'The only mouse in the world with its own little pair of fairy underpants.'

UFD

You can be the judge. Am I the biggest liar in the world or do I tell the truth? There is one thing for sure – Dad believes me. Anyway, I will leave it up to you. I will tell you what happened and you can make up your own mind.

It all starts one evening about tea time. Dad is cooking the tea and Mum is watching *Sixty Minutes* on television. Suddenly there is a knock on the door. 'I'll get it,' yells my little brother Matthew. He always runs to be first to the door and first to the telephone. It really gets on my nerves the way he does this.

We hear the sound of Matthew talking to an adult. Then we hear heavy footsteps coming down the hall. Everyone looks up and stares at this man wearing a light-blue uniform. He has badges on his chest. One of them is a pair of little wings joined together. On his shoulder is a patch saying ROYAL AUSTRALIAN AIRFORCE. We have never seen this man before.

'Yes?' says Dad.

'Mr Hutchins?' says the man from the airforce.

'Yes,' answers Dad.

'Mr Simon Hutchins?'

'No', says Dad pointing at me. 'That is Simon Hutchins.'

I can feel my face starting to go red. Everyone is looking at me. I think I know what this is about.

'I have come about the UFO,' says the man in the uniform.

'UFO?' say Mum and Dad together.

'Yes,' answers the bloke in the uniform. 'A Mister Simon Hutchins rang the airforce and reported a UFO.'

Dad looks at me with a fierce expression on his face. He is about to blow his top. 'This boy,' says Dad slowly, 'is the biggest liar in the world. You are wasting your time. He has not seen a UFO. He has dreamed it up. He is always making up the most fantastic stories. I am afraid you have come all this way for nothing.'

'Nevertheless,' says the man from the airforce, 'I will have to do a report. Do you mind if I talk to Simon?' Then he holds out his hand to Dad. 'My name is Wing Commander Collins.'

'Go ahead,' says Dad as he shakes Wing Commander Collins' hand. 'And after you have finished I will have a talk to Simon myself. A very long talk.' He gives me a dirty look. I know that I am in big trouble.

'What's a UFO?' butts in my little brother. Matthew doesn't know anything about anything. He is just a little kid with a big voice.

'It's an unidentified flying object,' answers Wing Commander Collins.

'Wow,' says Matthew with his mouth hanging open. 'A flying saucer. Did you really see a flying saucer?'

'Not exactly,' I say. 'But I did see a UFO.'

Wing Commander Collins sits down at the table and starts writing in a notebook. 'What time did you see it?' he asks.

I think for a bit and then I say, 'Seven o'clock this morning. I know it was seven o'clock because the boom gates on the railway line woke me up. The first train goes through at seven.'

The Wing Commander writes this down. I don't know if he believes me or not. It is true though. Those boom gates go flying up after a train has gone through. They end up pointing at the sky. When they hit the buffer they make a terrific crash. They wake me up at seven every morning.

The airforce man finishes writing and asks me his next question. 'Where did you see it?'

I point through the kitchen window. 'Out there. I was in bed and I saw it go past my window.'

'How big was it?'

'About one metre.'

He looks at me with a funny expression but he does not say anything. He just writes in his book. After a bit more writing he says, 'And what colour was it?'

'Black,' I answer.

'And what was it made of?'

'Skin,' I say. 'Skin and hair.'

At this point everyone in the room jumps to their feet and yells out, 'Skin and hair?' as if they have never heard of skin and hair before.

'Yes,' I say.

'And what shape was it?' growls the Commander.

'Dog-shaped. It was dog-shaped.'

'Dog-shaped?' yells the whole family again. I start to feel as if I am living with a bunch of parrots. They keep repeating everything I say.

'You mean,' says the Wing Commander, 'that you saw a flying object that was shaped like a dog and covered in skin and hair?'

'No,' I answer. 'It wasn't a dog-shaped object. It was a dog-shaped dog. A real dog.'

2

The Wing Commander springs to his feet and snaps his book shut. 'Good grief,' he shouts. 'You mean I have come all this way on a Sunday night just because you looked out of the window and saw a dog?' The Wing Commander is getting mad.

'It was not just a dog,' I tell him. 'It was alive. And it was flying. It flew past the window and up over the house. It came from down there, down near the railway line.'

Everyone looks down the hill but I can tell that no one believes me.

'Did it have wings?' says Matthew.

'No,' I yell. 'Of course not.'

'Or a propeller?' says Dad in a mean voice.

'No,' I shout. Tears are starting to come into my eyes. 'It was moving its legs. Like it was swimming in the air. Real fast. It was moving its legs and yapping.'

The Wing Commander is leaving. He is charging down the hall. Before he goes he turns round and barks at Dad. 'You had better teach that boy not to tell lies. Wasting people's time with this nonsense about a flying dog.' He goes out and slams the front door behind him.

Mum and Dad and Matthew all stare at me. I can see that they don't believe a word of my story. I run to my bedroom and throw myself on the bed. I can hear Dad shouting from the kitchen. 'You are grounded for two months Simon. I am sick of these stupid lies of yours. I am going to teach you a lesson about truthfulness once and for all.'

I am sick of being called a liar.

I have tears in my eyes.

Dad comes into the bedroom and looks at me. He can see that I am not faking it. I am very upset. He starts to feel sorry for me. 'Come on, Simon,' he says. 'You can't have seen a flying dog. It must have been a reflection in the window or something like that.'

'I did,' I shout at him. 'I saw an unidentified flying dog – a UFD. I'll bet you a thousand dollars that I did.'

'You haven't got a thousand dollars,' says Dad. 'In fact you haven't got any dollars at all.'

What he says is true. 'All right,' I say. 'If I prove that there is such a thing as a UFD you have to pay me a thousand dollars. If I can't prove it I will do the washing up on my own every night for three years.'

Dad thinks about this for a while, then he grins and holds out his hand. 'Okay,' he says, 'if you prove there is a UFD you get a thousand dollars. If not – three years of washing up. You have one week to prove it.' He thinks that I am going to back down and say that I didn't see the flying dog. But he is wrong.

I shake his hand slowly. I am not feeling too good though. If there is one thing I hate it is the washing up. I am sure that no more flying dogs are going to appear. I do not have the foggiest where the other one came from. Probably Mars or Venus. I wonder if there is a space ship somewhere looking for it – like in E.T.

3

'Come on,' says Dad 'Let's go down and get some ice-cream for everyone. We only have an hour left before the milk bar closes.'

We walk out the drive to Dad's precious new car. It is a Holden Camira. A red one with a big dent in the boot. Dad rubs his hand over the dent and looks unhappy. The dent happened a week earlier and it was not Dad's fault. The boom gates at the railway crossing dropped down in front of the car. Real quick. Dad slammed his foot on the brakes and – *kerpow* – a yellow

Ford ran into the back of our new Camira.

'Ruddy gates,' says Dad. He is still rubbing his hand over the dent like it is a personal wound. 'Someone ought to report them to the railways. Those gates go up and down like lightning. Don't give you a chance to stop.'

Dad is especially sore because there were no witnesses to the accident. No one saw it. If Dad had a witness he might be able to make the owner of the yellow Ford pay up. Now he has to fork out for the repair bill himself.

We drive down towards the milk bar. As we get to the railway crossing I see that there is no sign of any trains. I also see that Mrs Jensen is about to cross the line with her bull terrier. This bull terrier is the worst dog in the world. She has it on a long lead. This is good. It means that the vicious animal cannot bite anyone as they walk by.

Mrs Jensen's bull terrier is called Ripper. This is a good name for the rotten thing. Once it ripped a big hole in my pants. It has also been known to rip holes in people's legs.

Ripper snarls and snaps and tries to get off the lead as Mrs Jensen walks along.

We are driving behind a big truck. The truckie is looking at Mrs Jensen's dog Ripper. He is probably glad to be nice and safe inside his cabin. Suddenly the boom gates fall down in front of the truck. The truckie hits the brakes fast. Dad doesn't hit the brakes at all. Our Camira crashes into the back of the truck with a terrible grinding noise.

Dad groans and hangs his head down on the steering wheel. 'Not again,' he says. 'Not twice in the same month.' He looks around and then suddenly thinks of something. 'Quick,' he yells. 'Don't let Mrs Jensen go. She is our witness. She saw the whole thing. Run over and get her.'

The truckie is getting out. He is a big tough guy.

'Get Mrs Jensen,' yells Dad. 'Don't let her go.'

I take a couple of steps forward. Ripper is snarling and snapping. He recognises my leg. He wants to take another bite.

'The dog,' I say to Dad feebly. 'The dog will bite my leg.'

Dad is looking at the truckie. He really is a big bloke. 'Don't argue,' says Dad out of the corner of his mouth so that the truckie won't hear. 'Get Mrs Jensen.'

I walk over to Mrs Jensen and her savage dog. 'Dad would like to talk to you,' I say. 'But please don't bring your dog.'

Mrs Jensen is not too sure about this. She does not like me very much. In the end she slips the dog's lead over the end of one of the boom gates so that it cannot get my leg.

A train goes through the crossing and disappears along the track.

The boom gates fly up.

Ripper goes up with the boom gate. It flicks him and his lead high into the sky. Up over the trees and past the kitchen window of our house. His legs are moving like he is swimming in the air. He is yapping as he goes.

4

On the way home Dad is in a grumpy mood. He has one dent in the back of the car and another one in the front.

I am grinning my head off. I wonder how I will spend the thousand dollars.

P.S. Ripper lands in our neighbour's swimming pool. He is last seen heading for Darwin as fast as he can go.

EHEE! HAAHA!

Popping Off

'Disgusting,' said the man from the Rent Tribunal. He stared at my dog, Sandy. 'I've never seen an animal that does such loud ...'

He stopped speaking. He didn't seem to want to say the 'F' word.

'Farts,' I said.

'Bill,' yelled Dad. 'I've told you not to say that.'

'All right,' I said. 'Pops. Sandy pops a lot. So what? It's not her fault. It's his.' I pointed to Mr Skimpton. He sat there in his wheelchair saying nothing as usual.

Right at that moment Sandy let out another seven or eight rippers. *Pop, pop, poppety, pop, pop. Pop, pop.*

'Absolutely foul,' sniffed the male nurse. 'Terrible smell.' He was a tall, skinny man with a mean mouth.

The guy from the Rent Tribunal stared at me and Dad. He had a lot of power. He could kick people out of their flats if he wanted to. 'I'm sorry,' he said. 'But you'll have to find yourself another place. You can't expect your neighbours to put up with a noise like that.'

'No one gets a wink of sleep,' said the male nurse.

'We've already been kicked out of four rentals,' said

Dad wearily. 'Please don't make us move again.'

'Then get rid of the dog,' said the nurse.

Tears started to well up in my eyes. 'Sandy was a special present,' I yelled.

Dad nodded. 'Our other dog drowned. He was fifteen years old. Bill didn't sleep for a month after the accident. He just cried and cried and cried. Nothing would make him happy. Then I bought him Sandy. You should have seen Bill's face light up when I put the puppy in his hands.'

The man from the Tribunal smiled at me. Maybe there was a chance. Maybe he would change his mind and let us stay there.

'Why did you buy such an ugly dog?' said the nurse. 'I can't understand who would want a creature like that. Look at it. Its mouth is all twisted sideways.'

'Sandy didn't always pop off,' I said. 'She used to bark like a normal dog once.'

'At night,' said Dad.

'Why didn't you train her?' said the man from the Tribunal.

'We tried everything,' said Dad. 'She failed all the tests at obedience school.'

'It's a dumb dog,' said the nurse.

'It's not,' I yelled. 'Sandy is a genius.'

'So we got kicked out of our flat,' said Dad. 'We just couldn't stop her barking. The neighbours were always complaining.'

'Then he used a citrus spray,' I said. 'It was mean.'

'Better than getting her de-barked,' said Dad. 'I had no choice.'

The man from the Tribunal looked puzzled.

'Dad put this thing in front of Sandy's mouth,' I told him. 'And every time she barked it squirted lemon juice up her nose.'

Dad nodded. 'But Sandy learned to bark out of the side of her mouth. That's how her lips got twisted. In the end we had to use two sprays at the same time. One from each side.'

'That worked,' I said. 'She stopped barking and started . . .'

'Popping?' said the man from the Tribunal.

'Loudly,' said the nurse.

Everyone stared at Sandy. The poor dog. She couldn't help it. I put my arm around her and gave her a cuddle. She let a couple of small pops out of her bottom. Not very loud at all. Straight away Mr Skimpton fired back a long, loud one.

'See,' I yelled. 'He does it too.'

The nurse twisted his face. 'This poor man can't move,' he said. 'Not even a finger. The dog is teasing him. It's like a war. Watch this.'

He wheeled Mr Skimpton out of the door, along the corridor and into his flat.

'Don't, Sandy,' I prayed. 'Please don't.'

But she did. She ran straight over to the wall, turned her backside to it and let off five or six quick pops. They were loud ones. The nurse appeared through the door just as Sandy was finishing. 'See what I mean?' he shrieked. 'The stupid dog hates him. It does it on purpose.'

Just then there was a loud reply from the other side of the wall. Mr Skimpton was firing back.

'He does it even louder,' I yelled. 'Why should Sandy go?'

'It's his only weapon,' said the nurse. 'He's a defence-less old man.' He went out and wheeled Mr Skimpton back. I looked into the old man's eyes. What were they saying? What did he really think? No one could tell.

The man from the Tribunal stared at me sadly. 'I'm sorry,' he said. 'But a person is more important than a dog. You will have to find another flat.'

Right at that moment Sandy let out a barrage of furious pops. Mr Skimpton fired back.

Pop, pop, poppety, pop, pop. It was like two machine-guns. It was hopeless. We would have to leave. I hung my head. I tried not to cry.

'I'm sorry, Bill,' said Dad. 'But we'll have to get rid of her. We can't move. The whole thing will just start again.'

'Wait a minute,' yelled the man from the Tribunal. 'I used to be in the army once.'

'So?' said the nurse.

The man from the Tribunal squatted down in front of Mr Skimpton's wheelchair. 'Do that again,' he yelled.

Mr Skimpton tried really hard. At first nothing would come. But then he let out a series of long pops. He must have been eating baked beans for a month to get so much air into him.

'It's morse code,' shouted the Rent Tribunal man. 'Would you believe it? He says he loves the dog. He wants you to stay.'

Just then Sandy started popping like crazy.

'Wow,' yelled the Tribunal man. 'The dog can do it too. He says Mr Skimpton wants a new nurse.'

The nurse stuck his nose into the air and walked straight out of the door.

'Hooray,' I yelled. 'We can stay.'

It was too much for Dad. He didn't know what to say.

So he just popped off to the pub for a drink.

Next Time Around

It all started when I was reading a comic called ... what was it again ...? I forget now. Anyway, this comic reckoned you could hypnotise chickens by staring them in the eye and making chook noises.

Well, it was worth a try. See, Dad had this prize chook named Rastus. It used to win ribbons at the show. He kept it in a cage in the garage and gave it nothing but the best to eat. Dad loved Rastus.

It was a smart chook. I have to admit that. You probably won't believe me when I tell you that Rastus could understand English. 'Rastus,' Dad would say. 'Count to four.' Rastus would peck on the cage four times. No kidding. It could go all the way up to twenty-two without making a mistake. It sure was brainy.

Anyway, I wanted to see if the comic was right. It would be great to hypnotise a chook. I sneaked out to the garage and let Rastus onto the floor. Then I did what it said in the comic. I stared straight into Rastus' eyes. 'Puck, puck, puck, puck,' I said.

Rastus didn't take any notice. He just started scratching around on the ground. It didn't work. Things in comics never do. Still, I decided to give it one more try. This time I changed pitch. I made my voice higher. More like a chook's. 'Puck, puck, puck, puck,' I went.

Well, you wouldn't believe it. The silly chook froze like a statue. Its eyes went all glassy. It stood as still as a rock. Not a blink. Not a movement. It was out to it. Hypnotised. I had done it. Fantastic.

2

I walked around and around the staring chook. I poked it with my finger. It still didn't move. I grinned to myself. I could hypnotise chooks. Maybe this would make me famous. I could go on the stage. Or the TV. People would pay good money to see the boy who could put a chook into a trance.

Still and all, Dad wasn't going to like it much. He wouldn't win many ribbons with a chicken that just stood and stared.

The back door banged. I could hear Dad packing his fishing rod in the car.

I clicked my fingers at the chook. 'Okay, Rastus,' I said. 'You can snap out of it now.'

Rastus didn't move.

I tried something different. 'When I say bananas,' I said to Rastus, 'you will wake up. You will feel happy and well. You will not remember anything that has happened.'

I took a deep breath. 'Bananas,' I said.

Rastus stared to the front like a solid, feathered soldier.

I picked him up and looked into his eyes. 'Speak to me, Rastus,' I said. 'Puck, puck, puck.' I gave him a vigorous shake.

Rastus was rigid. The rotten rooster was out like a light.

Dad's footsteps came towards the garage. 'Oh no,' I said.

I grabbed Rastus and my school bag and nicked out of the back door. Dad was going to be mad when he found out that Rastus had gone. But not as mad as he would be if he knew what I'd done. I wasn't even supposed to go anywhere near the bloomin' chook. And if I couldn't get it out of its trance it might die of starvation.

3

I made my way slowly to school with the frozen fowl tucked under my arm. Its glassy eyes stared ahead without blinking.

'What have you got there?' said a loud voice. It was Splinter, my best mate.

'It's Rastus,' I said.

Splinter whistled. 'Wow. How did he die?'

'He's not dead. He's hypnotised. I can't bring him round.'

By now we had reached the school gate. 'Pull the other one,' said Splinter.

'No, it's true,' I said. 'I'm a hypnotist. I did it.'

'Okay,' said Splinter. 'Hypnotise me then.'

I looked around the school ground. Kids were staring

at me because I was standing there with a bit of petrified poultry under my arm. I could feel my face going red. 'All right,' I said. 'I will. But first I have to hide Rastus.'

We found a little trap door under one of the portable classrooms and hid Rastus inside. He looked kind of sad, staring out at us from the dark.

Splinter stretched himself out on a bench. 'Right,' he said. 'Get on with it. Put me in a trance.'

A group of kids gathered around. They were all scoffing like mad. They wanted to see me hypnotise Splinter. They didn't really think I could do it. Neither did I. A chook was one thing. But a person was another.

I took a silver pen from my pocket. 'Follow the tip of this pen with your eyes,' I said.

Splinter did as he was told. He had a big grin on his face. His eyes went from left to right like someone watching a tennis match. Suddenly the grin disappeared. Splinter's eyes went glassy. He stared to the front. Splinter was as solid as a statue.

Was he fooling? I didn't really know. I couldn't be sure. He was the sort of kid who was always playing jokes. 'You are a chook,' I said.

Splinter jumped to his feet and started crowing like a rooster. He was very good. He sounded just like the real thing; not like someone trying to copy a rooster. The kids around all gasped. They were impressed.

But I wasn't sure about it. I had a feeling that Splinter was tricking me. I had to find out. 'Splinter,' I said. 'When

I count to three you will be your old self. You will not be a chook any more. But whenever you hear the word "no", you will be a chicken again for thirty seconds.'

Splinter was just opening his mouth to start crowing again. I had to be quick. 'One, two, three,' I said. Splinter shook his head and blinked. He was back to normal.

4

The school bell rang and everyone made for the doors.

'What happened?' asked Splinter. He really didn't seem to remember. I smiled to myself. I was a hypnotist. From now on nobody could give me any cheek. I would make them think they were worms. Or maggots. Life was looking good.

But not for long.

We went into the first class. Maths. With Mr Spiggot. He sure was a mean teacher. If you hadn't done your homework you had to stand up and be yelled at. Or do a Saturday morning detention. Three girls were expelled because of him. Just for giving cheek.

Mr Spiggot looked at me. 'Have you done your homework, Robertson?' he growled.

I looked at my shoes. I was in big trouble. 'No,' I answered.

'No?' he yelled.

At that very moment Splinter jumped to his feet as if someone had just switched him on. He walked around the class pecking at the floor like a chicken. 'Puck, puck

puck,' he said. The class gasped. Some kids tried to smother a laugh. Splinter was in big trouble. You couldn't fool around in front of Mr Spiggot and get away with it.

Mr Spiggot started to go red in the face. I tried to figure out what was going on. And then I realised. Mr Spiggot and I had said 'no'. We put Splinter into a trance. Just like I'd told him. Splinter really did think he was a chook.

I can tell you one thing. It was the longest thirty seconds of my life. And there was nothing I could do except watch poor Splinter scratch around on the floor in front of the whole class.

Suddenly Splinter stopped. The thirty seconds were up. He looked around with a silly expression. Everyone was laughing. Except Mr Spiggot. He looked straight at me. He knew Splinter was my mate.

'Right,' he said in a very quiet voice. 'You two think you can get out of your homework by acting the fool.' He walked over to his desk and picked up two sheets of paper. He gave us one each.

I groaned. It was Maths homework. Twenty hard problems.

Splinter didn't know what was going on. 'Why?' he asked, 'I haven't done anything.'

'No?' said Mr Spiggot. 'What ...'

He didn't finish the sentence. As soon as Mr Spiggot said the word 'no', Splinter went back to thinking he was a chicken. He hopped up onto the front desk and squatted down. He put his elbows out like wings and flapped them. Then he sort of bounced up and down. He thought he was a chook laying an egg. 'Puck, puck, puck, puck,' he went.

Everyone packed up. The whole class was in fits. Mr Spiggot picked up two more sheets of sums. He held one out under Splinter's nose. Splinter pecked at his hand with his teeth. Just like a broody hen. Peck, peck, peck. 'Ouch,' shouted Mr Spiggot. He shook his hand and jumped up and down.

Splinter was still trying to lay an egg. Suddenly he stopped. The thirty seconds was up. He blinked. He stood up on the desk. Mr Spiggot was so furious that he couldn't speak. He staggered back to the desk and grabbed a handful of problem sheets. He gave us another one each.

'You two boys can leave my class,' he choked. 'And if those sums are not all finished, CORRECTLY, by tomorrow morning, you will both be expelled from the school.'

5

It was no good trying to explain. He wouldn't believe me. And he might say 'no' again at any minute. We walked sadly out of the room and into the yard. We made for the portable classroom. Rastus was still there – in a trance. I put him under my arm and we started walking home. It was raining and water dripped down our backs.

'Listen,' I said to Splinter. 'I have to put you into a trance. To stop you going into your chicken act every time I say "no".'

I tried to stop myself saying the last word. 'No.' Too late. Splinter started to scratch around on the footpath. Clucking and pecking. A couple of snails were making their way across the footpath.

Splinter was hungry.

He took a snail between his teeth and hit it on the ground. Then he swallowed it in one gulp. He did the same to another and another. 'Oh, no,' I yelled. Splinter was eating live snails. He looked around for more.

I had to do something. Quick. Before the thirty seconds were up. 'When I count to three,' I yelled. 'You will be your old self again. You will not be a chook when anyone says "no".' Then I added something else, just to be on the safe side. 'You will not remember anything about being a chook.' I took a deep breath. 'One, two, three.'

It worked straight away. Better than I thought. Splinter blinked. And winked. He rubbed his eyes. 'What happened?' he asked.

I didn't get a chance to answer him. Rastus flapped out of my arms and squawked crossly. He was his old self again. 'Rastus came out of his trance when I counted to three,' I shouted. 'It was the numbers. He understands numbers.'

Rastus looked up at me as if to agree. Then he pecked the ground three times.

Poor old Splinter wasn't interested in the chook. He waved the sheets of sums in my face. 'We have to do all of these by tomorrow,' he groaned. 'Or we're dead meat. My parents will murder me if I'm expelled from school.'

'Come round to my place after tea,' I said. 'We'll stay up all night and work on them.'

Splinter walked home. He dragged his feet as he went. I knew how he was feeling. And it was all my fault.

6

Mum and Dad were going out that night and I had to mind the baby. 'Mum,' I said. 'Splinter and I have to do homework. I can't mind the baby.'

'Rubbish,' said Mum. 'She'll be asleep. You just want to play records. Homework? That'll be the day.' She went off laughing loudly to herself. I couldn't tell her about the sums. Or being expelled if we didn't finish them. It would be like throwing wood on a bushfire.

The baby was asleep in her bassinet. She was only eighteen months old. But boy was she fat. She'd only just started to walk. She spent all day eating.

'Here's Splinter,' said Mum. She showed him into the lounge room. 'Make sure you don't make too much noise.' She kissed me goodbye even though Splinter was there. Talk about embarrassing.

The baby snored away making sucking noises. We sat

down at the table and tried to work out the answer to the first sum. It was something about water running into a bath at two litres a minute and out of the plug at half a litre a minute. You had to work out how long it would take to fill the bath.

'Strike,' said Splinter. 'How do you do it?'

'Search me,' I said. I looked at all the other sums. There were fifty altogether. Real hard ones.

'We'll never do it,' said Splinter.

My heart sank. I knew he was right. Tomorrow we would be expelled from school. We tried and tried for about an hour. But it was no good. We couldn't even work out one answer.

7

Splinter suddenly threw the papers on the floor. 'I'm sick of this,' he said. 'We might as well do something else.'

This is when Splinter had his brainwave. 'I was watching this show once,' he said. 'About a hypnotist. He could take people back in time. To earlier lives.'

'What do you mean?' I said.

He stared at me. 'Well, this bloke reckoned that everyone has lived before. Only you can't remember it. When you die, you get born again as someone else. If you were really good you might end up being born as a king or something. If you were bad in a past life you might come back as a rat.'

'I don't believe it,' I said.

Splinter was always wanting an adventure. 'Let's give it a try,' he said. 'You hypnotise me and see if I can tell you about an earlier life.'

I didn't want to do it. We were in enough trouble already. But in the end Splinter talked me into it.

'You are feeling sleepy,' I told him. Straight away Splinter started to nod off. I was getting better and better at this hypnotism lurk. 'You are going back,' I went on. 'Back to your earlier life. You are going back twenty years. It is the fifth of April at eight o'clock. Who are you?'

There was a long silence. Splinter had his eyes closed. He didn't say anything. He just sat there. It wasn't working.

Then something creepy happened. It made the hairs stand up on the top of my head. Splinter opened his mouth and spoke in a slow, deep voice. It wasn't his voice. It was the speech of a man. 'I am John Rivett,' he said.

It was amazing. I had taken him back in time. To an earlier life. I asked him what he did for a job.

'Fireman,' he said loudly.

'How old are you?'

'Thirty-two.' He was answering my questions very seriously. I wanted to know more. This is when I made my big mistake. 'What are you doing now?' I asked. 'At this very minute?'

'Fire,' Splinter shouted. 'No time to talk. Must put out the fire.' He sat bolt upright. His eyes were wild and staring. He ran over to the sink and filled up a jug of water. Then he threw it at the wall. It ran down Mum's best wallpaper and onto the floor.

'Stop,' I yelled. But it was no good. Splinter was back in an earlier life. He thought the house was on fire. I grabbed him by the arm but he was too strong. He had the power of a grown man. He brushed me aside as if I was a baby and ran outside.

To get the hosepipe.

'When I count to three . . .' I shouted. But it was useless. He wasn't listening. He dragged the hose into the lounge and started squirting the walls. And the sofa. And the carpet. The room was soon swirling with water. I tried to grab him but he was just too strong for me.

He kept shouting something about getting the baby out before the flames reached her. I grabbed the baby and ran into the back yard. Splinter had gone wild. He was wetting everything. He really thought the house was on fire. I had to stop him. But how? There was no one to help.

Or was there?

8

I stared down at the baby. It was sucking its knuckles and dribbling as usual. 'Baby,' I said. 'You are feeling sleepy. You are going back to another life. It is ten years ago on the third of November. Who are you? What is your name?'

The baby did nothing for a minute or so. Then it sat straight up in its bassinet. It boomed at me with this enormous deep voice. 'Lightning Larry,' said the baby. 'World Heavyweight Boxing Champion.'

'Please help me,' I said to the baby. 'Stop that maniac Splinter from flooding out the house.'

The baby jumped out of the bassinet and headed for the door. Splinter looked in amazement at the baby striding across the lawn. He didn't want an infant to get into a house that he thought was burning down. He slammed the door. The baby let fly with an enormous kick and knocked the door off its hinges.

I groaned. The house was being wrecked. The baby strode across the room to Splinter. Her nappy waggled as she walked. She drew back her arm, gave an enormous leap, and punched Splinter fair on the jaw. He dropped like a felled tree. Out to it.

The baby picked Splinter up and held him above her head. She carried him out to me and dumped him on the grass. 'How's that?' she boomed.

It was scary listening to that enormous voice coming out of such a tiny mouth. The baby gave a wicked grin and held her hands up like a boxer in a ring. 'Still the champ,' she shouted.

Splinter was starting to come round. He sat up and rubbed his jaw. 'When I count to three,' I said to both of them. 'You will forget everything that happened.'

And they did. The baby went back to being a baby

and started to bawl. Splinter looked at the fractured door. 'Gee,' he said. 'You're in big trouble.'

And I was. Mum and Dad were furious when they got home. They wouldn't stop going on about it. You know the sort of thing. On and on and on. They wouldn't believe that the baby kicked the door down. Wouldn't even let me start to explain about hypnosis. 'These lies just make it worse, lad,' said Dad.

Splinter was sent home in disgrace. I was sent to bed.

9

In the morning I woke up and hoped that it had all been a nightmare. But it hadn't. The sheets of unanswered sums were still on the floor.

When I got to school Splinter and I would be expelled. Dad and Mum would blow their tops. Life wasn't worth living.

I walked out of the door towards my doom. 'Make sure you behave yourself at school,' said Mum. I didn't answer.

I went out to check on Rastus. I stayed with him for so long that I made myself late for school.

Maths was the first class as usual. Mr Spiggot was just getting started. I rushed in right at the last minute.

'Right,' said Mr Spiggot in a low voice. 'Stand up, you two. Have you done your homework? Finished those sums?'

'No,' whispered Splinter.

'Yes we have,' I said. 'We worked on them together.'

'Okay, let's see,' said Mr Spiggot. He read out the first sum. The problem about the bath water. Then he looked at me for the answer.

'Three minutes,' I said. Mr Spiggot raised an eyebrow. I was right.

Mr Spiggot read out the next sum. It was about how many kilometres a car could travel in two days at a certain speed. 'Five hundred and two,' I said.

'Correct,' said Mr Spiggot. He read out all the sums. And I answered every one correctly. We were saved. You should have seen the look on Splinter's face.

Well, that's about all. We didn't get expelled but I was grounded for a month by Mum for all the water damage.

Looking back on it now, I would have to say that using hypnotism is not a good idea. I'm never doing it again. Never. It caused too much trouble.

If you asked me what was the worst bit, I would say it was when Splinter ate the snails. That was terrible.

And the best bit? Well, that was probably when I stopped to check on Rastus on the way to school that day. It was a great idea to send him back to an earlier life. It turned out that the silly chook had been a Maths teacher in a previous existence. I just read him the problems and he pecked out the answers. As easy as anything.

But I'll tell you what. Mr Spiggot's a Maths teacher. He'd better watch out. I reckon he'll probably be coming back as a flea next time around.

EHEE! HAAHA!

About the author

The Paul Jennings phenomenon began with the publication of *Unreal!* in 1985. Since then, readers all around the world have devoured his books.

Paul Jennings has written over one hundred stories and has been voted 'favourite author' by children in Australia over forty times, winning every children's choice award. The top rating TV series *Round the Twist* and *Driven Crazy* are based on a selection of his enormously popular short-story collections such as *Unseen!* which was awarded the 1999 Queensland Premier's Literary Award for Best Children's Book. In 1995 he was made a Member of the Order of Australia for services to children's literature and was awarded the prestigious Dromkeen Mdeal in 2001. Paul has sold over 7.5 million books worldwide.

His most recent books include *Paul Jennings' Weirdest Stories*, *Paul Jennings' Spookiest Stories*, *The Reading Bug . . . and how you can help your child to catch it* (2003), his *Rascal* storybooks for early readers (2004) and his much-anticipated first full-length novel, *How Hedley Hopkins Did a Dare . . .* (shortlisted for the 2006 Children's Book Council of Australia Book of the Year Award: Younger Readers).

This collection of twenty-five hilarious tales has been hand-picked by Paul from the *UnCollected* series and will have fans and new readers laughing out loud.

ALSO FROM PAUL JENNINGS

Also from the hugely popular *UnCollected* series, this special selection of tales showcases Paul's storytelling talents at their very best . . . and weirdest!

This special edition anthology boasts twenty of Paul's spookiest, fun-filled yarns, hand-picked by the author for a spine-tingling reading experience.